FEARMOJI

A QUEER HORROR ANTHOLOGY

EDITED BY

DAVID-JACK FLETCHER

SLASHIC HORROR PRESS

CONTENT WARNING
Content warnings are listed on the final page of this book.

OTHER TITLES BY SLASHIC HORROR

Raven's Creek by David-Jack Fletcher
The Gateway in Apartment 8 by Chisto Healy
The Vicious duology by Chloe Spencer
Pyramidia by Stephanie Sanders-Jacob
Haunted Places and Other Stories by Mark Allan Gunnells
The Desert Island Game by Cat Voleur
My Apologies to Tanya Grace by Cat Voleur
The Count by David-Jack Fletcher
The Thickest Soup You've Got by Nikki R. Leigh
Skeletons by Chisto Healy
Price Slashers by Chisto Healy, Michael R. Collins, Erica Summers
Dropshipped by Stephanie Sanders-Jacob
The White Harbor trilogy by Carlos E. Rivera
Sandower After Dark 1 & 2 by Elton Skelter
Waste Ground by Marc Ruvolo
Nobody's Savior by Wesley Winters
Somewhere Quiet, Full of Light by Henry Corrigan
Imposter Syndrome by Mark Allan Gunnells
Lesser Hungers by Rien Gray
He Will Have the World by David-Jack Fletcher

COMING SOON

The Familialists by TT Madden
The Shapes of Our Screams by TT Madden
Pieties by Marc Ruvolo
Summer 1973 trilogy by Dean Cade
Extremities #1: Deadbeat by Maxim Volk

CONTENTS

THE STERLING BRIDGE MONSTER

TT Madden

THE STERLING BRIDGE STREET MONSTER
TT Madden

The Fearsome Foursome Chat

Dani
They know. They know what we did.

Brianna
Shut the fuck up dont text that shit

Izzy
Dani thats impossible. They can't know.

None of us told so they can't know.

Brianna
Jesus Christ Im gonna leave this chat

Ryan
I haven't said shit.

Brianna
Guilty conscience much?

Ryan
thought you were leaving this chat.

BRIANNA
Fuck off, lezzie.

RYAN
Real rich coming from a girl who knows
what my insides feel like.

DANI
GUYS!

Don't you know where your parents are?

They're having a meeting RIGHT NOW to talk about it.

IZZY
What?

DANI
A pta meeting!

Oh my god, is what happened to Tristan our fault?!

Did we do this?!

IZZY
Dani, it's not our fault.

We didn't do anything.

RYAN
Fuck we didnt.

Izzy
So we fix it.

We can go back.

Erase it.

Dani
like scratch it out?

Ryan
I've still got paint left if that's the plan

Brianna
Leave me out of this

Izzy
Fuck that, bri, your coming

Brianna
I'm locking my doors and closing my blinds.

Ryan
I'm picking you up, bri

Rest of yall meet at the bridge?

Izzy
Burton ave

We go to the bridge together

RYAN
deal

DANI
ok

BRIANNA
fuck me fine

BLOCKED NUMBER

IZZY
Who's that?

BLOCKED NUMBER

BRIANNA
Who is that?

Who the FUCK is that?!

BRIANNA

BRIANNA WASN'T USED to her phone being an object of fear. She wasn't addicted to it, like plenty of the other people in her class seemed to be, always posting photos like the internet demanded constant proof of life. She was in plenty of those group shots though; blond-haired, blue-eyed, with the other cheerleaders, at parties (but always making sure she was never photographed with alcohol), school activities. Even without her adding to it, her phone was still a point of connection. Of happiness. But lately it seemed to bring her nothing but grief.

She stared at it, lying across the room where she had thrown it in fear after the group chat had come to an unceremonious conclusion with the intrusion of that strange, new number.

Those emojis.

The bridge.

Briana tried to think logically about the situation; ghosts weren't real, monsters weren't real. All those urban legends about killers hiding upstairs waiting to slaughter innocent babysitters or hook-handed psychos stalking lovers' lanes or what they said lived under the Sterling Bridge were just that. Stories.

Then why was this happening?

She wanted to blame her irrational fear on Ryan; they had watched so many scary movies lately, both with the other girls and on their own, sitting together on Ryan's couch in her parents' basement. Brianna thought about all the ghosts in those movies that could drive cars or communicate through television static or VHS tapes or voicemails from the future, and that terrified animal part of her brain convinced her that what was happening to them was completely plausible.

Of course there was some sort of monster that lived under the Sterling Bridge and of course they had summoned it That Night. All the times as a child she played Bloody Mary or tried to invoke the Hallway Man or parked in a secluded area to make out, she had never seen a ghost in the mirror or a specter standing in her doorway or found a hook attached to her car's door handle when she got home later that night.

But now something had happened.

Brianna's phone vibrated again and she jumped, only willing to look at the screen from across the room, standing on her bed, craning her neck to see the screen. This time it wasn't that strange, unknown number, those taunting symbols, but Ryan.

RYAN
Outside.

Brianna darted to her window, suddenly awash with a feeling she knew full well was more than simple relief. Sure enough, Ryan's battered, old boat of a Buick she got as a hand-me-down from her grandmother was out idling at the curb. Brianna couldn't see her through the dark—through the headlights or the streetlights reflecting off the windshield—but she recognized the shape and sound of the car and she wasn't so afraid anymore.

Brianna recognized the symptoms of a crush when she felt them.

Goddammit, she'd never hear the end of it if Ryan found out.

Found out? she asked herself. *You've already gone further with her than you have with any boy. You've let her put her fingers, her…her tongue inside you.* Not to mention all the stuff she did to Ryan. Was she still a virgin if she never had a dick inside her? But a crush was different than a simple hookup, and Brianna knew it was only because of those feelings that she could fight every urge telling her to stay home, lock her door, and stay under her covers forever. She headed outside, ignoring the curfew set in place, crossed the lawn, opened the door to the Buick, and slid onto the wide bench seat next to Ryan.

She tried to fight that stupid swell in her stupid chest when she saw Ryan's stupid face, but there was no fighting it, she knew. She let it wash over her, felt her face go red, felt that familiar flush between her legs. Why did she think Ryan was so pretty? Brianna had never before been attracted to girls, certainly not girls with pixie cuts and ripped jeans and muddy boots. Not girls with dark eye makeup and a nose ring and tank tops that showed off their muscles. Not girls at all. So why did she want to tell Ryan to forget about this whole thing, to drive them straight out of town, to find a motel where they could stop in under false names and lock the door and pull the curtains and shut out the entire world? Why was it she felt this feeling for Ryan and not any of the boys in her class?

Looking into Ryan's eyes, she honestly didn't fucking care why.

"I'm glad you decided to come," Ryan said, and put her hand on Brianna's bare knee just below where her sundress ended.

"Yeah," Brianna said, very nearly stuttered, not knowing what else to say, not knowing what else to do as Ryan pulled away from the curb, except to spread her leg a little bit, invite Ryan's warm palm towards the inside of her thigh. She kept it there the whole ride.

Izzy

Izzy DIDN'T KNOW how many more times and in how many more ways she could tell Dani it wasn't their fault; hell, she didn't know if that was even true. It might be their fault, but Izzy wasn't going to say that when Dani was in near-constant hysterics.

What she could say, though, what might help calm Dani down, was that perhaps they could fix it.

Perhaps they could stop it.

And if they could, maybe Izzy would never have to tell Dani and the others that she was sick. She tried to play it off, tried to tell herself it was just a normal sickness, but she could feel what was happening inside her body. She knew this was connected to Tristan. She knew this was part of what they'd done.

So, maybe if they stopped it, the sickness would go away.

Izzy and Dani sat in Izzy's mom's car, parked on the pull-off area of Burton Avenue, just before the entrance to the Sunderland Park nature trail which, after a short walk, would take them to the Sterling Bridge. This late at night, they were alone, and if the rumors were true about a curfew, they would continue to be so. Maybe Izzy should have pulled the car into the trail, tried to hide it. It didn't matter. If she was right and they could fix this, it would all be over soon.

Heading back to the bridge was Izzy's idea, and she prepared accordingly, dressed for a hike; her jeans tucked into boots, a beanie over her red hair, gloves, a jacket, a backpack with waters and protein bars because she was certain none of the other girls would prepare. Except maybe Ryan.

Given Dani's current mental state, though, Izzy was willing to give her lack of preparation a pass. Dani sat in the passenger's seat, fidgeting. She'd been a wreck ever since That Night; huge bags under her normally bright eyes, the color drained from her usually vibrant cheeks. Her long, brown hair, which she often curled and let flow free, was pulled back into a ponytail, and she was swimming in a giant pair of sweatpants and hoodie, both of which bore food and coffee stains. She had her phone in her lap, and Izzy could see her checking the lock screen again and again, pretending that she was either checking the time or awaiting a message from Ryan or Brianna.

But Izzy knew the urge Dani was really fighting.

She was tempted, was telling herself not to go into her files to find the picture, to rewatch the video.

All of this reconfirmed what Izzy had already told herself; she was going to keep her sickness to herself. She couldn't add to Dani's burden. Hopefully she'd never have to know at all. She already thought what happened to Tristan was their fault. The first kid in their class to get sick; they'd been talking about neolithic cave paintings in class when he'd bolted from the room. Mrs. Graner understood, realized sometimes kids got sick, but when he didn't show up by the final bell, she sent Todd Lindquist into the bathroom after him to see if he was alright, and Todd came back crying and heaving after what he'd seen.

All Todd could say in the moment was that something terrible had happened to Tristan, that he was hurt, that they needed an ambulance. He said he had a tumor, though no one could get much more information out of him since then. In the days that followed, the rumor mill spun, and word was that something horrid and grotesque had happened to Tristan. That he was *infected* with something. That it caused tumors, boils to grow across his skin. They said he was in a quarantined room at the hospital.

They said other kids could get it.

Izzy reached out and touched her girlfriend's bouncing knee, trying to quiet her, reassure her.

"It's going to work," she said, hoping she sounded convincing. Trying not to think about Tristan, and all the other kids who'd gotten sick since then. "Dani, I promise you, it's going to work and everything is going to go back to normal."

Dani squeezed Izzy's hand and Izzy saw a softness in her eyes. She couldn't tell if Dani believed her or if she was just grateful for her support, but either way she leaned forward and gently kissed Izzy on the mouth.

Which was the exact moment Izzy threw up.

She had enough wherewithal to pull away from Dani, to aim at the floor of the car (not quick enough to even make the door) and a fire-hose of smelly, yellow bile spewed from her mouth. It burned her nose coming up, and she felt chunks of something horrible she didn't want to know touch the back of her throat as she retched again and again.

When she was finally finished, Izzy looked into the puddle of vomit and saw half a dozen human fingers.

"Izzy," Dani said, her voice laced with sadness, but not shock. When Izzy looked up at her, there were tears in her eyes.

They didn't even notice the pair of headlights, the approaching car, the soft alt-rock music coming from the speakers. All they were aware of was Brianna's sudden, high-pitched screeching cutting through the night.

"Izzy, are you fucking *sick*?"

MICHAEL

"TELL US WHAT's happening to our children!"

The meeting had only just started and already the room was growing to a fever pitch. Michael wondered if this was how dogs felt before a storm, this sense of impending danger. Michael had once heard his daughter, Izzy, describe anxiety as you're playing a video game, just wandering around, and you hear boss music but there's no one in sight.

But given the circumstances, he could understand.

There was something happening at Beacon High School, something happening to the children. It was some kind of illness. Or at least that was what people were saying. Something serious had happened in the middle of class last week to a boy named Tristan, but there were so many rumors flying around it was impossible to figure out the truth. Some said a kid had gotten sick, some said he brought a gun to school, some said there was some kind of accident involving heavy machinery. The only thing that was certain was that Tristan Bishop, one of Izzy's classmates, had been sent to the hospital, was in some sort of special quarantine unit, and—

Michael's phone vibrated with a very specific rhythm, and he slapped his hand to his pocket because Jesus, did he really forget to mute his Grindr notifications at a goddamn PTA meeting?

He slipped his phone out of his pocket just enough to see the screen, but it wasn't Grindr. It was a text from an unknown number; a bridge, a heart, and two people embracing. What the hell was that?

The voices around him rose to a fever pitch and he shoved the phone back into his pocket, deciding to look at it later.

Christina

If Christina noticed, she said nothing. She never said anything, not about this part of Michael's life. There were some things, unspeakable things, that not even husband and wife discussed. They had a silent understanding about certain parts of Michael's life that was of a very specific generational attitude; a man had a right to be a man, and sometimes he needed to leave the house to do it. It was a deliberately nebulous definition, because such urges were not to be talked about on anything other than your wedding night.

They were urges that Christina, if she was being honest with herself, had never really felt strongly in her entire life. Maybe at all. Ever. The desire for someone else's flesh was something that felt completely alien to her. And if she were being even more honest, she found the entire thing disgusting. She remembered very vividly the first time she ever saw a penis; in a magazine full of them she'd stumbled upon when playing hide-and-seek. It was decades later that she realized the implications of it being under her father's side of the bed.

In real life, a penis had been even more frightening, poking out of Jacob Gold's jeans at the drive-in theater. She was supposed to fit that entire thing inside her? She remembered looking down, past their torsos, and watching in muted horror as he slid his *thing* inside of her. There was a moment where the head entered, and it looked like the two of them were connected by some sort of flesh tether, a terrible, foul connection, and then with a single hard, desperate thrust he pushed forward and disappeared inside her. After that moment, Christina resolved to always have sex under the covers, or to simply hike up her skirt, or to turn around and let her partner take her from behind. Anything so she wouldn't have to look upon that grotesque sight.

Idly, she once overheard Izzy saying there was a word for people like her; *asexual*. Christina didn't really know what that meant, and had long ago swore to not type anything even remotely sexual into the internet after she tried to find some golf clubs for Michael's fortieth birthday by going to dicks-dot-com. This generation had so many new words—and so much stuff beyond the usual slang that changed every couple years—it was impossible to keep up.

Izzy would call that *conditioning*.

Brainwashing if she were feeling like a little smart-alec.

"We believe it's best to institute a curfew for anyone under the age of eighteen," the sheriff said, who was on the stage with a microphone, helping the parents discuss the strange incident—and possibly incidents—that were happening to their children, this unidentified sickness running through the school. The sheriff seemed to reconsider his statement, and then added, "Hell, anyone, really. Just to be safe."

Most of the senior class of Beacon High School was over eighteen, including Izzy. She and all her friends were legal adults. Well, adult enough to go to war, but not adult enough to have a beer, Michael always grumbled. The idea of a curfew reminded both so many parents of those PSAs from their childhoods: *It's ten o'clock. Do you know where your children are?*

"We believe the best course of action at this time," the sheriff continued, "is to discuss this frankly and openly with your children."

Which, to many of the parents, but especially Christina, seemed like the greatest terror of all.

Izzy

THE STERLING BRIDGE was categorized as a truss bridge, with those big, metal beams almost spiderwebbing up high above. When it was first constructed it much more resembled its namesake, the metal glinting in the sun. But over the years, natural wear, weather, and, of course, graffiti had taken its toll, and now it was more of a rusted brown.

The bridge was one of those places that had a stranglehold on the rumor mill of their parents' generation. It was supposed to be a nice, removed, woodsy landmark, but if the urban legends of the time were true, it was one of the most hopping places in all of Beacon, especially for the bizarre or paranormal. It was the hiding place of an escaped mental patient, a suicide hotspot, where you could sight a local ghost, where sewer mutants went to hide when the sun was up.

But for Izzy and her friends' generation, it was just a bridge, a way to get from one side of Beacon to the other. Most of them didn't even know the reason it was named what it was anymore (after its architect, not its design). All they knew was that it was a secluded place, some-where they could go to get away from their parents, from authority of any kind. Sure, cops sometimes patrolled the park and the bridge, but the trail was angled so that you could see any incoming cars from plenty far away, gave any loiterers more than enough time to scatter into the woods and hide, only to return when the prowler had passed.

The four girls reached the Sterling Bridge without issue. That was the easy part, the part of Sunderland Park that had wide, mostly paved, walking trails. The hard part was going to be climbing down into the valley, especially since Izzy was sick.

Brianna walked far ahead, refusing to help carry her, and even more vehemently refusing to be downwind of her, still covering her mouth and nose despite being a hundred feet ahead.

Izzy wasn't offended. She understood. She'd puked again halfway down the trail, this time spewing up a handful of human teeth. There was a wetness in her panties, and she didn't even remotely want to look and see what it was.

"We should stop and rest here," Dani said once they reached the bridge. She leaned Izzy up against the railing, who looked like she might heave again at any moment. The other three girls stood coiled, like they were preparing for an inevitable jump scare in a movie, the strings of the soundtrack tensing and moaning.

When their phones vibrated at the same time, they refused to look.

"Fuck!" Brianna yelped, jumping in place.

"It knows we're here," Dani said, and she couldn't resist; she reached into her back pocket and pulled out her phone. It was the group chat.

"What's it say?" Brianna asked, looking away from them, up over the rusted hulk of the bridge.

On Dani's screen were four hugging emojis.

"In a few minutes it won't matter." Ryan looked at Izzy. "You gonna be able to make it down the hill?"

Izzy didn't know, if she was being honest. She felt like another bout of sickness might come at any moment. And what if it did when she was near Ryan or Brianna? Dani was already surely infected, and Izzy couldn't bring herself to look at her. Dani, who felt the most guilt out of all of them, was now going to join Izzy in her sudden suffering.

"Look, we can do this without you," Brianna interrupted. "We can go down there and cover it up and then we can come back for you." But for some reason none of them could articulate, that felt wrong. No, not just wrong, but like it wouldn't work. It felt like they all needed to do this together, as a group, a unit, otherwise what was happening would keep on happening. They couldn't explain why, but it felt to them like the sickness would keep on spreading, and who knew how far it was already.

Ryan turned around and got down on one knee in front of Izzy.

"Hop on," she said. "I'll carry you."

Brianna huffed in protest but said nothing as Izzy slumped forward onto Ryan's back.

"Damn, Izzy, you lose weight?" Ryan asked, and then the awkwardness settled over the moment as they all realized what was meant as a complement was an indicator of something else. Something terrible.

"Forget it, let's go," Ryan said, standing, trying to hide the grimace on her face—shit, she hoped they weren't already too late for Izzy, "let's get this done. Bri, stop ogling my muscles and lead the way."

The chuckles that rippled their way through the group were forced, but they were better than nothing.

"Why did I wear these stupid goddamn flats when I knew we were going through the woods?" Brianna asked aloud.

"The faster you move," Dani said, "the sooner this will be over." Brianna hurried, periodically looking back over her shoulder to make sure the others were still there. Dani was right on her heels, and Ryan wasn't lagging behind with Izzy on her back.

They made it to the bottom of the hill, splashing into a low portion of the creek, and when they could finally take their eyes off the precarious ground in front of them, they looked up to the Sterling Bridge high above. It looked different from beneath, its metal bars less resembling supports and now evoking in them the image of the ribcage of some giant skeleton, just as it had on That Night. It looked less like a place and more like a thing, a being, something that was once alive, and they could imagine some ancient creature falling down here and dying long before time became time. The underside of the bridge was about fifty feet above the river, dotted with skinny catwalks and railings that were ostensibly meant for repair crews, but were much more often used for teenaged hangs. The metal of the bridge was connected to land on either side by concrete foundations that, to them, looked like the skin of the earth peeling away to expose the bone of the bridge, and it was in the shadows of those overhangs, specifically the one to the north—the far side—that they had to go.

Dani checked her phone. There was no service now that they'd moved into the river valley, and that was a small mercy, but the danger was about to leave the digital world and enter… Well, not the real world, because that was equally real, but the world of flesh and bone, muscle and blood.

"Come on," Ryan said, pushing past them, Izzy still on her back, "let's end this."

Dani and Brianna followed, hoping that ending this was exactly what they were about to do.

The Parents

"Who's doing this?" someone from the crowd cried.

"We're not at liberty to discuss any suspects in an ongoing case." The way the sheriff said it was so robotic, a line he'd regurgitated a thousand times and surely would a thousand more. Probably in relation to this case specifically.

A hysterical voice spoke up and said the senior class's reading material was no doubt responsible for this current wave of events. So many books about sex and violence could only bring it about in real life, yes? And what about video games? Or the music they listened to? Someone else suggested hackers, but Michael didn't think it was hackers, didn't think it was anything so benign as a prank. This felt different. It felt like before. Michael remembered AIDS in the 80s and 90s, and though he was married at that time, wasn't as exposed as some other men he knew, he still remembered that feeling, that specter. This felt like that, but for the children.

During the hysterical shouting, more than one person excused themselves. It looked like they were going to be sick; hurrying out of the room with their hands over their mouths or on their stomachs or clapped to their heads.

"What about the picture and the video?" someone from the crowd called.

"I'm sorr—the what?" the sheriff leaned forward. Michael and Christina did too. They hadn't heard about any video.

"It's all over the internet!" the crazed mother who ranted about the curriculum screamed, and as if on cue phones all around the auditorium began buzzing. Parents began checking their pockets. Michael and Christina did too, and when they saw what was there, all three minutes and forty-six seconds of it, the thought that they might rise to that same level of hysteria didn't seem so far-fetched at all.

"They have a secret language to talk about this sort of thing without us knowing!" a different hysterical mother called from the crowd.

Michael still reeled, and Christina stared down at her feet, the memories of that video still playing behind their eyes. That couldn't have been real, could it? No, no, it was impossible. They had computers now that could make all sorts of fake things. Just look at any superhero movie. Now peoples' phones even came with AI that could make goofy images like Abraham Lincoln slam dunking against Ronald McDonald with the press of a button.

"Those little…pictures on their phones," that same shrill voice called, "there's a whole world in there we don't know anything about!"

Michael almost chuckled at the woman's hysteria, but then he remembered something. Something he'd long thought forgotten. He remembered being a teenager himself, remembered spray-painting graffiti on the side of the Beacon High School gymnasium, remembered how its featureless brick wall seemed like a canvas begging to be filled. He remembered teachers standing out next to the gym, wondering the meaning of what he and his fellows had painted there. They weren't offended so much as confused, and Michael remembered the shock at how out of touch these adults were.

But now he was one of those adults, and in that moment he knew he couldn't dismiss what he'd seen out of hand.

Brianna

THE SYMBOLS THEY'D spray-painted That Night were still there, hastily scrawled onto the foundations of the bridge; a bridge itself, a heart, two people embracing. The last one was a little more complex, and the girls must've been drunker than they thought when they'd done it, because it looked like two people fusing, trying to become one, to crawl inside each other. Or, at least, that was their interpretation.

"Do you think this is why?" Dani asked, looking at that last symbol. "Do you think things wouldn't have happened the way they happened if we'd gotten it right?"

Ryan breathed heavily as she sat Izzy down. Brianna still stayed a good distance away from all of them.

"I think in a few minutes," Ryan huffed, reaching into her bag and pulling out the spray paint, "it's not gonna matter." She handed Dani a can, held one out for Brianna, offering but not expecting her to take it. But she darted forward and snatched it out of her hand, eager to risk it if it meant ending it.

Dani looked down at Izzy. "Don't worry," she said, "we'll stop this."

The three girls turned to the graffiti. The source of it all, or so it seemed. Or so they hoped. Because if this was the source, then this was also the way to stop it.

They covered it unceremoniously, as fast as they could, huge swaths of color swallowing the symbols just like how they hoped their memories and the effects of That Night could be wiped away.

EVERYTHING CHANGED THAT NIGHT. The girls didn't know it at the time, of course. When you're a teenager, there are very few times you're consciously aware you're in the middle of a life-changing moment, a crossroads that will forever alter you. Higher thoughts are not always present when you're lying on your back, the boy who you think is the love of your life on top of you, telling you he's gonna come and he wants to come inside you, and you think *I love him so I'll let him, but just this once, one time won't hurt* because you're on birth control, only to be anxiously peeing on a stick two months later. Your brain isn't working the way it should on prom night when you think *I've only had three beers, I can totally drive to the afterparty*, only for your car to end up being the one parked in the school's front lawn next year, crumpled like an aluminum can after a frat party.

No one was thinking of the consequences when they were beneath the Sterling Bridge That Night. Stomachs full of liquor obtained from the store on Seventh that never ID'd, the air full of cigarette and weed smoke and the laughter of dozens of partygoers, Ryan had pulled cans of spray paint from her backpack. She shook the can, the little ball bearing inside rattling, getting everyone's attention.

"Are you gonna do what I think you're gonna do?" Dani asked, smiling, because at that moment it was fun. At that moment she hadn't yet experienced the consequences. She was a little drunk, a little high, and Izzy was holding her from behind, arms wrapped around her shoulders, and everything in the world seemed perfect.

With only a mischievous smile, Ryan rattled the can, turned around, and painted a symbol against the foundation of the bridge; a bridge.

"Anyone else?" she asked over her shoulder, shaking the can.

Giggling, Izzy and Dani held the can together and painted a heart.

"Bri?" Ryan asked, looking at her.

Brianna rolled her eyes and completed the ritual, took her turn and painted two people embracing, and she let out a breath and then laughed because this all felt stupid and fun, but what happened after was not stupid.

Nor was it fun.

What happened after was they all suddenly felt even more drunk and even more high, like the booze and the weed was working on some sort of time-delay in their systems, only to detonate right then and there. They all felt loose, and they all felt aroused, and none of them noticed the shape in the dark beneath the bridge because they were all so preoccupied with their own feelings, and with each others' bodies. That strange feeling swept over them, and what happened to them was what the parents gathered in the Beacon High auditorium saw on video, because there was someone there with a cell phone who didn't want to participate, but wanted only to watch, and they figured why not hang on to these memories for later?

The recorder watched, and the parents gathered in the Beacon High auditorium watched the echo of what happened to their children, beginning with Izzy. She held her arm out before her, watching in mute amazement as her skin peeled away. Unaffected by the forces of gravity, it hung there, suspended, as if underwater. Her muscle went next, hovering around her, exposing bone, droplets of blood levitating in the air around her in a kind of spontaneous vivisecting, like an anatomy textbook, muscle and organs and bone laid out for the world. The condition spread to the rest of her body as the student with the phone recorded, as everyone watched in breathless awe.

They watched Izzy peel her own clothes away and the flesh flay itself from her chest, exposing her beating heart beneath its ribcage. With each thump, the floating layer of skin and muscle around her expanded and contracted, and Dani reached forward, eager to touch Izzy's heart, eager to be inside her. The moment she crossed some invisible barrier, the skin and muscle that hovered around Izzy closed around both her and Dani, drawing her in, making them one.

As Izzy's body splintered, others converged, their bodies colliding together and melding into one like two waves meeting, their seams now impossible to find. Ryan and Brianna crashed together like this, smashing together like lovers reunited after a war, their lips melding into one, the places where their skin touched searing together. All around them, the rest of the students gathered for the party experienced the same things; skin melting, colliding, mixing as easily as separate rivers converging. From the sounds the adults heard in the auditorium, it was impossible to tell if they were experiencing pain or pleasure, though there were a few parents in the crowd who, from experience, knew the answer to be both.

They were all so preoccupied with their children that none of them saw the dark shape under the bridge, the shape that had been summoned forth, which came from somewhere deep and dark and red, drawn into this place by three simple symbols.

Three symbols that now appeared in the phones of every single adult in the auditorium.

Somewhere in the crowd, someone checked their phone. And they screamed.

THE DRIVE BACK into town was just as quiet and somber as the drive out to the bridge.

Before they got into their cars, Dani asked, "Do you think we did it?"

No one said anything. They were too afraid to jinx it. After what they'd experienced, jinxes could be real too.

They drove back into town in their separate cars, in silence, and though they weren't all together, they could all sense each others' tension, knowing something was wrong; there was not a single person on the streets.

Ryan slowed down and allowed Dani to pull up alongside her as they hit the light at Seventh and Wilson.

"Where is everyone?" Ryan asked.

"The curfew?" Dani offered, but even saying it, she knew it wasn't true. Even with the curfew, there would always be *someone* out on the street. Someone breaking the rules.

"They're at the meeting," Izzy breathed. She couldn't tell if she was feeling better because they'd lifted the curse—or whatever this was— or if she was drifting closer to passing out.

"Let's go see," Ryan said, leading the way towards Beacon High. They drove through abandoned streets, reminded of their eerie freshman year of high school they spent in COVID-lockdown. But the farther they went, the less it looked like everyone was simply inside, and the more it looked like something had gone wrong. There was a car parked askew in the fire lane, its hazards on. The door to a deli hung wide open, someone's groceries spilled across the sidewalk.

Dani wasn't looking in front of her, screeched to a stop and nearly smashed Ryan's fender.

"I can't see," she said to herself more than Izzy, and put the car in park and stepped out to look around Ryan's huge Buick.

They had made it to the high school, but they were too late, either in their arrival or in their attempt to fix what they'd done under the bridge. The school's front doors were open and something impossible was spilling forth from them; a tidal wave of stitched-together flesh, just like the thing they'd become under the bridge That Night. The parents of almost every child who attended Beacon High were brought together, had become one, a swirling mass of multicolored limbs and skin, a wave of flesh spilling out of the high school and into the street. Features haphazardly arranged themselves on this massive blob, a single eye here, a mouth full of too many teeth there. Limbs and cocks sprouting out at terrible angles, the orifices of mouths and assholes gaping. The blob surged out of the many sets of front doors, spilling in every direction, but coming towards the two cars faster, knowing through some strange sense that there was life there, that there were their children there.

Ryan reversed, slamming into the front of Dani's car, but there was nowhere for them to go, nowhere for them to run. Dani leapt back into the car, but the wall of flesh came too fast, and it grabbed her and yanked her out like floodwaters, barreling both past and in, surging towards Izzy, swallowing her. Ryan and Briana held onto each other as the windows shattered with the weight of the flesh, and the skin surged inside. Effortlessly, the wave washed over them, the cars, the streets, the buildings, the town. And it kept going.

THE BEAVER WEAVES AS THE BEAVER WILLS

A. Max Traphagan

THE BEAVER WEAVES AS
THE BEAVER WILLS

A. Max Traphagan

I'D BARELY MADE it to Belton when I noticed the air conditioner in my car was blowing blistering heat like an air fryer.

Guess it didn't just need freon.

Great. Just fucking great.

It wasn't enough that I was stuck on I-35 in August on a day when it was probably 108 in the shade. It wasn't enough that I was surrounded by all my worldly possessions in this piece of shit car. It wasn't enough that I was going back to my parents' house in Dallas with my tail between my legs after making a miserable failure of myself in Austin. Now I had to do it without air conditioning.

Fuck.

I had at least two-and-a-half hours left of this drive. That's how long it would be with no traffic, but on I-35 that definitely wasn't happening. Not now that the highway was going down to one lane thanks to the endless construction. My car was already hot enough inside to make me feel like a rotisserie chicken. I rolled the windows down, but that didn't do much in this traffic except make everything smell like car exhaust. I wriggled my arms out of the little plaid shirt I was wearing over my tank top and shorts—sweat was already making it stick to me. That didn't make me feel much cooler either. This was going to be a long day.

I thought back to the reasons I was in this predicament. A couple of years ago, when I'd just finished my computer science degree at UT Dallas, my friend Jason suggested I come to Austin and help him start a company. We'd been good friends since elementary school, pushed together by virtue of being the two main targets of our school's bullies. Jason was the only Asian kid at our otherwise lily-white school and, well, the bullies knew there was something up with me well before I figured out I was trans ten years later.

Jason and I bonded over typical nerd shit, but Jason was the smarter of the two of us. I was like regular nerd smart and he was something else. So, when Jason had an idea, I tended to go along with it. This idea for a company was no exception. Besides, his idea sounded way cooler than anything else I had going on. I had a little money saved up since I'd lived with my parents while I was in school. I was also barely into my 20s; I hadn't done much of anything in life other than go to school, and I was so eager to get out of there, do something exciting, and really be myself.

My parents had been *fine* about the whole trans thing—they were both teachers and typical NPR tote bag liberals—but I found myself chafing against their pity. They treated me as if I'd told them I had some terminal illness instead of that I was trans. It was an exaggerated gentleness that made me feel nothing but weak and burdensome. I had to do something to prove to them, and to myself, that I wasn't a burden.

Jason's idea was called DAMSync, short for Data-Assisted Momentum Synchronization. It was supposed to consolidate everyone's digital lives. It was meant to be something like a cross between a productivity app, social network, health tracker, and personal AI assistant. It would track your behaviors, anticipate your needs, and nudge you toward optimal outcomes. It sounded pretty creepy to me at first, but Jason's rationale had convinced me.

"Come on, Cleo, do you really think you can keep anything private anymore?" he said. "Your information's out there. Everyone's got it.

Nobody's really using it responsibly. We might as well make it work for people, right?"

When I thought about it that way, it sounded like a good idea. I knew I could use some help getting my life on track. I didn't know much about living in the world outside of my parents' home and it seemed like a waste of time to make a bunch of mistakes just to figure out how to do that. I was sure so many other people would need that kind of help, too. I figured it was better than just having my information used to give me weirdly-targeted ads for stuff I had talked about in passing. Weirder still when it gave me ads for things I'd only *thought* about. With Jason's vision and my coding skills, maybe we really could change the whole information game.

Well, it hadn't exactly gone that way. We'd gotten pretty far in developing the prototype, and it was turning out pretty cool, but we ran out of money fast, and investors seemed to be allergic to the whole idea. Eventually, Jason came to me and told me it was time to pull the plug on DAMSync. Jason ended up moving to San Francisco after that to work for one of the big tech conglomerates. He promised he'd try to hook me up with a job once he could, but I never heard from him again.

I probably should have tried to bounce into doing something else in Austin, but I just got so depressed. The failure of DAMSync hit me so hard and I couldn't imagine myself as anything other than a failure. I struggled to get out of bed for weeks, and when I could, I realized I was being evicted from my place and I had no friends I could stay with since I spent all my time in Austin busting my ass at DAMSync.

So, there I was, stuck on I-35 going back to my parents' house, sweating from places I didn't even know I had. And I was thirsty. So fucking thirsty. I didn't bring any water because I didn't want to try to pee somewhere in the middle of nowhere, but the lack of AC and this traffic were both putting a wrench in that plan. I was going to have to stop soon if I didn't want to pass out, so I would just have to risk it somewhere.

The traffic let up enough to allow my car to start crawling forward again and a familiar billboard came into view. Staring down at me was the face of the Buc-ee's beaver. As always, he looked to the side, slack-jawed, in that dumb red hat. **CLEANEST RESTROOMS ON I-35**, the billboard proclaimed, as the beaver looked stupidly awestruck by this declaration.

I never understood why people were so obsessed with Buc-ee's. It was like getting excited about a Wal-Mart just because it had a creepy logo and made scatological puns. But the restrooms were clean. I'd give them that.

My playlist switched to the next song, from Mitski to Roy Orbison. "A candy-colored clown they call the sandman…" Of course, I thought about *Blue Velvet*. I admit that's the only reason I knew that song in the first place, from my requisite college cinephile David Lynch deep dive phase. I thought about Frank Booth, looking monstrous and fragile all at once, looking like that song was the only thing tethering him to the world, and Roy Orbison's androgynous, unnervingly beautiful voice. I'd been a little obsessed with the song after that, and it was really hitting now in this weird moment. I was no Frank Booth, of course, but I felt on the brink of being truly untethered just the same, and Roy Orbison's voice felt like the only beautiful thing left.

The back of the car in front of me looked blurry, like all the exhaust and heat around were distorting things a little bit. It looked heavy and strange, like the way the air felt around me. As sweaty as I was getting, I felt like I was swimming. Really, it was almost starting to feel like drowning, like I was breathing in too much humidity and sweat and exhaust along with all the oxygen. It was making me dizzy.

I started to laugh. The writers of this season of my life were really heavy-handed, weren't they? Some amateur critic would have a field day writing an essay about this scene for their Substack. "Our protagonist's life was melting in the heat much like the makeup on her face, as Roy Orbison's voice sang out a warning, much as it did for those who encountered Frank Booth, the split self, the raw nerve of violence underneath suburban politeness, the same suffocating politeness the protagonist finds herself driving toward…"

It wasn't long before I saw another Buc-ee's billboard. **TOP TWO REASONS TO STOP: #1 AND #2**, it read, with that dopey beaver once again looking amazed by this statement. Something about this billboard pissed me off, no pun intended. I didn't have time for the beaver's juvenile bullshit. I was just into Temple now and I was beginning to feel like I was going to throw up from this heat. My pulse was pounding in every part of my body. My skin was tender and angry. The way the backs of my thighs were sticking to the pleather seat was so gross and unbearable. It was so stupid of me to not bring any water. I worried my throat was going to close up.

"A candy-colored clown they call the sandman…"

How was this song still playing? It was restarting, I realized, just like it had, well, I didn't know how many times at this point. How long *had* it been playing? I didn't remember putting it on repeat. Why would I even do that? I was getting kind of sick of it; it was just too much right now. I needed something lighter. But, every time I picked up my phone to turn on something else, all the text on the screen seemed to start swimming. I couldn't make sense of how to change the song anymore. It was too fucking hot.

I had to get through this. I just had to keep driving as long as I could. The traffic would let up soon, and maybe then my air conditioner might blow cold again, or I could at least get some airflow through the windows.

That song was really getting to me. Just too fucking heavy right now. I was starting to cry; even my tears felt dry and dehydrated. I was feeling so far away from my dreams, so far from everything I thought I should have. I tried so hard, and yet here I was, boomeranging back to exactly where I was before. I was going to be a useless failure forever.

I took a glance at myself in the rear view mirror and quickly pulled my eyes away. In that split second, with the number the heat had done on my makeup, I saw myself looking like a melted wax sculpture, or some kind of early 2000s J-Horror cursed ghost. It was really hitting me just how wrong everything felt. And every time I even thought about putting on a different song, everything felt worse and worse, and nothing felt harder than changing to a different song. It felt like the song was taking over, and it was punishing me for trying to resist it.

But that couldn't be true. This heat was really getting to me, that's all it was. I had to focus on the road. The traffic was starting to move faster. I tried to remember to take deep breaths to calm myself. This was the same drive I'd taken like a million times. Nothing was wrong about it. It was just the heat.

My eyes fell on that slack-jawed beaver again. Another Buc-ee's billboard. Why did they have so many? I could swear the beaver looked a little different on this one, though. He didn't look as slack-jawed and out of it as he normally did—there was something a little knowing in his eyes. It was less of a smug type of knowing look and more one of concern. I couldn't help but feel he knew I was suffering somehow. But that couldn't be right. The logo was always the same.

NEED TO COOL OFF? the billboard read.

I chuckled to myself. I sure did. Way to hit the nail on the head, beaver.

Okay, I'd stop in a little while. But right then, I had to keep moving.

Before I passed the billboard, from the corner of my eye, I was sure I saw the beaver wink.

I sat up as straight as I could. My skin was so stuck to the seat that it felt like pulling off a Band-Aid. I gritted my teeth through the pain and put my hands at a perfect 10 and 2 on the steering wheel. I gripped the wheel until my knuckles were white, like I was trying to use it to pull myself back to reality.

My mind started to drift. My stomach rumbled and I saw steam pouring off the pavement, like steam coming off reheated food. It made me think of being back at my parents' house. I saw us having a meal after I got there. We sat at the old table, with plates full of Kroger rotisserie chicken, gritty mashed potatoes, and soggy green beans.

"I was talking to Michelle today," my mom said, oddly pointed.

"Your sister? How's she doing?" my dad said, in that same way he always did.

"She's good," she replied, followed by an awkward pause. "You know, Cody's still doing great at Google."

Fucking Cody. My cousin. The family's golden boy, despite all his bigoted bullshit. It had been a couple of years since I'd talked to him, ever since I chewed him out for getting my name wrong—obviously on purpose—for the millionth time. But I was being too hard on him, my family thought.

My mom looked straight at me with a gaze that felt as uncomfortably warm as the steam off the rotisserie chicken and continued. "You should talk to him, Cleo. Maybe he could get you a job there. You know, as a company, they're very, um, accepting."

I blinked until I was out of my head and back to reality. This heat was making my daydreams way too vivid; it had been like I was actually there, like I'd shifted in time, in reality. I switched into the right lane, just in case. There was another billboard ahead.

That fucking beaver.

This time he looked smug to me. The concern was gone and he was all arrogant eyes and too-toothy grin.

IT'S ALWAYS COOL INSIDE, CLEO.

I felt so certain that's what it said, but there was no way the billboard had my name on it. I drove past before I could get another good look, so I couldn't be sure, but I had to be imagining it. This heat really was driving me insane. It had to be.

And this song. I couldn't take it anymore. I focused as hard as I could on the act of picking up my phone and changing the song. It felt like I was moving through quicksand. The seat felt like it was burning my skin. But I had to keep on. Finally, I got my hand on my phone and the screen lit up.

"In Dreams – Roy Orbison (∞ Repeat Version)" it read at the center of the screen.

Above that was a notification, from the old DAMSync prototype app. *You're on track, Cleo!* it told me, followed by a winking emoji and a thumbs up emoji. After that, the text continued. *Estimated time to optimal outcome: 42 minutes.*

I was so startled, I dropped my phone onto the floorboard. I'd deleted everything DAMSync from my phone. I didn't even remember coding those emojis in there. None of this made any sense.

I looked up and saw another Buc-ee's billboard. The beaver's teeth were jagged in his too-toothy grin, and his eyes narrowed with menace.

WE'RE TOGETHER IN DREAMS.

My vision started to go dark. The last thing I remembered was hearing Roy Orbison's voice. "It's too bad that all these things, can only happen in my dreams…"

WHEN I WOKE up, I was still in the driver's seat of my car, parked in what looked like a huge parking lot. There were just spots all full of cars all around me. At first, I thought it might be some kind of hallucination, but as the fog lifted from my brain, the cars remained, and I started to notice people walking to and from their cars. I had no idea where I was, how I'd gotten there, or how long I'd been out. I didn't feel injured, and my car still looked to be in one piece.

What happened?

I felt on the verge of heat exhaustion. My skin felt like it was drowning in sweat, but everything inside felt dry like old forgotten cotton. I was sure I looked as disgusting as I felt, so sure that I couldn't bring myself to look in the mirror.

I picked up my phone off the passenger seat and looked at the time. I'd been out for about a half hour. My music player wasn't on the lock screen. But, there was another DAMSync notification.

Congratulations, Cleo! Optimal outcome imminent! the notification read, followed by the same winking emoji and thumbs up emoji. When I tried to swipe the notification away, the screen was filled with a large blinking thumbs up emoji that I definitely did not code into the original app.

I started laughing, my dehydrated body spasming as I lost too much control. "Yep, real fucking optimal!" I said out loud once I regained some composure.

It was time to try to figure out what was going on. I put my phone in my shorts pocket and got out of the car. I felt like I was made of lead. I looked around, trying to get my bearings, and when I saw it, I started laughing all over again.

The beaver.

I was in the Buc-ee's parking lot.

Well, there was no use staying out in the heat. I'd already gone this far into the weirdness. I walked toward the entrance on slow, heavy, wobbly legs. Outside the sliding doors, there was a large sculpture of the beaver. He was making a thumbs up gesture. Did he usually make that gesture?

"Hey, buddy," I said as I passed him and went through the doors. A part of me thought I saw some recognition in his eyes. A part of me saw the eyes following me.

I didn't think anything on Earth had ever felt better than the air conditioning did once I walked into Buc-ee's. I paused right inside the store and basked in it. The air conditioning was so cold, so deliciously cold, my body felt lighter and more energetic in an instant. I knew I still didn't look great, but I felt a million times better. After a few moments, I walked a bit further into the store, and it was then that I heard it playing over the store's loudspeaker.

"A candy-colored clown they call the sandman…"

My heart started beating faster. Not only had the song found me again, but now, something sounded strange about it. I couldn't put my finger on it, but something was off about it, like it was a second or two out of time or bent or…something. Just be overheated brain playing tricks on me, though. Right? It's not like it was so weird to hear an old country song at Buc-ee's.

Right?

My eyes fell on the huge refrigerators across the store holding every kind of cold drink available in Texas. That's what I needed. I needed to get some water in me. I was so dehydrated that nothing made sense. Just some water, and I could make sense of all of this. I walked as fast as I could to the refrigerators. I wanted to run, but I didn't want to seem too weird. I didn't think I had ever wanted anything as much as I wanted a cold drink right then. When I reached the refrigerators, I found myself overwhelmed for a few seconds. It was the choices. Water was water until you stood in front of a fridge like this. How many different brands of bottled water and sports drinks were there?

Out of the corner of my eye, I noticed the faintest flash of green light. My eyes reflexively moved to where I thought the light was coming from, but there didn't seem to be any light there—just some 1.5 liter bottles of electrolyte-enhanced ionized alkaline purified water that looked cold and delicious. That was exactly what I needed. I opened the glass door, and the cold air that blasted out felt as delicious as the bottle of water I was going for looked. I grabbed the bottle and barely got the refrigerator door closed before I opened the bottle and started chugging it down right there. Right after I finished it, I noticed that same song starting over, sounding still weirdly out of time, Orbison's voice drawling a little. It was almost as if two recordings of the song were playing at the same time that didn't quite sync up.

"A candy-colored clown they call the sandman…"

My heart started to beat fast again, and I knew I had to get the hell out of this place.

I turned and started to run, then slammed into some poor red-shirted soul restocking Beaver Nuggets.

"Sorry," I muttered as the Buc-ee's employee turned to look at me.

When I saw his face, I couldn't believe my eyes. "Jason?!"

He stared at me with not even a flicker of recognition. He was expressionless, didn't even acknowledge that I'd shouldered him. Maybe it wasn't Jason. Except…the longer I looked at him, the more convinced I became. It was him. It was my old friend, who'd abandoned me for some amazing tech job. "Jason, what the fuck are you doing here?"

"Excuse me?" he said, then moved to continue restocking the Beaver Nuggets.

I couldn't believe this. After all this time and after everything we'd been through together, why was he treating me like this? "Jason, come on. It's me, Cleo. I know, I look like shit, but you've seen me look a lot worse. Why are you acting like this?"

Jason turned just for a moment, just long enough to glare at me with confusion before returning once again to the Beaver Nuggets. "I have to restock the nuggets…" He spoke without inflection, without emotion. Just kept adding bags of nuggets to the rack.

A rush of heat spread through me; different to the dry heat outside. This was pure rage. Before I knew it, I pushed him and he toppled over with strange ease. I stepped back, hands over my mouth, and began to apologize, but before I could, I heard a voice behind me.

"Is there something wrong?" the voice said.

I turned around and found myself looking straight at the Buc-ee's beaver, or rather, someone dressed in a mascot costume of him. Despite the silly costume, there was something oddly intimidating about the beaver's presence.

"Uh, no, I guess not," I stammered. "Just thought I saw someone I knew, but I guess I…"

The beaver gave me a stern look and spoke again, his voice clear and unmuffled despite the mask he wore. "We don't take kindly to people assaulting our team members."

I swallowed hard, and as if I needed more reason to be afraid, the beaver smiled big enough for me to see that it had very real, very jagged teeth. As soon as I saw those teeth, I ran for the door, my body reacting before my brain could tell me that wasn't a fucking costume.

I didn't get far before two more red-shirted Buc-ee's employees grabbed me. I tried to struggle out of their grasp, tried to call for help—there had been people around before, right? Now the place was empty. Just me, the two staff grabbing at me, and that fucking beaver. I saw the employees' faces, and I couldn't believe my eyes.

They were both Jason.

I saw the beaver swaggering toward me with the original Jason beside it. "And now you're shoplifting, too," the beaver drawled in a low, menacing tone. "I expected more from you, Cleo."

My adrenaline spiked and I was on autopilot again. I broke free of the two staff members with a move I vaguely remembered learning in a self-defense class I'd taken years ago, kneed the nearest one in the groin, and bolted in the opposite direction. The staff members tended to each other while the beaver ran after me, but I was faster than he was. Since we'd been in front of the door, I was headed deeper into the store, but it was better than nothing. I burst through a door labeled STAFF ONLY, with the beaver's face taunting me from between the words.

The area behind the door was stark and gray. There were no decorations except random boxes everywhere. I could still hear the Roy Orbison song. It was quieter, but somehow even more warbly. There was a hallway ahead of me, lined with identical red doors. When I stopped to look around, my head started to spin. I was so tired. Still, I had to keep moving. I ran down the hallway, toward the door at the end of it. That had to be the exit, right? The door was heavy, which seemed like a good sign. I pushed it open as hard as I could and braced for more of that relentless heat, but it never came.

Instead, I was in a massive high-ceilinged room that appeared to be a high-tech factory, but smelled rotten. People in clean room suits were working on an assembly line with their backs to me. A large portrait of the beaver took up one wall. Over the sound of Roy Orbison, I heard strange crackling sounds that reminded me of insects. I backed out of the room as quickly as I could. No one here could help me, and my body was feeling heavier by the second. It took almost all of my strength to keep the door from slamming.

Back in the hallway, I hid behind a stack of boxes and took my phone out of my pocket. The screen still blinked with the thumbs-up emoji. I couldn't even tell if I had service. I tried with shaky hands to get it off the screen, to restart my phone, to get it to do anything, but nothing worked. Just then, I heard voices.

"Don't worry, boys, there's no way she could have made it that far," the beaver said.

Shit.

I wobbled toward the nearest of the red doors and tried it, but of course, it was locked. My heartbeat was getting so loud I could barely concentrate. I tried another door. It opened into what looked like a break room. There was a woman in there wearing a Buc-ee's employee uniform eating a sandwich. When she raised her eyes to look at me, I saw she looked just like me. My ears started ringing loudly. The woman put her sandwich down and stood up.

I felt someone grab me from behind. It was one of the staff members who looked like Jason. I almost managed to break free and run again, but the woman lunged at me and pushed me toward the Jason, flipping me around in the process. The two of them grabbed me tightly, and I saw the beaver walking toward me with another Jason. I kept trying to struggle free, but the closer the beaver came, the harder it became to move. I barely managed to sputter out a "How…" before my mouth wouldn't move either.

The beaver smirked, giving me another tiny glimpse of those teeth. "There you go. I knew you were a feisty girl, so I put out that special bottle of water just for you. It's going to make everything so much easier."

I was desperate to run, desperate to scream, desperate to do anything to be far away from whatever the fuck was going on here. But there was nothing I could do except stare at this creepy beaver and the face of my old best friend.

The beaver nodded at the staff members holding me. "Do y'all wanna help me take her back now?"

My eyes closed and everything went black. The last thing I remember seeing is my phone on the floor where I dropped it in the struggle, its screen now blinking with an enormous winking face emoji, and the sound of that song over the loudspeaker.

"If I cry, I remember that you said goodbye."

I'M SITTING IN the break room eating my pulled pork sandwich, just as I do every day. I can't remember a day when I didn't had a pulled pork sandwich for lunch. This time, it takes me 10 minutes and 51 seconds to eat it. I frown. 51 seconds too many. Not optimal. The Beaver Nuggets need me.

Quickly, I run to the bathroom. I look in the mirror, then take off my Buc-ee's hat. Some strands of hair were falling loose from the bun I'd put my hair into that morning. I was already running late, but I can't risk hair getting into the Beaver Nuggets. They can't be corrupted like that. I carefully redo my hair, reapply my lipstick, and wash my hands. Now it's time to get back to work.

I walk out and see the beaver walking down the hallway. Oh, my dear sweet beaver.

"Working hard or hardly working?" the beaver says with a chuckle.

I smile. "Oh, you know."

"Oh, I sure do!" the beaver says.

We look at each other for a moment. I think to walk away, since I need to get back to work, but something is missing.

"A candy-colored clown they call the sandman," the beaver sings in its mellifluous tenor.

I smile. There it is. "Tiptoes to my room every night," I continue.

"Just to sprinkle stardust and to whisper," the beaver sings.

The beaver and I join our voices for the next line. "Go to sleep. Everything is alright."

THE EMOJI CHALLENGE

Niko Lapidus

THE EMOJI CHALLENGE

NIKI LAPIDUS

RAIN WAS STUCK.

Their eyes, a warm chocolate brown that might have been called pretty if not so bloodshot, danced across the computer screen, the harsh blue glare making their eyes water. Still, Rain kept looking. They had found that the best way to deal with being stuck was almost always to buckle down and just work. Dig in the dirt enough, and you might find diamonds. But after around fifteen minutes of fruitless scanning on true crime forums, hoping for something creepy-crawly enough that they could submit before their deadline slammed down like a guillotine, Rain had to admit that this blog post might be a bit late.

So, Rain shut off the monitor, trying to blink exhaustion away. They looked around their side of the cramped room, Steve still dozing on his side. Steve made for a good roommate. He wasn't much in the way of conversation, but at least he paid his share of rent—even when Rain couldn't, which was more often than both of them would have liked— and kept things clean, which Rain rarely did.

Rain spun in their swivel chair, the wheel catching up against a sock marooned from the drawer. Case in point. Rain's side of the room could be better, but it was cozy. A few sock puppets lying on the unmade bed.

A cursed puppet, maybe? No, it's been done.

Besides, Rain didn't do crappy horror like that. They preferred to operate…with class. The rest of the room, save for the sock puppets, offered up little inspiration for something. Two flags hung on the walls, haphazard—a large rainbow pride flag and a Dade College pennant.

"Go, Sharks," Rain said, voice sounding like someone had shoved a back scratcher down their throat. It sort of tasted like that as well. Rain reached for a water bottle, and as they did, their elbow bumped into a copy of *Carrie* lying on the bed, which fell to the dorm floor with a thump.

Steven stirred in his bed in response, but Rain was occupied, googling *Snake incident death scary story true.* A few things popped up and Rain sifted through them, but as far as Rain could tell, there were no possessed/rabid/cursed snakes out there. And if there were, someone has probably gotten to them already. They bookmarked a page about a four-headed snake found in India, just in case they couldn't think of anything better.

"Shit," Rain murmured. The window next to their desk rattled in the night breeze.

Rain slumped back in their chair, ran a hand through thick, soft hair that might have needed some shampoo, and thought about how they had gotten to this point. A few months earlier, their little horror blog had been in the top 10 most visited LinkedIn blogs. They had written a great article on the biology of vampires. Rain couldn't care less about the non-blood-sucking and sometimes sparkly aspects of vampires, but as it happened, their readers did, and they had gotten more views on that one article than all of their other posts combined. Their fall from relative glory had been swift, losing readership not with a bang but with a whimper. The only thing that popped out nowadays when they googled *Rain's Nightmare Emporium,* something they were addicted to, was a comment on R/Blogs praising *Emporium.* That was sort of cool, even though that comment had gotten downvoted to hell.

Since that one article, Rain had resumed hunting for that white whale of a story that would elevate *Emporium* to stardom. Among the topics they had looked into were a copy of Dante's *Inferno* that could open a portal to hell, HP Lovecraft's haunted mansion, and a woman who had been feeding people to her pet snakes. The book had just been a library copy that somebody had spilled ketchup on, making it illegible but not extradimensional. The Lovecraft in question had been a *Harold* Lovecraft, not at all related to the author, and the haunting he was complaining about had proven to be nothing more than a starving raccoon.

As for the snake-lady, that one was true (though it had only been one guy, and according to reports, the snake didn't even eat him). Unfortunately, some Next-door group had jumped all over it before Rain could. Leaving Rain optionless, and with a deadline closing, they were about to lose a sponsorship deal with a local tea brand, actually called TeaBrand, something that Rain found painfully unfunny. Rain was never clear on whether they were sponsoring TeaBrand or vice versa, but it wouldn't matter. The folks over at TeaBrand had made it clear. One more missed deadline, and their deal was done. Nobody wanted to sponsor/be sponsored by a blogger who had regular readers in the double digits and couldn't meet deadlines. Leaving Rain working the graveyard shift.

Graveyard shift…

Rain sprang up in their chair, inspiration hitting them hard. If the murky yellow bulb above their head still worked, it might have almost switched on. Rain slid off the chair, or maybe just fell off of it—either way, adrenaline ensured there was no difference.

Right now, Rain's uncle, Andrew Saint Peter, was working at his late-night diner, Saint Eater's. Uncle Andy always had the best stories. Anyone who worked at a diner open at two in the morning always had a good story. Maybe it was a patron who had an empty look in his eyes and paid with a blood-spattered twenty. Maybe someone found a human tooth in their taco. Either way, if it happened to anyone, it had to have happened to Uncle Andy.

Rain clicked on his contact, scrolled past fishing photos he had sent Rain and received a thumbs-up emoji for, and gave him a FaceTime call. The line rang once, twice, then Uncle Andy's face filled the camera, yellowed but friendly tombstone teeth flexed into a smile. "Rainy? Not that I don't mind the call, but what are you doing up so late?" Behind him, rain lashed dirty windows, while neon light from a sign glowing ST. EATER'S bounced across the linoleum floor.

Rain shrugged, sinking back into their chair. "I'm, you know, writing. I was hoping you could help me out. You always have good tips."

Uncle Andy smiled, but it seemed forced. There was a flicker of lightning in the window behind him, then a massive crash of thunder. "Right now, Rainy?" It was only then that Rain noticed it was not just lightning flashing behind him. Outside, flickering dancing patterns of red and blue, and under the scream of the storm, Rain heard the howl of a siren. "I, uh, have a work thing."

Rain put a hand over their mouth. They imagined they must have looked like a lady in a silent film, about to faint. "Wait, what's going on at Eater's? Did someone get hurt?"

Uncle Andy nodded, then waved someone in the background away. "You talk to the guys, Tess. I'm busy right now." He turned back to Rain, face grim. Normally, he was a jolly, pink-faced Santa type, a man who had always had a sweet for Rain when they were little and always had a joke for them now. But today, he looked…haunted. Cheered for a moment by Rain's call, but the cheer was fading back into something darker. His eyes looked shell-shocked. "Listen, Rain, I've got to go. What happened was, some kid on the night shift was taking a break, and he, uh… Ah, *fuck.*" Uncle Andy swallowed, his Adam's apple at its zenith. "He cut himself by accident. Badly."

Uncle Andy's camera bobbed as he looked around the room, chatter coming from EMTs behind him. One of them had the front of his rain jacket painted with dark red liquid. Rain felt their stomach lurch. They had seen a lot more blood than most in movies and comics, but this was so much worse. It looked like a splatter painting in one color, like blood had been pumped out of a hose. Before rain could take a closer look, Uncle Andy turned back to them. He was just as sick about all this as Rain.

"Still don't know what happened. My first thought, he was playing with a knife or something, but nothing sharp near him, not even a fork." Uncle Andy scratched a scraggly brown beard, flecked with breadcrumbs. "Before he went on break, he said he was gonna do… I don't know, a game or something. One of those online things?"

"A challenge?" Rain asked. There were all sorts of those challenges that floated around the internet, bobbing up in the vast, trendy ocean. Dances, trick shots, filters. Nothing that could ever…do that.

Uncle Andy nodded. "Yeah. The 'emoji challenge.' I don't know. Bye-bye, Rainy."

"Bye, Uncle Andy." The phone shut off as the call ended, the light disappearing from the room. And Rain was left in the dark. They craned their head up to look at the lightbulb, murky with time, filled with bugs. "Ding," Rain whispered.

Steven snored on the other side of the room.

FIVE MINUTES LATER, Rain had a jacket on over their *Looney Toons* printed pajamas and was walking outside, laptop and phone in a bag at their side. They found a soft, dry patch of grass, then sat down and flipped open the laptop. Rain worked best outside, and it was a nice, quiet night. Besides, they didn't want to wake up Steven with some blaring video. Rain was prepared to do plenty of research on whatever this emoji challenge might be, diving deep into the annals of every platform out there.

It didn't even take them a minute to find it. The first thing to pop up was an article labeled: **WHAT YOU NEED TO KNOW ABOUT THE INTERNET'S NEW 'EMOJI CHALLENGE**. Rain placed their notebook beside the laptop and began to take notes. They'd write out an outline longhand, then type up the story in the morning. They'd sleep until at least noon, but right now, adrenaline and more than one monster would be enough to carry them all the way to the finish line. A thousand or so words on some dumb trend.

Easy.

Maybe it wouldn't be their best work, but it would be enough to keep them afloat until a better topic came their way. Besides, research was easy enough. So far, what Rain had found out was that it was one of those 'cursed dare' creepypasta things. You were supposed to do it late at night—Rain already had that covered—and you needed a phone. What would happen was, you texted a certain number, 666—

Subtle.

666-542-3492. Then…something would respond. Sources differed. Some videos or bloggers said it was a ghost or a demon. Others thought it was some murderer or escaped asylum patient. Rain suspected it was either a chatbot that someone had set up or somebody manning the line, clout-chasing and trying to build mystique for their dumbass little urban legend. Either way, it was working. Rain felt a shiver crawl up their spine, but dismissed it as the cold of the night, and tugged at their jacket. They began typing on the computer.

There are lots of challenges out there, and a lot of them seem pretty dangerous to me. I'm sure we've all heard of the ice bucket challenge, which I've heard—Rain did a quick Google search—**has led to loss of consciousness in those taking heart medication while doing the challenge. One I just saw was the Corn Drill Challenge, where apparently, you eat corn that's spinning on a drill. Problem is, you might get teeth damage so bad you might as well pack up and move to London. Anyhow, with all this dangerous shit out there, something as innocuous as emojis might seem harmless. And yet, due to this new 'emoji challenge', people are for-real getting hurt. I've seen it happen myself, when a guy doing the challenge almost lost a hand.** Well, that was what it looked like from Rain's perspective, anyway. **Needless to say, when I heard about this through research, I decided to dig deeper on my own. Apparently, the emoji challenge is a step-by-step process to communicate with supernatural forces.**

1. It needs to be dark out to get in contact with the spirit.

2. You need to text this number: 666-542-3492.

3. Whatever emojis you text the spirit, they will come to life.

Rain shut down the computer. They had done enough research at this point. Now, it was time to get to the actual fieldwork. They produced a phone, clicked the side of a grimy pink case, and it came to life, showing a background of Rain typing at their desk, giving the camera the middle finger. Rain was just about to finish punching in the number.

Should I be doing this?

Rain had never believed in the supernatural. They knew for a fact that they would cheer if they saw a UFO or found out their dorm was haunted. But that was wishful thinking, and at the end of the day, Rain was a realist. Of course, they didn't believe this number would call up malign spirits. And yet, it sort of felt like that. Perhaps it was just the power of suggestion, reading about it while sitting out there alone, in the black of night, but Rain felt almost as if they were being warned to turn back. Their finger hovered over the SEND button for their first message—*Are you a ghost?*—but refused to go downwards. Around Rain, the breeze rustled in the night air, fluttering around them like the wide black wings of a crow, croaking out into the starless night sky.

In Rain's mind's eye, a warning flashed, not a haunted house sign twisted with rusty spikes nor a message of dripping blood. Rain pictured more of a grey text message, bordered by grinning jaundiced faces, ghoulish and black eyed, and between them, *All hope abandon, ye who enter here.*

Power of suggestion, Rain reminded themself. That, or a STOP sign put up by some primitive instinct. The primal, lizard brain amygdala, between its dying gasps, had issued a warning to Rain that their modern brain, accustomed to everyday miracles that would give a lumbering *Homo Erectus* a heart attack, could not comprehend.

The finger lowered upon SEND, and the message appeared on the screen. For about a minute, no response. Rain had thought a GPT model would be faster, so it was probably somebody screwing around on a landline. Then, in a blink, bubbles appeared on the other end. Someone was sending a response.

666-542-3493

Are YOU a ghost?

Rain chuckled a little, ill at ease. This didn't sound like anyone Rain had ever texted, nor did it sound newly generated. It was like something trying to imitate human speech…and failing.

"No," they wrote back.

666-542-3493

Good to know. ☺. What's your name?

Rain's thumbs, rapidly working at the miniature keyboard, paused for a second. This person was asking for their name? So that implied the entire emoji challenge was some data-theft thing. Rain didn't want to be doxxed. But neither did they want to lose this story, unfolding like origami before Rain's disbelieving eyes. "Steven," Rain wrote.

666-542-3493

YOUR NAME IS RAIN.

The text appeared on the screen less than a second after Rain had finished.

Rain half-gasped; a low rattle of surprise came from the back of their throat. They had given a fake name. They had taken precautions. But this bot, person, *whatever* had IDed them. So, fuck the story. Fuck *Rain's Nightmare Emporium*. They'd find a haunted house to write about. Maybe just ask ChatGPT. Either way, this little game was over and done. Rain switched off the phone, then threw it to the ground as if it were ablaze.

Except the phone didn't fall from their hands. It just stayed there, hanging by the fingertips of each hand except the thumbs, like there was glue on Rain's fingers. Another message illuminated the black surface of the phone.

666-542-3493

Are you ready to do the EMOJI CHALLENGE? 😼

Rain heard the noisemaker's sound. Not an effect coming from the phone, but as if the air was humming in concert with the text.

Rain yelped in sudden instinct, pulling away from the glow of the phone. Their voice was the only sound in the dead of night save for the crickets, but it still sounded shrill and small. They beat their hands onto the ground, swung their hands back and in the air, doing everything they could to shake off the phone.

Nothing.

It was suspended in the constant position of Rain's response. Rain yanked their hands away, but nothing worked. The phone wouldn't move. Another message popped up, and Rain paused their frantic thrashing to look at it. There was another finger pointing forward at Rain, and then, a yellow emoji face, twisted up in an exaggerated wince of pain.

Rain screamed. White-hot sheets of agony raced up their arms, starting from their hands locked onto the phone and blasting into their body.

Rain thought they had gotten hurt before. One time as a kid, Mom had been making spaghetti and accidentally scalded Rain. Years later, Rain had been at the gym and dropped a 35-pound barbell on their foot. Then, a few months later, when their foot was healed, a knee had been dislocated.

Every time something like that happened, it felt like the end times to Rain. Now, those were bee stings compared to this. Rain's back arched and legs hammered at the grass beneath them as they tore their hands back and forth, droplets of blood blooming to life as their fingertips nearly tore off their hands. One fingernail, before painted with blue and now painted with red, almost tore loose as a ravine went through the fingernail, welling with blood. Rain's eyes bulged, sight disappearing in flashes of white light. Rain's throat felt like it was being clawed as they screamed and screamed and—

Stopped.

The pain was gone now, just as fast as it had come. Rain half-gasped, half-sobbed, shaking. Their hands were still stuck, unwillingly poised to respond to the texts that they just now noticed were popping up. All of them read the same thing.

666-542-3493

Are you ready to do the EMOJI CHALLENGE?

Rain's breaths were shaky, but they managed to growl in frustration, angry tears welling in their eyes. Of all people, this had to have happened to them. But…there might be a silver lining, one now glinting in Rain's mind. This was no urban legend or internet dare.

This was *real.*

Rain had discovered an actual spirit. And even if nobody believed them, the story was great. Rain could tell. It knocked all of that ghost hunter bullshit out of the park. And if Rain had to play the game, they'd get something out of it. They'd make sure. Another message had popped up, a break in the endless stream of identical questions.

666-542-3493

Ready to PLAY? Or do you want MORE? 🫠

The melting face emoji smiled at them, even as its face dissolved and poured on the ground. In Rain's head, a vision of themself flashed—not as a person, but as a gelatinous blob, flesh sloughing off the bones like tender meat, eyeballs bursting into pools of white jelly shot through with burst red veins. Rain saw their entire body popping like a blister and foul smelling, gelatinous blood bursting out of what used to be human, as bloated maggots, fat with pus and blood, swam through the soup of what used to be Rain and crows descended from the slate black sky, gorging themselves on Rain's melted corpse.

That was, at the very least, an unpleasant thing to think about, and hopefully not a threat 666-542-3493 could actually carry out.

666-542-3493

I'm waiting

Rain fumbled with the keys, typing out a response as fast as they could. "I'll play, but you need to answer some questions first." A thumbs up was the only response that they got, but it was better than more melted faces. "What are you?" Rain typed again, the phone screen smudging with blood with each tap. Rain's fingertips still stung. After they sent the text, Rain scrolled upwards, then began to take rapid screenshots of the conversation. They needed to document this. This was their Bigfoot, their Loch Ness monster, their very own figure in the back of the photograph. This could propel *Emporium*… No, it could propel Rain to stardom. And all they had to do was play a game of Russian roulette, played with smiley faces instead of bullets.

It took a little while for the bubbles to pop into an actual answer, like the person on the other end was considering the answer.

666-542-3493

Here's how THE EMOJI CHALLENGE is played. You send me the SYMBOLS. They become real.

"Symbols?" Rain responded. Their heart beat faster and faster. Whether it was fear or excitement, Rain themself couldn't say. *This is my white whale.* "I thought it was just emojis?"

666-542-3493

EMOJIS are the same thing as SYMBOLS. Hieroglyphs. Pentagrams. Runes. A shrugging emoji. I've played my game for a long time, RAIN. Lately I've been getting a lot of traffic.

"What are you?" Rain asked again. "A ghost? A demon?" They had given up any ideas they might have had about this being just a person with a cruel sense of humor. Another screenshot was snapped.

666-542-3493

I'm the VOICE on the other end of the line. I'm the guy the Egyptians AND the Norse AND the cavemen before them CHOSE to play the game.

666-542-3493

YOU chose, and now YOU need to play.

Seconds passed, then a minute. Then another. Rain kept typing, deleting, trying to think of what to write.

666-542-3493

YOU CHOSE.

666-542-3493

YOUCHOSE.

The phone vibrated and buzzed.

666-542-3493

YOUCHOSEYOUCHOSEYOUCHOSE.

Cracks began to run through the screen. A tiny shard of glass sliced into Rain's fingertip.

"What do you want me to do?"

A text dinged in response.

666-542-3493

Play the GAME. Do the CHALLENGE. Send it to me.

Rain cleared their throat, then spoke with text-to-speech, the words forming in the textbox. This would be faster, and Rain felt being slow would be dangerous. "After I do that, can you answer a question?" Rain felt the same way crisis negotiators must have felt when a terrorist had a hostage. *But there is a hostage, Rain. Yourself.*

666-542-3493

Send me the EMOJI, the SYMBOL, the YELLOW pulp, SEND IT TO ME, and I'll think about it. But pick. Pick and CHOOSE❗❗❗❗❗

Rain nodded, stomach churning. A memory of the EMT, rain jacket covered in blood and dangling strands of skin, flashed in their vision, alongside a melted body. They scanned the wall of different emojis, searching for an answer, their heart pumping with adrenaline. The thing had said that the emojis would become real. But what did it mean by that? Rain sent the thing a dog, and suddenly, there would be a dog in front of them?

666-542-3493

CHOOSE. CHOOSE or… 😵

It didn't take much thinking on Rain's part to figure out what that meant.

They scrolled through the emojis, frantic. What would be the least dangerous? The crying one? No, Rain didn't want to have some sort of breakdown if they picked that. The bucktoothed, bespectacled nerd emoji? Would glasses just appear on Rain's face? No, not that one. Rain knew they should shy away from anything that looked like it might mess with their body. At that moment, Rain was considering the wedding ring… Would it just appear in their hand? Or would something else happen?

3. Next to the message was a bomb emoji, and next to it, two string emojis, then a flame.

"Shit!" Rain yelped. What to pick, what to pick, what to pick… "Okay… Heart, no, clown, no, skull, definitely not…"

2. One of the strings was gone, and the flame was one step closer to the bomb.

Rain sucked in breath, fingers trembling, moving rapidly across the digital keys. What to do, what to do…

1. The flame was right next to the bomb, and though it was just colored pixels, Rain realized that the phone was growing hot and shaking. They could feel blisters beginning to form.

Rain didn't have time to think. They just acted, punching down the first smiley-face that they saw and clicking send. But not in time.

BANG, the phone read, hot as if it was over a flame. Rain threw themself backwards as they shoved themself away from the blast, as there was a fiery pop.

Rain opened their eyes, expecting to see nothing but ash and their own blood and gore. What they saw, instead, was colorful confetti, drifting down to the ground in front of their face. A party popper glowed cheerfully on the screen.

666-542-3493

Good CHOICE.

Rain sighed in relief…but even as their face was sagging down in exhaustion, something else happened. Their lips and teeth pulled themselves upwards, the edges of their mouth straining at the skin, forcing them to smile wider and wider. Rain could feel their chapped lips beginning to split, and on the screen they could see their smile, huge and white and terrible, like the rigor mortis of a corpse. The smile hurt, but Rain *couldn't stop* smiling. They tried to speak, to scream, but when their mouth opened, it just pulled wider and wider, an impossible gesture of hideous, fevered joy.

And then the pressure stopped. Rain's grin slackened, and their burning facial muscles seemed to melt. "What the fuck was that?" Rain yelled, typing words with their voice into the text box. "Exclamation mark," they added, swore again, then clicked SEND.

666-542-3493

The symbol YOU CHOSE. The smile.

Rain raised their sweaty hands to run through their hair, but the phone was still in their grasp, and it knocked against their forehead. Their face still hurt…but they had plenty of screenshots at this point. They had the story. Besides, the smile-trick had been painful, but it was better than what had happened before. *And a small price to pay for encountering a real demon, and even better, getting to post the story.* Even if nobody believed them, this was still fantastic as a work of fiction. With the right branding, Rain could create a new urban legend, something people would talk about around a campfire. "Can I ask you a question before my next choice?"

666-542-3493

ASK away, FRIEND.

So they were friends now? Well, better for it to consider Rain a friend than an enemy. Anyhow, Rain was starting to figure out the rules. This thing wasn't exactly responsive to questions, but Rain had figured out how the game worked. If you played the game, things happened to you, things severe, to say the least. But if you played it right, sending the creature the emojis, it played nice. You could ask questions, but you needed to play the game. If you played the game, it wouldn't or perhaps *couldn't* harm you. It was structured so that both parties involved in the exchange had to play nice. Rain could work with that.

"What is your name? Where did you come from? And are you, well, real? I'm not hallucinating this?"

666-542-3493

That's THREE questions.

"Then you can just answer one."

It took a long time for the creature to reply.

666-542-3493

To name me is to DEFY me. To INSULT me. I am not NAMED, it goes against my very nature. ☹ I am called the MAGNUM INNOMINANDUM. I came from the WHERE. The space BETWEEN space. I am half as real as YOU are, half REAL and half less and more than UNREAL. This is not a DREAM, no more than all of life is a DREAM.

Rain looked above, and noticed that the number now had a contact. Magnum Innominandum, and for the profile picture, a white cloud on a black field. This didn't tell Rain anything other than the fact that this Magnum Innominandum wasn't playing with a full deck here. Either that, or a different set of cards. Another message popped up, and Rain's heart skipped a beat when they saw the bomb emoji once more.

666-542-3493

You know the... 

"Clever," Rain muttered, then began scanning the screen. They could always pick the smile again… Painful, but not dangerous. But when they went to send it, they saw that the smiley face had a large X over it. They could only do each one once. Another text appeared, and the flame moved one space closer. The first thing their mind went to was the frowning face, but they remembered how the smile had hurt. They could find something better. Rain ran through their options until something caught their eye. A red-faced swearing emoji. Rain looked through their other choices, but none seemed quite as riskless as this one, even as the clock ran down. Babbling a few curses was bearable. The flame inched closer, but before the confetti or something worse could come, Rain sent the swearing face. Nothing happened.

And then, Rain's mouth hinged wide open, painfully wide, just as the smile had been. An invisible force wrenched down the jawbone, and Rain felt the muffled cracks of their own jaw fighting to expand around the words that came from Rain's unwilling voicebox. "*Vyragh!*" came the first word. "*Vyragh lechyirsh vantlestri! P'hapf mgha, sulrch mgha, shrorir mgha, yhrogah xylst shrkro h'hlaghf zrei zrei vantlestri Yeb andpha'hrk slrk yhrogah MH'PHAGHN MGHA HRE'LESQ QUESYRA ZREI VANTLESTRI VYRAGH! P'HAPF MGHA!*"

A trickle of blood traced its way down Rain's face. They didn't notice. They didn't stop the chanting, nor could they have if they wanted to. There was a mad ecstasy in the words spoken, as Rain was lost in the swirling sounds, written in the dark spaces between stars. In the grass below Rain, roots withered, moss blackened, and tiny critters scuttled away, before the words tore through what passed as auditory organs and turned their beetled heads to jelly, hot and shuddering beneath shells.

The words came on. "*Phra'P'Hyrgh, zrei zrei mgha fchu vantlestri! Nug vy'orch fhagn shoi droxel yrt'samar, v'reo vch'hcu, phraghf'M'lyirztz!*"

And then it stopped.

Rain came to, blinking light out of their eyes, though it was black as pitch in the night sky, even darker than it had been before, as if something had caused a star or two to wink out above. They looked down and saw that they were sitting in a circle of dried, brown grass. The circle went outwards, stretching across maybe fifty feet originating from Rain, and Rain could see that there was more than just a perfect circle.

Alien shapes spun out in whorls of pattern, hieroglyphs and letters that hurt to look at. Like a crop circle, Rain realized, and shuddered.

The memories of the dread words they had spoken were gone, blown away like dust in the wind. Rain couldn't have replicated a single syllable even if they had tried. And now, the swearing face emoji was Xed out, used up. Rain grimaced, trying to swish out a bitter taste in their mouth, and wiped a smear of red from their lip. They coughed violently, their body doubling over as their throat fought to get the last physical remnants of those words out.

They turned back to the screen at the sound of a fresh ping. One new message. The Magnum Innominandum had sent Rain another emoji, two hands clapping.

666-542-3493

WHAT will be your next one? I'm waiting.

Rain cleared their throat and coughed, a thick black liquid spattering across their lips, white shapes that writhed amongst the deep, torturous bile. Their dark eyes were bleary yet fiery and alive, glowing like volcanic rock in the blue light of the phone. Their hands were no longer locked in place on the keyboard, but it was no longer necessary. The device pulled them and held them better than any chains or super-glue could have. Across the case, lines twisted and broke off, shattering conventional geometry, arrow straight into the air, or dancing like smoke, a writhing mass around the flat, glowing blue-white screen.

Rain took another couple of screenshots, even though as they pressed the buttons, their own fingers dived into inky pits between the boundaries of the rubber. Then they spoke, the words forming on the screen without any action by them. Rubber tendrils crawled their way up Rain's arm. "I need to know more about the challenge. For my story.

You need to tell me!"

The phone buzzed, a violent tremble.

666-542-3493

That isn't part of the GAME. I don't like that.

"If you tell me more about the game," Rain countered, face shiny with sweat and blood and bile, "more people will play. You want that, don't you, Mr. Magnum?"

666-542-3493

Don't try to make ME play a game. I don't like THAT. I'M the one who makes the rules of the game. It's MY GAME! Mine, not yours!

The screen was slick with ice, and below the glowing white rectangle that was once the phone, rubber melted and ran, sliding up Rain's arm, reaching, reaching.

Rain clutched what remained of the phone tighter and tighter. Lines of agony shot through them, as their cracked and bleeding fingernails pressed into the broken glass, but they ignored it. They needed the story; they *needed* it. They had the pictures, but dammit, they could have so much more than that—but first, they had to get the fucking story. "One more emoji, but then you have to tell me more. You have to get me the story, you understand?!"

Thick white mist whirled around Rain, and in the mists, things moved, dark writhing shapes that skittered and swam through the thick white air. Rain saw the things, but their eyes, sweat dripping down in front of them, were focused on the phone, shaking and smoking and melting upwards. Their thumbs pressed down so hard into the screen that the glowing blue screen began to break, driving shards into their hands.

666-542-3493

Fine. ⚡ One more emoji. One more SYMBOL. And then, you will know. My secrets. My database will tell you, all the knowledge of the Great Old Ones. Octopus emoji. Eibon, Necronomicon, De Vermis Mysteriis. You will KNOW. KNOW it all. But you NEED TO PLAY THE GAME!

The words on the screen bubbled and fizzed against the cracked, obscured glass. Rain could barely see the screen, but that didn't matter. Their finger went down, clicking on the first face they could see. It never occurred to them, that there might be worse things than words or smiles. They realized, only after it had appeared in response, which emoji they had sent to the Magnum Innominandum. Eyes and mouth wide open on the yellow face. And on the top of the head, a yellow explosion ripping through the cartoonish head.

A deep throbbing came into the back of Rain's head, and all at once, they knew what was coming. Something hammered at their skull, pressure building, fighting to escape and winning. The phone dropped from their hands. Rain looked up towards the sky, cold and starless in the thick pulsing mist. Something seemed to move in the mist, something huge and fractaled beyond the limits of Rain's brain. Their eyes bulged with terror, and before they could scream, the back of their head shattered into a red explosion of grey, mutilated brain matter, white bone slicked with blood, and their eyeballs burst outwards, leaving their sockets as dripping red pits and the top of their head smashed like an egg with thick red yolk. Their mouth hung open, wide and confused.

It looked a lot like a smiley face.

The phone pinged once more, not that anyone could see it.

666-542-3493

GAME OVER.

SCULPTING

gaast

SCULPTING

GAAST

THE CEILING DOESN'T look so interesting anymore. I sit up, shake my head, and open a hookup app.

It's the sixth time I've come out to my friends. How was it the *hardest* time? The way their faces twisted ever so slightly, the changes in their demeanors, the subtle ways they tried to get out of addressing me, talking about me… They'll come around, I think. I don't know. I remember Chelsea saying some nasty things about it/its users.

I've been expecting texts ever since I got home. Words of support maybe or, more likely, repudiations. But I've gotten nothing. Nobody has anything to say. Maybe it's because it's my sixth go-round. And that's fair.

But what I need right now is to forget about them. I need to lose myself in someone else. Forget *me*. Work on pleasing somebody who I don't know. Someone who doesn't care that I'm a *thing*. Someone who just wants to use me.

Luckily, I have no shortage of interested parties. My body disgusts me, but it seems to attract handfuls of people, especially when they learn it belongs to a trans person—if a person I am. Chasers are fun to tease, if nothing else. And at least they make me feel *wanted*.

But what I *don't* want is to talk. I just want a quick fix. I want to go to someone's place and find them naked and hard and waiting for me. I don't care who they are or how they look. I just want to forget everything else that happened tonight.

Most of the people in my inbox are yappers, but there's a few promising leads. Like this guy, Samson76. Clearly a dad and clearly cheating on his wife. His opening line to me is a terse: "?"

ME

Then I follow up with:

ME

SAMSON76
Now.

ME

Before he even sends me his address, though, I'm off the couch and out the door.

IT TAKES ME a while to get there. I decided to jog the whole way. It's for the better. I don't think I'm sober yet.

He isn't too far from where I live. I was already going in the right direction by the time he sent me his location. At least something's going well tonight.

Samson76's house is a pleasant two-story building with a yard, a driveway, and a garage. A car sits outside; it looks like a station wagon. No lights are on upstairs. I knock on the door, then notice the doorbell and ring it.

Before I can even start to catch my breath, the door is open, and huge hands yank me inside. He wastes no time, pressing his mouth against mine and exploring my body with his paws.

He lets go of me for long enough to get me a glass of wine. He leads me into the living room, where he's helpfully laid a towel on the couch.

Samson76 sits me on his lap and has me drink my glass. It's a cheap red, but it's better than nothing. The more I drink, the more of my clothes he takes off, with one particular motion jarring me so roughly that I gasp. He rewards me with a powerful caress, and I melt against him.

My head is swimming, but only a little. His living room is nice. There's some pictures of him and his family, and one of him in a fishing boat, staring out across the water. He places a bottle of lube on the coffee table, next to a porcelain figurine of a rabbit.

He lifts me up. I take a look behind me and see the incredible heft of his cock, slick and shining, and my eyes pop. He smiles at me, then puts a finger to his lips.

"Be quiet, boy," he whispers. "My son's got school tomorrow."

WHEN HE WAS done with me, I rolled off of him onto the floor. He walked over me and tossed a fresh towel at me. I'm still lying here, staring at the ceiling. At least it's not mine.

Boy, he'd called me. *Boy*.

I feel around for my pants and fish my phone out of them. I have a message, but thankfully it's not from any of my friends. Well, it is, but my long-distance one, the one who's known for a while about my latest gender update.

ELENA

How'd it go?

ME
Bad.

ELENA
What happened?

ME
Tell you when I get home?

ELENA
You're still there?

ME
No, I'm… You know.

ELENA
😄

ME
This dude… 🥒➕➕➕. I want it.

ELENA
Didn't you already get it? 😜

ME
No. I mean, like… 🔪🥒🍽️🥒🥒

ELENA
You want *more*? You can have mine.

ME
Sure.

ELENA
lol

A loud thud comes from the kitchen. I wonder if he kicked something by accident. Or maybe he's working on opening another bottle of wine. Either way, I better get going. I don't want to spend any more time here.

I wipe myself off and start to gather my clothes when Samson76 reenters the living room. Blood is pouring down his legs. His dick isn't between them anymore. It's in his hands. I stumble backwards and fall onto my ass. He follows me down, spreads my legs, and shoves the base of his severed cock into my crotch. He presses it hard—and I can feel my skin break open, melt, accept his offering, seal itself around it. And my blood pours in.

When I look back at Samson76, he's unconscious in a pool of his own blood.

I throw on my clothes, bolt out the door, and run all the way back home.

As SOON AS I get home, I tear off my clothes and stare at my crotch in front of a mirror. It's still there. And it's on there good. I yank it, trying to tear it off. It went on so easily, I think, it must come off just the same. But no. All I manage to do is get myself hard.

What the fuck do I do?

I fumble for my phone. Elena's last message to me was sent twenty minutes ago. "You okay?"

How am I supposed to respond? Or act? Or think? Or *feel*?

For the first time, I'm grateful that Elena doesn't like to talk on the phone. Whatever I say to her, she won't hear the fear in my voice. But if that's what I'm thinking, then I need time. I need to process all this. I need to figure things out. So I just answer, "Home safe. Exhausted. Talk tomorrow."

I toss my phone away and shut my eyes tight.

It takes a while, but I eventually calm down. My breaths come easily, and my mind ceases to race. I open them and gaze quietly at my genitals. As expected, two dicks, sizes and colors mismatched. Looking at them now, I don't panic. My chest doesn't even tighten. They're just my dicks. Mine.

And I like it.

He called me *boy*, despite everything. No matter how clear I make it that I'm no such thing, my body will always be read in that one specific way. Actually, that's not true. Some of the people in my inbox clearly saw that I'm trans, but took that to mean that I'm a girl. And that's all I can be, one or the other, never neither, never both. This fact has always caused me to despise my body, from its slender frame, its defined musculature, its hair, its bones. But to say that others' apprehension of me is the true cause of that animosity would be to give strangers far too much power.

No.

The problem is that I cannot see my body as anything other than a man's. HRT would never help. It would end up being a woman's, or an androgyne's, or anything else, and it would always resolve back to one unfortunate, immutable truth. And *that* is the concept that has always made me revolt against my body, against its shape and form and movements and affordances and parts.

It took me until recently to distill all my dysphoria down to that root. As soon as I had the answer, I told Elena. "I don't understand," she said. "But in a way, I do."

It was the most wonderful thing anyone had ever said to me.

If Samson76 is dead, the police will come for me tomorrow, not long after his son gets up for school. They'll find his phone, figure out my identity, and take my prints off the wine glass. But they won't find anything on whatever he used to emasculate himself. They'll never think to check my crotch for his missing dick. And besides, I don't think anyone would believe that I could somehow overpower him and, without a struggle, lop off his—hah—manhood. I'm maybe a third of his size.

Otherwise, he'll be alive. His son will be no less traumatized, I'm sure. But Samson76 himself will protect me. He wouldn't want his wife knowing, would he? He'll tell her he got drunk and had an accident while making something to eat. I wonder if he'll have the wherewithal to hide my glass before the ambulance gets to him. I wonder if he'll ask me for him back?

I'm good. Nothing to worry about.

Even so, if danger comes, I think I have ways to get out of it. I touch my phone, feeling its coolness in the dark of my bedroom. I'm about to sleep, but I decide to give my hunch a try.

I start a text conversation with my own number.

ME

Suddenly, a pulling sensation yanks on the tip of my dicks. I check both. They've gotten longer. Fatter.

I can't help but smile.

"You hear about the dude who chopped off his own dick?"

Carter is sitting across from me in a local brunch place. He's the only one of my friends to contact me since last night. He's wearing a half-binder as a crop top, his favorite way to challenge *anyone* to give him a hard time about how he's dressed. So he's definitely in a good mood.

He invited me to breakfast because apparently he feels like shit about last night. "I should have been more supportive," he said. "Especially because you *rule*."

But we've both known Chelsea since middle school. She has this incredible power to radiate her mood to others, like she forces empathy onto us, but only for her. When she's happy, everyone's happy; when she's disturbed, everyone is. Carter and I in particular have gotten into enough arguments over this ability of hers that he and I decided in high school that we're not allowed to use her as an excuse for the ways we may treat one another.

"Is this a setup for a joke?" I ask.

Carter laughs. "It happened last night, a few blocks over. Kid found his dad in a pool of blood in the living room and called an ambulance. Guess he got wasted and, you know." He made a hacking motion with one hand.

"Jesus."

"No kidding."

"Could they put it back on?"

"What, his dick? Get this: they couldn't find it."

"How the hell does that happen?"

"Like you haven't done stupid shit when you're drunk."

"Never once."

Carter laughs again. I've always loved his laugh. He keeps talking, but I'm not listening. I'm just thinking about how badly I want to take his laugh for myself.

My phone vibrates and shakes me out of my reverie. Samson76 has sent me a message. I consider deleting it unread, but take a look. "sorry 4 last night. In hospital now. Don't know what came over me."

That's okay. I do.

I DECIDE TO tell Elena about only my latest coming out. She commiserates with me and writes, "Those bastards. Except Carter. He seems chill."

I'm back in my apartment after brunch. The food hasn't done much for my hangover. I don't work until tomorrow.

You know, I've never thought until now about what my ideal body would look like. I just assumed I'd never have it. After all, there's limits to the body, boundaries you can't cross. At the same time, there's always been parts of other people that I've admired—maybe an expression, a way of moving, a curve or an angle, or, of course, a size.

The point is that I never let myself dream of what I could be. I can't be *other*, and I can't have what they have, and I certainly can't have both. In the meantime, I let the world press in against me, from my inboxes to my clothes to the ways I get spoken to, each and every look and conversation and apprehension and exchange pressing me into myself, defining me, writing upon me. What's left of my imagination? I can hardly think of where to start.

My phone is in my hand and my finger hovers over the keyboard. What do I want to be? Or, rather, what *am I*?

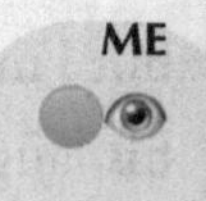

I chuckle to myself. Then I type it in a note app. I check my reflection on my phone screen. No change. I must have to send it. So I send it to myself. And, sure enough, my eyes change color. I watch as the green invades my irises, leaks into them, fills out the blue, eradicates it.

I walk into the bathroom and scan my face in the mirror. I scroll through emoji after emoji, trying to find anything that seems appealing, trying to concoct combinations that could work, trying desperately to think of what I want to become.

Maybe I'm overthinking. Maybe I just need to focus on a goal. Maybe I just want to start with making it so that nobody ever calls me *boy* again.

Each message brings with it searing pain. My forehead cracks open and my skull pushes through my skin, twisting upwards, splitting, coiling, branching, winding, solidifying into many-pointed horns made of bloodstained bone. My fingers—my new ones—pierce the flesh of my armpits; my nails claw through me, ripping me, making hideous noises as blood gushes and dermis splits. I fumble for purchase on the rest of my body and once I find it, I pull, digging myself deeper into my skin as muscle and bone creak, fresh arms bursting from the holes made in me, hairless and smooth and dripping with pus and blood. My knees snap and my thighs break; they bend themselves into new patterns, making or changing joints. And my shoulder blades erupt from my body, the torn flesh left in their wake rising, stretching, lengthening, dripping, thinning, until an enormous pair of wings flap delicately at my sides.

I look like a child's drawing. I look stupid. I look like dog shit.

I look *amazing*.

THE EUPHORIA WEARS off quickly. I may be an emo teen's wet dream, but I still look…*masc*. How the hell am I gonna rework my jaw, my build, and my voice with *emoji*?

A knock on the door. Quick, strong raps. I know that knock anywhere. It's Chelsea.

I look at myself in the mirror.

"Coming," I say. I open the door, naked and bleeding. She's alone, and she barely glances at me before she walks past me into my apartment.

"Hi, Chelsea," I say.

"So, what the fuck? An *it*?" She crosses her arms and glares at me. She's seeing what she wants to see. And I don't think it's me. "I didn't say anything last night—you're welcome—but come on. You're being ridiculous. That's not a thing."

"Yeah it is. You know it is."

"Look. We've been friends a long time. I've always known you're a freak. But you're not a freak like *this*."

"What are you saying?"

She sighs, shifts, intensifies her glare. "Look, around the fourth time you had something going on with your gender or whatever, even *I* could tell you were confused, all right? And, okay, maybe I don't get the whole gender thing to begin with, with you *or* Carter. But, I thought, whatever. Whatever! Who cares! Girls, boys, neither, I don't give a shit! Leave me out of it! But now it seems like you're, you're just—I don't fucking know—*denying* something, something you can't actually fucking deny. There's *fundamentals*. It's like self-delusion. You can't *stop* being, being, whatever it is you're trying to stop being. *Human*, I guess." For the first time, she seems to take in the changes I've made to myself. No, for the first time she decides to *regard* them. *Acknowledge* them. Hate them.

"I knew you were gonna be this way."

"Because you know how self-denial affects me. You know the kind of shit I went through with my parents. You know how much I had to lie, and lie, and lie, pretend and pretend and pretend that I was *straight* just to keep them from… from… And you *know* how many attempts I made because of it."

"This isn't *denial*, Chelsea. It's who I *am*."

Every single inch of my body where she looks at it burns violently hot. I almost wince under her gaze.

"Besides," I continue, "this isn't about *you*."

"Clearly. It never fucking is."

We stare at each other. It feels like we're motionless for an eternity. Both of our eyes blaze.

Eventually, she scoffs. She glances between my legs, looks back at me, then glances down again. She's thinking. Something has occurred to her. She looks back into my eyes.

"Where'd you get that?" she asks. "Because I don't think it belongs to you."

"Same place I got everything else."

"Yeah. The news didn't mention that man cut off his wings and arms, too."

"Reporting in this town has never been the best, has it?"

"I think you need help. A *lot* of help." She pulls out her phone. "And since we are friends, I think I'll call it in for you."

"Wait, Chelsea." She hasn't dialed yet. She's giving me a chance.

"I—Fine. It's just… It's hard to say aloud. Can I—will you let me text it to you?"

She considers it, then lowers her hands. "Fine. But it better be what I want to hear."

"Phone's in the bathroom. I'll be right back."

My mind races. I spoke without thinking. I have no idea what to do, what to say, how to act. As always, she's being unreasonable—isn't she?—and I know she's being dead serious about calling in "help." I can feel it. I know it. The way we always know what she's feeling. The way she can rewrite the world itself. That power of hers I've always envied. The power that made me miserable through all of her school years, as miserable as she was. As if Carter and I didn't have to drink just as deeply of the pain she forced us to share.

It doesn't take long for me to write it out.

ME

Send.

SHE DOESN'T EVEN look at the message. Her eyes glaze over. She looks at me, and her feet move.

The thick, heavy pall she cast over the room vanishes. Dozens of atmospheres of pressure lift off of me. She approaches me, walks up to me, keeps walking. Her flesh melts into mine, and mine into hers. Every ounce of us liquefies. We become puddles, fleshy and swollen, clumps of hair drifting on us. We mingle, merge; our nerves scream in biting agony, not with heat but with chill, each point of contact, of intermixing, searing each with frostbite. We are becoming an absence together, or rather, I am becoming an absence of Chelsea. An inversion of her.

Slowly, my body forms itself out of our clay. Bones, muscles, sinews, tendons, organs, flesh—all pull themselves up, stacking themselves atop one another, resolving into their locations, settling there, swimming in the sea of existence.

When I can see again I walk to the mirror and stare.

A layer on top of my skin, or maybe just beneath it, seems to swim. It swirls, eddies of mismatched tones abutting each other, pressing against each other. In the light, it shimmers.

My face is softer now, rounder. My horns have broken, no longer antlers but potentials. My wings have shrunk, grown tattered. Flesh hangs off them like clothes on a line. I have to search myself for evidence that I am me, and when I find it, I'm not sure who it is I'm finding. Only in the places now most foreign to me do I spot Chelsea.

"What the fuck did I do?" I moan. My voice is no longer my own.

My apartment feels unfamiliar now. I have changed size, though I can't tell whether I'm taller or shorter. The colors and shapes of things feel off, as though I'm seeing new aspects of them, or as if I had forgotten each object and am reacquainting myself with them. An unfamiliar dull pain seeps through my body and lodges in my joints. I reek of rot, a product of the destroyed skin hanging off my back.

What was my plan? To go to work tomorrow? To act like I didn't turn myself into a fantasy creature? Was I going to make it all vanish, and only get it back when I was alone in my fucking apartment? Was I just going to play dress-up?

These thoughts claw at the inside of my skull. I know their source.

Maybe that's just what I would have done. Maybe I was exactly the deluded coward she thought I was.

But not anymore. I've gone much too far, now. I'll have to go farther still.

"I'm so jealous of Carter," I text Elena. "Nobody clocks him anymore, you know?"

"Good for him."

"Yeah. But still. You think they'll ever see me how I wanna be seen?"

"I guess that depends on how you wanna be seen. As a thing, right?"

"Maybe. But what kind of thing?"

"You'll have to figure that out for yourself, huh?"

"What if… What if I want to be a monster?"

"Go for it."

"What if I *am* a monster?"

"Aren't we all?"

"What if I told you I ate Chelsea. What if I told you I merged her body with mine."

"I'd probably call you based."

"You don't mean that."

"I said we're all monsters, right? Look, you don't know how many people I've wanted to kill to get my hands on what they have—or just to take away their power over me. Honestly, I don't know what stops me. I guess because I still buy into the idea that this is *their* world. And in their world, we don't get to do that, to take from them, hurt them, kill them and fuck their corpses, breed inside of them like maggots and hatch brand-new terrors that can stalk this world and hunt them down."

"What if I could cast a spell on you, on us? What if I told you I could bring you here, turn us into the kinds of things that can lay eggs in their torn bodies, watch our young teem and fester and drink their rot?"

"I'd tell you to do it. I'd tell you to do it *now*."

As if an incantation just completed, I feel a certain power swell inside of me. A ritual energy, unmistakable in its wild force. It has been summoned and now must be unleashed.

The materials, the media through which this energy must act is our bodies. And it will act upon the world that is not yet ours. It is for me to command, direct, enact. Untold voices begging me to begin my work, to channel them, to become a revelation.

Through fucking *emoji*.

ME

The air around me seems to crackle, and the space there bends and twists until it can't take it anymore and splits open. Someone is thrown through the tear, striking me, bowling us over, tumbling us to the floor. And in another instant, it all fades, quiets, until there's nothing left to suggest that I tore a portal through the world.

Atop me, Elena laughs. "Holy *shit*."

We disentangle ourselves and stand. She stares at me, smiling at the modifications I've already made to my body. "Damn good start. But I think we can come up with something *much* better."

"No. I want something *worse*."

ARMS LITTER THE floor. Vast clumps of skin blanket them. The rug is caked with dried blood and bile. Our bodies ooze pus and stink of death.

We're never satisfied. Anything we grow we love for moments, but as minutes pass our features seem too human, too comprehensible. We tear them off with our claws and huddle around my phone, thinking of the combinations that might obliterate whatever remains human about us so we can violate the world with our monstrosity.

ME

My skin seems to boil. Whatever magic the emoji work on it has its own opinions about what to do with my body, and it always suggests boiling, generating growths and lumps and bones to protrude from them. Fingers, arms, faces press against my flesh from the inside. "Give me that," Elena says, and I oblige.

ME

I bite off an errant cock, severing it from her body as she fine-tunes the complex genitalia she's always dreamed of. My face elongates, protrudes; my jaw grows to fit the jagged fangs pushing violently against my blunt omnivore's teeth. I can't speak anymore. I moan when she touches me, lops off a part of me, holds me close as the pain of breaking ourselves over and over threatens to drag us down. Through ragged, rotten breath, we exhale new meanings into each other.

We learn that while the emoji make their distortions, we can use our hands to shape them. I help her smooth out the wings that burst from her back, elongate them, ensure each inch is covered by a feather.

Anything, anything at all, we try. We hit the limits of the palette available to us. The human forms of human symbols lock us into humanity. I am beastly, bestial—but am I a beast? Elena examines herself in the mirror and smiles. "Now *this* is what a girl looks like." Teeth and claws and spines protrude from every inch of her. She too is digitigrade, and the rectangular pupils in her eyes narrow down to almost nothing. She is all horn and bone and protein; she has discarded her skin, and left herself a body of chitin, mold, muscle.

She looks at me and smiles. "Do it," she says.

I grin. Drool pours down my lips.

I pounce, push my cocks inside her. We lose ourselves in the ecstasy, until she pushes SEND for me on my own phone.

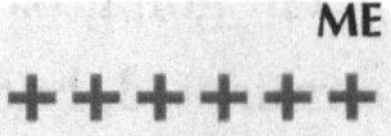

I melt. I become acid. I dissolve her. She becomes liquid. What we are becomes me. I am us. I rise from the mess of us and I am something else, not what I was before, not what I'll be after.

I don't recognize myself in the mirror. Nothing about me is mine, I think; nothing I was still is.

What am I now?

That doesn't matter. I'm missing pieces. I need to go collect them.

I need to go and unfinish me.

CARTER RECOGNIZES ME, somehow. Well, we've been friends for decades.

Even so, he cowers. His apartment is as small as mine is. The two of us barely fit.

I approach him silently. He laughs nervously.

I can't wait to make it mine.

MY MONTH IN the woods was fruitful. I've added so many new forms to myself. When I see my reflection in the pond I drink from, I can't tell what I'm seeing. It's something alien, yes, but I can still trace in my features my human bodies and the animal influences upon them. Maybe, I think, maybe Earth can't produce a monster.

But I shouldn't think like that. I've worked so hard. I'm about to be a debutante. My tongues lick my tattered lips.

I'm going back to work tomorrow. Oh, I'm sure I've already been terminated, but I figure I'll drop by. I should show my boss what I've been up to for the last month, shouldn't I? I'm sure she'll understand. But, I wonder, who should I visit next? Where should I go?

SCULPTING

Oh, I'm sure I'll find somewhere to dance. I'll only move more wildly when I hear the sirens and screams. Maybe they'll try to shoot me! Maybe they'll try to *reason* with me!

No matter what they do, I'll forgive them. I'll hug them. I'll melt them all. They're all welcome. They're all so very welcome. And together, we'll rewrite what it means to be human.

THE HIGH ROAD

Carlos E. Rivera

THE HIGH ROAD

Carlos E. Rivera

> *"I will no longer put up with this shit!*
> *I have been beaten. I've had my nose broken.*
> *I have been thrown in jail. I have lost my job.*
> *I have lost my apartment for gay liberation,*
> *And you all treat me this way?*
> *What the fuck's wrong with you all?"*
> — Sylvia Rivera.
> Trans LGBTQ+ rights activist.
> 1973 NYC Pride. Being booed by gay people.

THE GLOB OF blood and spit hit the white porcelain surface of her sink, reddish black under the ferocious white light of the light bulb over her head. Its high-wattage luminosity increased the contrast of the world to an unflattering degree. It drowned all color in stark shadows, making those very angular features—her cheekbones, her jaw, her chin— seem drawn in charcoal.

Two red lines raced down the porcelain toward the black hole of the drain, racing to get lost forever in oblivion. Betty didn't catch who won. Her eyes rolled up toward the mirror, and she flinched, unprepared, the second she beheld her face

(*It's a dude!*)

and the deep red scar that now adorned her right cheek. It looked like a check-mark, a red line with glossy, dried lines of blood, all pointing straight down toward

(*Yo, bro! It's totally a dude!*)

that blocky, square jaw she hated so much. Years of hormones had done wonders for her skin, her body hair, and overall self-image, but it had done nothing to de-neanderthal that rugby-player jaw she'd inherited from her dad.

That familiar feeling came over her then. Pressure. Jagged pressure. Blunt teeth biting into her, perpendicular to every inch of her skin. Inside, she felt like one of those heartburn medicine commercials with the transparent upper body and the red arrow going up from the stomach, with the opposing blue arrow going down to extinguish it, except, for her, both arrows were fiery red. Both burned against each other while two more huge arrows pressed from the sides of her ribcage, creating a single point of boiling plasma between her breasts.

(*Check out his tits, bro! They look like he tucked two oranges under his skin! That's so gross!*)

In her reflection, her jaw widened, hardened, turned to rock, turned to metal, grew rivets. She thought of all the other dolls, the ones who "passed", the ones who didn't get clocked at first glance. She felt a tinge of envy, of hatred. She felt her breath grow shallower, quicker.

Pressure. Teeth. Arrows. Fire. Plasma.

(*Whatever. A dude's a dude. And if it's a dude, it can take a punch*)

Two black eyes. Her eyeliner was almost invisible under the swollen skin. Many more inflamed, darkened areas covered her brown skin in tight lumps and splotches, pulsating with pain. Her nose was bent, bleeding, two drying dark-red smears pointed to either side of her upper lip, like a grotesque mustache. There was a nasty split diagonally across her upper and lower lip, as if she'd made out with a sushi knife. She'd lost her left canine; her incisor swung back and forth—she might lose that one, too, widening the gap. Her left cheek was a blackened ball of hot fluid; that stretched balloon look reserved for girls with filler injections or recent bruises, and she hadn't had the former. Her forehead felt bumpy and uneven, not to mention the patch of bare, bleeding scalp where Clay—one of those assholes—had pulled her hair up and back, believing it to be a wig. He'd been quite amused and emboldened by the realization it had been her own hair—most of it wouldn't rip away as they held it taut while punching and kicking her.

As she pressed a towel soaked with alcohol against the cut on her cheek—the one that would certainly leave a repugnant scar—and it burned white hot, she could picture it sizzling like a steak.

Travis Martin and Clay Shepherd had dragged her out of the women's restroom on the first floor of the engineering building on campus. They'd beat her without mercy. All because that bitch, Rebecca Hagel, had started screaming that there was a man in her restroom trying to touch her. Travis had burst through the restroom door like a giant battering ram, chest puffed, acting all macho to defend his girl, followed by that closeted piece of shit, Clay.

Oh yes, Clay. He wasn't too straight to have been dicked down by half the local Grindr population—always on the DL, of course. She'd once caught "the ringtone" coming from his phone, to his embarrassment. He'd hated her since then for the simple reason of knowing. He idol-worshiped Travis, overcompensating and playing straight like a caricature.

Each blow landed without mercy as Betty screamed for help. People all around only watched. Some didn't even do that much. They just kept on walking, as if afraid to get involved, as if the simple act of looking would get them ostracized. Then, came Ernesto, the building's middle-aged security guard. Hearing the commotion, he'd come check on what was happening. He regarded the scene, wide-eyed, then his mouth closed, his jaw clenched. The man in uniform turned around and walked back the way he'd come. It was surreal, like something she would've never imagined seeing in real life. A hasty "this is a bad guy" moment in a soap opera. Yet, there she was, living it, having her canine kicked loose with a shoe to the face, then watching it shoot out of her out in a geyser of blood as another kick sunk into her abdomen. She'd felt like a piece of stringy old beef being mauled by two angry dogs. She was meat. She was nothing. Nothing.

Her phone let out a loud *ding!* It echoed briskly in her bathroom, breaking her out of the accelerating doom spiral.

She glanced down at it, sitting on the cold white surface beside her sink.

A message. Two emojis greeted her from the text preview:

She didn't recognize the phone number.

Awareness floated up from the crimson haze of rage that had been overwhelming her mere seconds earlier.

That's impossible, she thought. *It can't be.*

"Have a drink first," her dad said, pushing a tall beer mug covered in drops of condensation across the table. "Let that cool your throat."

Betty sat across from her dad at Cunningham's bar five years earlier. She'd just recently come out as trans, and for two days, her old man had been brooding and quiet, making her worried he'd kick her out of the house.

Instead, before he'd been able to breathe a word on the subject, that afternoon, a mob of her high-school classmates had forced the subject. They'd pursued her from school all the way home, throwing rocks at her, calling her a faggot and a tranny. She flew up her porch just as her dad emerged from the door to see what the ruckus was all about. She pushed past him in teary desperation, leaving him to gawk at the frenzied, taunting mob.

Rather than closing the front door, though, her dad ran inside, picked up a baseball bat, and rushed into the crowd, swinging in wild arcs, not caring whom he hit, not caring about the consequences. He chased the entire pack of high school kids away, managing to graze a few arms and shoulders, sending the group scattering in panic.

He'd walked inside to find Betty weeping, hugging her knees to her chest in a corner of her bedroom. She noticed his trembling hand clutching his keys. "Get in the car," he commanded.

Now, a cold beer sat in front of her, coloring her confused as her dad's hand slid away from the mug.

"Go on," he urged.

Betty surveyed the area. Only old Chuck was in the deserted bar, wiping glasses and acting oblivious. She was an underage high-school senior. Chuck could get in trouble, even lose his license, if anyone saw her there. Old Chuck didn't seem to mind.

"Bennett," her dad said in a firm voice, using her deadname, earning a look of indignation from her. "What, you're old enough to decide one day you want to chop your dick off, but not old enough for a beer?"

She was ready to stand up, flip him off, tell him to go fuck himself, and stomp away, but before she could, he put his palms forward, big hands raised, not in violence but in appeasement.

"I'm sorry," he said in a softer tone. "Beatrice… Alright? I'm sorry. I didn't think. This is hard for me to make heads or tails of, alright?" He surveyed her face. "I'm here, ain't I?"

She returned his scrutinizing gaze, saw no ill intent, only worry, only love, and she let out a long breath, claws retreating.

"It's just…you still look like…" He waved a hand in her direction.

"Like an 18-year-old Russell Wilson?" she said, her voice coarse from shouting at her classmates, the lines of heat across her chest from her dysphoria making her feel like she would spontaneously combust.

"I feel bad now for saying you looked like him," her dad said, blushing. "I just liked the Seahawks, and I saw you, and thought, maybe someday, you might…" He shot her a bashful glance. "I'm fucking it up again. I'm sorry. Drink, please."

She glanced at her father, then the beer, lifted it, and took a steady sip, its icy bitterness unfamiliar but oddly steadying in the empty bar. He did likewise with his own mug. This felt like a ritual for the old army vet—more for his benefit than hers. Some antiquated way to turn this into an adult conversation, or perhaps a rite of passage: having a drink with his daughter in remembrance of whom he perceived as his dead son.

"Michelle Obama," he said, confusing her anew with the seeming non-sequitur. "She said, 'When they go low, we go high.'" He examined her eyes again to see if she was following. "The high road." He cleared his throat. "This whole idea that those…animals…those *fucking* animals will act the way animals do, but we're better than that, so we should do better. We must educate, use love, practice the tolerance we preach."

Betty took another quick drink, unprompted. Nodded nervously. This pull didn't taste as good as the first.

"Well, look how good it did them," he said. "Hyenas can't be trained. Acting all high and mighty only tells these evil fucks they can do whatever they want, because we won't put a bullet in their foreheads, like they deserve. They can break the rules because we'll only slap their wrists, but won't actually knife them in the throat…like they deserve." He shook his head, taking on a countenance of pure disgust, which he washed down with a long drink of beer. "Fuck the high road," he said in a flinty growl. "Fuck it to Hell."

His eyes were brimming, smoldering with hatred when they again met hers. "Thank god the first thing I got a hold of was that baseball bat. If I had made it all the way to the kitchen and gotten hold of a knife, I don't know how many of your classmates would be lying in front of our house right now with their throats open and their blood drying on the asphalt."

Betty swallowed hard and was at once too aware of her Adam's apple rising and falling. She hated it. The tension of the day had made her hyper-aware of every single thing she hated about her body.

Her dad was a war veteran. God knew the things he'd done in Afghanistan. She'd never asked. She'd never wanted to ask. He'd only said he'd worked in tech—he was a software engineer, after all—but his job wasn't just that. Couldn't be. There had been "wetworks" over there. Things he wouldn't tell her or her late mom—the scars on his hands and arms betrayed it hadn't just been a computer geek's job, or even "clean" kills with bullets. There was this ugly, moist, crimson idea in her mind about her dad she refused to give shape to. He kept no pictures from his time in the military.

"What those beasts did to my baby girl…" he continued. "I don't care what you look like. You're my baby. Your mom entrusted you to me when she died. You say you're not a boy, you're a girl. Fine, then. It's all the same to me. They hurt my baby. They deserve to bleed."

"Dad…"

"Don't get me wrong. I'm not saying the moment someone talks to you the wrong way, to choose violence. Try reason when reasonable.

But if one of these animals comes for you and won't stop, you have to choose: stay a defenseless victim, or make them bleed." His face took on the most terrifying expression she'd ever seen on him, but it somehow didn't feel scary to her, it felt reassuring. "You're my blood. If anyone hurts you, I'd shed blood for you. No hesitation. I would kill for you."

A DROP OF blood and a knife. In that order.

To other people, it might seem threatening; some stranger saying, "I will kill you." But that wasn't it. A threat would've been a knife, then a drop of blood, or a different more horrible and creative combination of otherwise innocuous examples of the modern hieroglyphic.

It was a drop of blood and a knife. "You are my blood. I would kill for you."

Disturbing as it sounded, it was her dad's little reassurance every time she told him about someone treating her like shit, someone making fun of her, or yet another of the many indignities this world, its religions, its politicians, or even a next-door neighbor had put her through. At the end of every chat, or every phone call, without fail, a text would come: A drop of blood. A knife.

You are my blood. I would kill for you.

Except her dad had passed away a year earlier. The ever-unfulfilled reassurance, and the warmth and safety that came with it, had disappeared the moment her dad had let out a single whimper and clutched the left side of his chest with a trembling hand. Her bastion of safety had tumbled down in front of a crowd of onlookers at a bad Italian restaurant.

Who are you? she thought at the phone.

In a hurry, she washed the sticky blood off her hands, reached for the phone and unlocked it. As she opened the messaging app, another message came in. A link to a file ending in .apk.

An app? No fuckin' way I'm that dumb, asshole.

BETTY
Who are you?

The reply came almost immediately, without the three little dots indicating the other person was typing.

UNKNOWN
Click on the link, Baby Girl.

"Drop of blood. Knife." Again. Her breath caught in her throat. The tip of her tongue touched the back of her teeth, almost ready to say, "D…ad?" but she stopped herself.

BETTY
I'm not doing that, you fucker. This isn't funny. Especially not today.

UNKNOWN
Read the filename.

The message popped up immediately, again without typing.

Her eyes glided up to the link. The file was named "The_High_Road.apk", and as if her body weren't weak enough from the beating she'd taken, she felt herself swoon, her head feeling swimmy. Swimmy enough that, against her better judgment, she tapped on the link. She watched as the thin little bar popped up, showing her the download progress of The_High_Road.apk

It downloaded quickly. She opened the file, received a security warning about installing apps from external sources. As if in a trance, she disabled the security block on external apps, and now it was installing.

The_High_Road.

10%

43%

64%

95%

100%

An app icon popped up right on her home screen. A drop of blood and a knife. Her finger hovered over it.

What the hell am I doing? she thought, clarity piercing the madness. Her face throbbed, ribs aching—likely broken—and yet, instead of calling a doctor, she was falling for some scammer. Some creep who'd hacked her old chats and picked the worst moment to trick her into installing malware. Her bank account would be drained in seconds. *Hope you enjoy the fifty bucks I've got, you asshole.*

She considered for a few more seconds. Another message popped up.

UNKNOWN

I made this for you, Baby Girl. This is what I wish I'd had instead of a baseball bat.

(*You are my blood. I would kill for you*) *Fuck it.* She tapped on the app. A loading screen came up: The High Road by Manuel Ballestero. *Dad? How is this possible?*

Gradually, a word in red appeared over the app name, and now, the title screen read: "FUCK The High Road."

Four video feeds popped up, from cameras that couldn't even be there. Like the POV of someone standing just a few feet away from the subjects. To her utter shock, she realized the people were Rebecca, Travis, Clay, and Ernesto.

Her eyes flew toward Clay's video feed. She noticed he and Ernesto were in the same room, Clay's dorm room, but their feeds were from different angles, like two invisible voyeurs were standing there in the room with them. This wasn't as shocking as the fact Clay was giving the big security guard—a forty-five-year-old married man with three children, as far as she knew—the most furious, hungry blowjob she'd seen in her life.

What the fuck?

In the other feed, Rebecca was in her bathroom, drawing a bath and ready to get in, admiring her gorgeous face in the mirror. Unwittingly, Beatrice ran a finger over the edge of the scar on her cheek, which would mar her forever.

Travis stood outside the Economics building, chatting up a brunette in leggings so tight they looked painted on. He was flirting with no shame, while on another feed, his girlfriend struck poses in the mirror, unaware.

Betty watched both video feeds, caught between disgust and fascination. She didn't question how she was seeing this anymore—what she couldn't fathom was how, less than an hour after nearly beating her to death—or enabling it, in Ernesto and Rebecca's case—they could just carry on like nothing happened. Travis still had scratches on his knuckles from punching her, and here he was, flirting like it meant nothing. Meanwhile, she was left with pain, rage, and a trauma that would haunt her for years.

As if fueled by her anger and indignation, words appeared at the top of the screen: CHOOSE WHO'S FIRST.

WHAT AM I doing? What am I doing? What am I doing? Her finger moved with a life of its own toward Clay's camera feed.

DAD

WHO WILL BE FIRST?

The name had changed. The moment she opened the app, the name on the texts had changed. Then came the memory of the first message: the drop of blood and the knife. *You're my blood. I would kill for you… Who will be first?*

She lightly tapped on it, as if tapping softly would cause it to not do anything and she could just put the damn app away. She would have done nothing to anyone. She would've… *Taken the high road?*

The feed from Clay's bedroom filled her screen. Clay on his knees in front of Ernesto, gobbling away at his cock, as the security guard held his shirt up with one hand and his boxers down with the other.

The words CHOOSE THEIR FATE now appeared at the top of the screen, and at the bottom, three emojis, seeming discordant in this entire situation: 🔪, 😬, 💧.

She stared at the three, knowing in her heart that nothing pleasant would come of either. The whole situation was too bizarre and ominous for "pleasant". Something would happen if she chose. Maybe she should test it first, look for the more harmless-looking one—not that either of them deserved her mercy. A test was a good idea. If she changed her mind, there was always Ernesto's feed in the same location. This was assuming anything *actually* would happen.

I mean…how could *anything happen?* This was just a dumb voyeur app. A clearly advanced one, with ridiculously powerful U.S. spy technology backing it, based on the camera placement. An invisible tiny drone, maybe. *Maybe it will just be some augmented reality thing in which I'll see some AI rendering of what I wish would happen to them. Right?*

She held her breath.

Right?

The pen looked sharp—not a ballpoint, but the pointed inkwell pen emoji. She grinned at the possibilities, then reminded herself: stick to the test. Harmless. An egg seemed harmless enough… until she remembered her Spanish-speaking dad calling testicles "huevos." Ernesto's clearly exposed, middle-aged huevos flashed in her mind. What if Clay did something to his huevos?

Shit. No. Focus. The test. Just the test.

The drooling face with its salacious grin and purely ecstatic joy seemed like the obvious choice here. Especially given what Clay was currently doing. Maybe it would be some harmless little shameful "choking on Ernesto's cum and puking all over" rendering and that would be that.

She tapped on the drooling face.

Clay's facial expression changed so drastically it was even obvious with a big dick in his mouth pushing his cheek out. It was like his eyes had gone dead. Expressionless. A zombie.

What the f—

Without hesitation, Clay bit down on Ernesto's dick, and blood gushed all over his face from the bleeding gash left over from where an erect penis used to exist.

She could hear Ernesto's desperate wails of horror and pain as he staggered back, bleeding all over the carpet, and at the same time, spraying piss out of his urethra in an uncontrollable spray. His feet caught in his pants and fell on his ass. He rolled on the floor wailing for help as blood and urine flooded the area around his body.

Clay, his cheeks puffed, mouth closed, blood all over his mouth and neck, still in a trance, raised his two hands toward his face. He pressed the palm of his right hand tight over his mouth and with the other he pinched his nose shut. It was then Beatrice saw awareness come back to his face, but only his face. His hands didn't come off his mouth and nose, and she now saw terror brimming in his bulging eyes. She saw him roll on the floor, veins throbbing in his neck.

"Oh my god!" Betty said out loud, and for a second, just a second, she wished she could stop what was unfolding before her eyes, but the thought passed. A flash, then gone. She wanted this. She wanted to see this. She wanted to *enjoy* this. *Fuck the high road!*

Clay thrashed, moaned, and gurgled as he quite literally choked on a dick—his own hands, no longer his, given new meaning to a two-handed blowjob. The absurdity of it all made Betty burst out laughing. She watched as tears streamed down Clay's face, the same kind of tears she'd cried when he'd ripped her hair out by the roots. And in the background, still howling, still writhing on the floor, was the newly dickless security guard.

Little by little, Clay's convulsions waned. He stopped moving. In a slow, lazy motion, his hands slid away from his face, bloodied and limp, and fell to his sides. He lay there, face bloody, eyes red and teary, mouth slightly open, showing just a bit of the bloody end of Ernesto's cock, and a long wet strand of blood dribbling down the side of his mouth.

Beatrice watched the phone, dumbfounded at what she had just witnessed, but so entertained she could almost forget about the pain coursing through her body.

Seconds later, she was taken back to the main screen where a green checkmark now showed over Clay's camera feed. Egged on by the morbid excitement of the moment, she tapped on Ernesto's feed.

CHOOSE HIS FATE

The screen prompted her again. This time, the three emojis were: 🔫, 🔪—like replacing real guns with that plastic one had ever made a difference—and 🎃. The gun felt obvious; the man had been armed, so maybe that would just give him a quick out. The jack-o-lantern? That one was murkier. Images of carving pumpkins, scooping out their guts, slicing eyes and mouths, flashed through her mind. Tempting, but that wasn't what she wanted. This man had lived in the world for forty-five years. He'd chosen to work security, which wasn't exactly like being a cop, but still came with a duty to protect. And he hadn't. He'd turned away while she was beaten bloody. No, he didn't deserve an easy death. He didn't even deserve a grotesque, messy one—enticing as that might sound. He deserved to survive, to live with what he'd let happen, and its consequences. The wheelchair emoji was the only choice that fit.

She tapped on it.

Despite the excruciating pain the guard was in, she saw the same dead expression as Clay's spread over his face. He stood up, the ragged hole with a half-inch piece of his severed penis continued to bleed.

As if he'd just made it home from a hard day's work, he removed his shoes, his pants, his underwear, and as he stood on top of the patch of blood and piss in the carpet, he seemed to regain consciousness. Coming back to his senses, he once again began screaming in pain, but his body didn't obey him from the neck down.

Betty saw him turn around on the spot and face the window.

The POV changed now to outside the second-story dorm window, just three seconds before Ernesto flew backwards in an explosion of broken glass. His arms were firmly at his sides, causing him to land on his head, which bent to one side. Beatrice thought she'd heard his vertebrae snap, but that would've been impossible from this distance. The man's body fell limp like a bag of sand.

People around Ernesto screamed as they saw the man with no pants, no dick, and a broken neck lying on the concrete at the building's entrance.

It was even more shocking but satisfying when she heard, seconds before being pulled to the main screen, Ernesto's garbled voice, screaming what sounded like the word "Help" but blurted by someone who no longer had full knowledge of how language worked. She saw his head shake a little, but his body lay still.

As Beatrice looked at green checkmark over his video feed, she savored the fact Ernesto had a real chance of someone calling 911 and saving his life, sentencing him to never being able to move again, or perhaps, even talk.

Who knows? Betty thought. *It might give that piece of shit a chance to become a better person someday.*

BETTY'S FINGER NOW hovered over the three emojis under Rebecca's video feed. The irony wasn't lost on her that whatever disgrace she was about to bring down upon that blond bitch would happen to her in the safety of her own bathroom, in the privacy of her own home, after she'd been screaming in a public bathroom about the "man" that had threatened her safe space.

The first emoji seemed fun:

Would she sew her mouth shut? Her mouth and eyes? Fun. It had potential.

The second one felt obvious:

While she would love to watch Rebecca wiggle and dance in an electrified bathtub, she'd seen that a million times in movies already. How boring.

Wait. She paused. *Is it wrong that I'm having so much fun with this?*

Her dad's voice floated up from the ether in her mind and said the magic words: *Fuck the high road.*

She tapped the remaining emoji, one she hadn't seen before, but it was because she'd only ever seen the male version of it: This one had with blood in her mouth, and very long straight black hair. It was a gamble, but she felt like being surprised.

The dead look on Rebecca's face was visible in the bathroom mirror as she opened a drawer, pulled out a curling iron, plugged it in, and cranked the temperature dial to max, and if there was something Betty was familiar with it was curling irons; she knew their temperatures could reach up to 400 degrees, which was insane for something a woman too put that close to her skin.

She counted the seconds. Rebecca stood still as a mannequin, waiting for the curling iron to reach peak temperature. The view moved and zoomed in, closer to her, as if commanded by some unseen director wanting to get the most suspense and the best shot out of the upcoming scene. Then, Betty let out a startled gasp as, in one swift motion, Rebecca clutched the curling iron, opened her mouth wide and took the whole cylindrical thing deep into her mouth, just as her eyes regained awareness.

Rebecca's muffled screams echoed, bouncing all around the bathroom tiles, but try as she might, she couldn't make herself pull the burning piece of metal out of her mouth. Beatrice could see her lips bubbling, burning, almost melting around the curling iron. She watched steam, blood, and boiling saliva, mixed in a frothing pink ooze, running down her nose and the sides of her burning lips. She pictured all the soft tissue in the cavern of her mouth, the inside of her cheeks, her uvula, her throat, cooking as the fluids boiled. Her face went red hot with strain as she continued to let out gurgling moans.

Then she turned. Her whole body spun on the spot in a swift motion, facing the tub.

Rebecca, her screaming head almost independent from her body, grabbed her plugged-in hair dryer by the cord and let it hang about halfway down her shin.

"You've gotta be kidding me," Beatrice whispered in shock, realizing what was about to happen.

Curling iron still deep in her mouth, boiling her head alive, still squealing in helpless desperation, Rebecca jumped, looking for a second like she was pulling a skateboarding trick of some kind. Her towel fell off her body in midair as she landed with both feet in the tub, followed by her hair dryer not a second later.

The curling iron came unplugged, yielding the closing act to the hair dryer, which obliged by sending violent jolts of electricity through Rebecca, who shook like a naked rag doll, hot iron still in her mouth, pinkish blood dribbling down her mouth and running down her breasts, until she finally collapsed into the tub water, a few bucks and jerks still coursing through her from time to time, and a curling iron sticking out of her mouth, covered in gore.

"Fuck you, you TERF piece of shit," Betty said. "Good riddance."

She thought, a little underwhelmed, she would've preferred the thread and needle.

ONLY TRAVIS REMAINED now.

It felt strange to think she felt a little sad that the experience—whatever it was—was about to end. What if this was a one-time deal? Did she actually want it to keep going?

Mrs. Li from across the street keeps threatening to make her six dogs maul me to death. A dog emoji on her… Just sayin'.

No. Why would she continue? Even though they were technically killing themselves, she was the one giving the commands, and that felt wrong. Did that make her a murderer?

After everything she'd gone through, did she even care?

Fuck the high road!

"Three emojis stand before me," she mumbled and smiled so wide the cut in her lip split again and blood started seeping down her chin. Without thinking much of it, she licked it off and dabbed at it with the alcohol-soaked towel. She continued studying the three emojis before her. No time for pain when the excitement of giving Travis his just desserts was literally at her fingertips. "This is your last chance to impress me and entertain me with your elimination."

Travis sat on a bench outside the Economics building, getting cozy with the nameless girl he was cheating on his now-dead girlfriend with. Betty grinned, savoring how clueless he was of the doom floating above him: 😾, 🐵,   🇺🇸 .

The exploding head felt obvious—brains all over the girl—but also weirdly dull for the closing act. The monkey? Now that one intrigued her. Ear trauma, maybe? Pencils jammed in his eardrums? Or something more creative—ripping them off, eating them, choking on them? But that'd be the third choking death… Too repetitive. Still, damn, she wanted to know.

Then her eyes landed on the American flag, and something in her twisted. A familiar surge of rage burned through her. Was the U.S. the most dangerous place in the world for a trans person of color? Maybe not. But it sure as hell felt like it nowadays. America hated her. America wanted her dead. It had dangled the illusion of safety, of joy, of being seen as human in her face—just long enough to give her hope. And that's what she hated most: the hope. Hope that had been stomped out and spat on. That cruel bait-and-switch, where she now stopped being a person and became a target. Trans. Latina. The two things this country despised most. The U.S. had made it open season on people like her, handed badges and guns to monsters, and wrapped them in immunity. She felt disgusted by the place she'd been born.

As she stared at the screen, Travis's smug face lined up with the flag so perfectly that they blurred together—one and the same. America wanted her dead. And for the first time, she felt like maybe she wanted to—at least symbolically—kill it right back.

Fuck. The. High. Road.

She gave such a hateful tap to the tempered glass of her phone screen it almost broke.

She watched with fascination the way Travis's eyes went dead, prompting a confused look on the nameless girl's face. He stood up straight. He almost looked like he didn't know where he was.

He turned on his heels and walked toward the large entrance of the building and swiftly climbed up a chest-high wall at the side of the entrance, and he reached up, looking like he was about to climb up the side of the building.

Beatrice didn't understand what he was doing at first. She watched him with the same baffled look the nameless girl wore. Then the POV tilted up, and she saw it—a big American flag flapping in the wind. He wrestled with it, the fabric whipping around his face and arms, but eventually yanked it free. He stood there, holding the metal pole like it was something sacred. Then, slowly, almost reverently, he ran a finger along its sharp, spear-like tip, eyes wide with a strange awe.

Holding the pole in one hand, he unbuttoned his jeans, and digging his thumb under his briefs, he pulled down twice, three times, until his tiny, limp dick wiggled free, and his ass cheeks were bare in the wind. She heard the nameless girl scream, "What the fuck?!" and people around Travis gawked, murmured, and laughed at the spectacle.

"What the fuck?" Beatrice echoed.

Travis bent his knees, arched his back, and something shifted in his eyes—awareness, horror—as he pressed the sharp tip of the flagpole against his asshole. At first, just a little entered, making him squawk in pain. Then the entire pointed tip disappeared inside him. The pole thickened near its base—about as wide as a vodka bottle. Travis screamed, wild with panic and confusion. Blood began soaking his white briefs, trickling down his thighs in rivulets. As if possessed, he shoved the pole in a few inches deeper for good measure.

"Help me!" he managed to scream, as if he were shouting while anesthetized, but Betty knew he was feeling every bit of pain. It was clear on his face. "HELP ME!!!"

Phone cameras all around pointed at him as people laughed and groaned but did their best to stay away from the dangerous lunatic.

Standing on the edge of the raised wall, Travis turned around, giving the crowd a high-definition, 4K look of his bleeding ass with a seven-foot pole sticking out of it—the remaining foot buried deep inside him. The onlookers gasped.

He was weeping, shaking his head, sensing what he was about to do. "Please…" he begged to some unseen force. "No…" He begged, like she had begged him to stop kicking her.

Travis jumped backwards, hands crossed over his chest, legs up in the air.

The bottom end of the flag hit the concrete and pushed the flagpole, flag and all, into his guts with such violence, the lance tip emerged just under his belly, his intestines curled around the flag like a snake, soaking it in blood and shit.

He lingered at a shaky, unnatural angle, supported by his legs and the remainder of the flagpole that hadn't made it inside his body, as a chorus of screams filled the air. He gasped, unable to utter a word or a scream, his mouth opening and closing like a dying fish, then he fell sideways and lay there, dead, in front of a screaming crowd.

The camera lingered for just a few more seconds before it returned to the main screen. Four green checkmarks on four images. No more revenge to dish out.

For a moment, she felt a little empty. How would she feel that night? How would she feel tomorrow?

It didn't matter, she thought. She felt no guilt. She felt no remorse. They'd gotten what they deserved, and they'd done it to themselves. All she'd done was tap a button and sit down to watch, not knowing what was going to happen. As far as she knew, it might not even have happened. *Officer, I thought this was just an AI generated video game. How could I have known?*

A message appeared on screen.

DAD

Good job, Baby Girl.

"Thanks, Dad," she whispered with a smile, missing him more than ever, wishing he could give her a hug and promise everything would be alright. He gave her something else.

Another message appeared.

DAD

One for the road? 

She tapped on it.

SHE KNEW WHO she was looking at. Who wouldn't?

It was *HIM*. Capital HIM.

Standing behind a podium in his ridiculous, oversized blue suit and a red tie meant to hide his belly. Reporters, microphones, and cameras pointed at him as he rambled on about how he was the best this, and the most that, and everyone else were the worst this, and the most unpatriotic that.

She'd seen this so many times, and it never failed to turn her stomach.

There was a poop emoji in the middle of the screen.

Just one emoji. A simple prompt: no choice, just act.

She didn't care what it'd do. Anything would be less boring than letting him die of something lame like vascular disease or old age. Without hesitation, without caring about consequences, pushing back the thoughts of masked agents with guns breaking down her door. Agents who wouldn't care she'd been born in America, like her parents before her. They'd just see her brown skin—and that square jaw, damn her dad's genes—and they'd put her on a one-way flight to a concentration camp, never to be seen again.

Let them. I'll proudly go to my grave knowing I took this one down with me.

She tapped on the poop emoji.

The man—the clown—didn't get the zombie look on his face like the others. He doubled over with a loud groan, clutching his abdomen, teeth bared, comb-over sliding off slightly to reveal a bit of his bald head. He could see him wincing and twisting. Screams issued in intermittent, pathetic staccato from him.

She saw his belly swell and swell and swell. Buttons flew out like bullets as the man's bodyguards rushed to his side, but there was nothing they could do. He ballooned, he grew, the visible pale skin of his torso began to stretch and break and bleed.

What happened later was recorded by every camera there.

In seconds, it spread across the internet like a virus. The ludicrous horror and death of a ludicrous, horrible man.

No matter how much they tried to contain it, to delete it, to ban it, to outlaw it, it would never disappear. Years later, it would become nothing but a funny animation to be shared by high school kids as a meme in text applications, too ridiculous to be taken seriously. All they'd need to do was tap the emoji button on their keyboard, slide over to GIFs, and search for "poop explosion". It was so popular it was always the first result.

Fuck the High Road.

BLOOD DROP REACT

Fendy S. Tulodo

BLOOD DROP REACT

Fendy S. Tulodo

At first, everyone assumed this was planned. The act appeared intentional to them. LickHaus was packed like a sealed bag of wet glitter. The walls throbbed with fluorescent tongues, their animations licking the darkness on repeat. Bass lines slapped across skin while sweat and smoke blurred edges. A scream pierced through near the bar, muffled by some drink. Nobody cared. Tonight's crowd came for Dana alone.

From the edge of the pole stage, you could see her moving like heat. Legs wrapped, heels scratched high on metal, the neon casting blood-orange reflections across the floor.

Then it happened.

She jerked back, arms wide, mouth open… Not in rhythm, but in rupture. Her nose bled suddenly, thick and dark, staining her lips and chest. Nobody moved. No one shouted. For almost ten seconds, the crowd thought it was art.

Then she fell.

The sound her spine made when it hit the stage cut through the music like a wrong word in a confession. People began to back up fast, knocking drinks, toppling chairs. Someone slipped on the blood…and finally, the music stopped.

A series of emojis were pulsing behind her on the LED display: 💧
👀

It blinked once more, then faded.

After Dana's body was taken, after the mop buckets rolled out and the bouncers locked the front, Marley sat with me in the restock room. His fingers dug into a can of expired lychee soda while his other hand refreshed Dana's last post again and again. His knee pressed against mine, the way it always did when he was scared, and I didn't move it away.

She had captioned it simple.

Wish me luck 🦋 💧 👀

That combo was on every screen across the city now. Some people shared it like a candlelight vigil. Some as a meme. Others as a dare.

It didn't take long for someone else to drop.

A drag king in Munich lost consciousness halfway through a slow strip tease. A pole artist in Cape Town coughed blood during a spin and never woke up. Their last posts were the same.

Wish me luck 🦋 💧 👀

Marley kept saying it had to be coincidence. That algorithms were just copying each other.

But the emojis…

The blood drop didn't match the standard Apple one. The shape appeared sharper. A faint shimmer emerged when stared at too long, like something trapped beneath thin glass.

Reina texted me four days after Dana's funeral.

REINA

You want to understand it? Come to Glitchside. Don't bring him.

The shop she led me to had no signage, no brand. String lights barely brightened the dim garage, their glow catching on vintage Japanese pop records covering the walls. Burnt metal tinged the stale air.

On a sunken beanbag, a figure in a Hello Kitty hoodie scrolled through a device that had been ancient even when we were born. Their eyes never lifted from the screen. "Late," they noted.

Reina didn't speak.

The hoodie person tossed a cracked flip phone onto the floor between us. "This emoji isn't Unicode. It's not standard. You know what that means?"

I didn't.

"It's regional. Experimental. From before the apps got sterilized. There were underground updates… Secret emoji patches designed for niche communities. This one came from a dance platform. FlowTok."

That rang a bell. FlowTok was banned five years ago for being "emotionally manipulative". Mostly because it let users link dances to mood algorithms.

"This emoji was used to mark high-energy expressions… Peak moments. It flags intensity. But somewhere down the line, it got corrupted. Or…redirected."

"Redirected to what?" I asked.

They looked at me, then stood. "To who."

Reina stepped forward. "You mean someone's controlling it?"

"Not someone," they replied. "Some*thing*. And it's feeding."

"Feeding on what?"

They pointed to my chest. "Performance. But not just physical. Emotional output. If you post the combo at peak intensity, it locks onto you."

I said nothing. They left without another word.

That night, Marley called me. "I posted it," he said quietly.

"You what?"

"I didn't mean to. I was archiving Dana's post and hit share by mistake. It's down now. It was up for less than a minute."

I stayed quiet.

"I feel weird," he added. "My ribs hurt… Like I ran too far, too fast." My fingers twitched, almost reaching for his. I stopped halfway. The space between us felt loud.

"Where are you?"

"My place. Sitting by the shelf. The one with the trophies."

I remembered the shelf. Tilted, packed with medals from all those choreo battles.

The door was already half behind me when I left.

Above a noodle shop that never thawed, Marley's walk-up waited, narrow and cramped. His door was unlocked. Inside, the air felt thick. The lamp kept flickering on its own.

His bare chest moved in circles before the mirror, fingers working hard like some stubborn mark needed scrubbing away. In the glass, his body shrank smaller than real life.

Above the mirror, drawn in red… A heart. Below it, the combo. A stupid, broken heart. Not mine. Not his. But it hit me like it was.

"What the hell is this?" I asked.

He looked confused. "I don't know. I didn't do it. I don't even own lipstick."

I searched the room. Chair near the desk. Bed. Old posters. Shelf. That shelf… I climbed up and felt around. There, tucked behind a frame, was a FlowTok sticker. It glinted with holographic shimmer… and then dripped. Real blood. From a sticker.

My hand jerked back.

Marley sat down, both hands on his chest now. "It feels like it's pushing from the inside."

I stepped back. Drops kept falling from the sticker, staining his floor. Words failed me.

His glassy eyes lifted toward me. "What if I dance?" he asked. "What if I release it?"

I stared. "You think this is about dancing?"

"I think it's about attention. Movement. Ritual."

"You sound insane."

He smiled, weak. "Something real includes me now. Doesn't that scare you?"

I didn't answer.

That night, I burned the sticker. The flame started blue, then green, then black. As it curled into ash, the blood trail it left behind on the floor dried instantly.

But the combo kept appearing on Marley's feed. Automatically. Hidden in backgrounds. Blurred into shadows of photos. Like something was trying to remind us.

And we were starting to believe it could see us back.

The sound of breath changed in Marley's apartment.

It wasn't just his. It was mine too. Like both of us had forgotten how to inhale. Every little motion felt sharp, like the air was watching. We didn't speak for a while. He sat hunched in the corner, arms around his knees, watching me burn the remains of the FlowTok sticker in his sink.

I poured a bit of old soda on the ashes. The foam bubbled. The fizz hissed like warning.

"I think it's done," I said.

Marley didn't move. His body looked softer than usual, but his eyes… They were tight. Alert. Awake in the wrong way.

"You should stay somewhere else tonight."

He nodded, slow.

"You can crash at mine. We'll figure this out."

"Sure," he said. But I knew he wasn't listening.

I left the window open when we walked out. The air inside smelled like old wire and sugar.

We didn't talk the whole walk home. My place was smaller, but safer. I didn't own anything cursed. No trophies. No old apps. Just a couch, a fake plant from Reina's old booth, and an overused heater that buzzed when kicked.

Marley dropped onto the couch without even taking off his jacket. His head knocked my shoulder. Heavy. Warm. I didn't move. "I keep thinking," he said, breaking the silence, "what if this thing doesn't just kill… What if it *changes* first?" His voice cracked. He hated cracking. Only let it slip when it was just me.

"Changes what?"

"People. Like rewiring. You ever feel like it's watching *through* the emoji?"

I stared at him. "You're not making sense."

"It makes sense to me." He reached for his phone, screen dark. I slapped it out of his hand without thinking. It landed screen-down on the carpet.

"Don't touch that thing."

He looked up, startled. "You really think it's in the phone?"

"I think it's in *you* now," I said. My voice was shaking.

Marley didn't reply.

We both sat in silence. The only sound came from the heater clicking every ten seconds. That stupid rhythm.

Click… click… click…

Then the power cut out.

I froze. The room dropped into low-blue from the hallway's emergency lights outside the door. Marley's face was barely visible.

Then his phone lit up again.

His hands weren't on it.

A single vibration shook the object. It inched forward on the carpet before freezing.

I stepped back.

The screen turned on by itself. On it: a video. Blurry. Vertical. It looked like someone's POV walking down a hall. Steps. A mirror at the end. The sound was distorted, like breath and bass overlapping.

The person in the video lifted their hand. Reached toward the mirror.

Written on the glass in dripping red…

🐾💧👀

"Marley…" I said. "Is this live?"

He didn't move.

I reached for the phone. It locked instantly. On the black screen, one red dot blinked. Right in the top corner.

Recording.

I dropped it.

This thing wasn't in the phone. It was in the *camera*. The lens.

It was looking for faces.

It was learning.

We spent the rest of the night with the battery ripped out. I wrapped the phone in tinfoil, stuck it in a metal tin under the sink. I didn't care if that was paranoid. It made me feel better.

Marley didn't sleep. I could hear him breathing fast even with the blanket over his head. At some point, I think he started humming. Something off-key. Something slow.

At sunrise, I checked the mirror.

Nothing was written. But my reflection didn't look quite right. Like the angle was off. Too flat. Too centered.

I stepped back.

"Don't go near it," Marley muttered, wiping sleep from his eyes.

I turned. "What?"

He was already sitting up, eyes bloodshot. "It's spreading through reflections now. You saw it, right?"

I said nothing. My chest was too tight for words. His hand disappeared into the bag, emerging with a crumpled sheet. A printed screenshot. One I hadn't seen before.

A post by someone named Jae_K. Dancer. From Seoul. The caption was different.

Felt cute, might bleed later 🐎 💧 👀

Posted two months ago. Same emoji combo. Same order.

She was found collapsed outside a theatre the same night. But here's the weird part. In the comments, under the first few "RIP" replies, was one that stood out. Just a single red drop emoji.

💧

Posted by: [null]

No profile pic. No link. No username trail. No source. Just the emoji. Sitting there like a full stop at the end of a sentence nobody wanted to read.

"Have you seen that before?" I asked.

Marley nodded. "It shows up under *every one* of them."

"Like…it's watching?"

"Like it's counting."

Later that afternoon, I went to Reina's. Her place always smelled like burnt incense and nail polish remover.

"You brought him, didn't you?" she said when she opened the door.

"No," I said. "He's resting. Probably."

"Resting or broadcasting?" She waved me in.

Inside, her desk was covered in ripped magazines, glitter palettes, and old emoji design guides from the banned years.

"I traced the blood emoji," she said. "It doesn't just exist on Flow-Tok. It got ported. Shared. Smuggled into updates through cracked libraries. I found it attached to a downloadable dance generator called MoodBeat. The file's gone now…but the source code tagged it as RE-ACT-BX-23."

"What does that mean?"

"It means it was written as a reaction emoji, not an input. Like…you can't post it manually unless it reacts first."

"But people *are* posting it."

"No," she said. "They're *thinking* they are. The code rewrites your memory of typing. It just slides in."

I shivered. "So what now?"

"You need to isolate him. Before he performs again."

"He's not going to perform again."

She looked up at me with that dead-serious expression she only used during breakups and ghost sightings. "You sure about that?"

I wasn't.

When I got home, Marley was gone. The tin under the sink was open. The phone was missing. So was my mirror.

He had unscrewed it from the bathroom wall, and on the floor, in lipstick, again:

🐝💧👀

I checked my feed. A new post was live from my account. A selfie of Marley in the mirror, shirtless, eyes wide.

Ready for the show tonight. Let it pour 🐝💧👀

Thousands of likes and no way to delete. The blood emoji blinked every five seconds. The app wouldn't close and I couldn't navigate away from it. And somewhere under the post, sitting like a signature…

From: [null]

I ran.

Down the stairs. Into the street. No coat. No socks. My mind couldn't focus on anything except one word: performance.

The emoji didn't care about logic. It didn't want a puzzle. It wanted an audience. And Marley was giving it what it wanted.

I reached LickHaus first. The metal shutter was down. A sign in marker read, *Reopening Tonight at 9pm – Tribute Showcase for Dana.*

Tribute.

That word made my stomach clench.

I called Reina. Twice. No answer. Sent her a message. No reply.

I called Marley. Straight to voicemail.

I checked his public feed again. Three new posts. Same blood emoji. Same tone like he was hyping an event.

I typed a comment: *Where are you? Call me. This isn't funny.* It wouldn't post. My hands shook as I typed again. *Stop. Please.*

The screen froze.

Then went black.

Then flashed red.

Then showed a close-up of Marley's face. Eyes closed. Breathing heavy. Background pulsing with pink neon. His lips moved. No sound came out.

The post disappeared.

I got what I needed from it, though. He wasn't at the club. Marley was at the *Studio.*

The Studio was where we used to rehearse together before he got good and I got scared. A wide room above a car rental spot. Mirrors on three sides. One speaker system. A pile of water bottles by the door and a cheap ring light on a cracked tripod. It had been shut down for a while, but we both had keys. For old times' sake.

I ran all the way. My legs hurt halfway, but I didn't stop. When I reached the door, I heard it. Music. A slow build. Synth and heartbeat.

Inside, Marley was dancing.

Alone. Shirt off. Sweat running down his spine. Movements sharp but…too smooth. Like he was being guided. Like someone was puppeting from inside.

The emoji was on every mirror. Lipstick again. Bright, wet, raw.

🩰💧👀

Written once per panel. Over and over. Repeating. Perfect spacing.

He didn't see me enter. I stepped in quietly. Watched him spin, freeze, slide. He turned, landed in a drop, flung his arms wide. Blood sprayed.

Real blood, wet and thick and red. From his nose. His ears. His palm.

I shouted his name.

He didn't stop.

The music got louder. The mirrors began to flicker. Reflections doubled. Tripled.

Twisted.

In the reflections, he was bleeding more. Dancing harder. But his real body paused. Looked at me. Whispered, "It's feeding off them now." He collapsed.

I dragged him out of there. His skin was hot. His breath shallow. He kept muttering strange lines. I pressed his face against my chest.

Whispered his name. Over and over. Like saying it might anchor him. Nothing full. Just broken things.

"Filter… Rhythm… It likes pattern… Don't fight the loop… Let it end."

I brought him back to Reina's. She opened the door without asking questions. We laid him on the couch. She pressed cold rags to his face. I wrapped his hands. The blood wasn't thick. It was watery. Too thin.

"He's not dying," she said. "But he's not really here either."

"What the hell does that mean?"

She pointed to his phone. Still in his back pocket. Still recording.

I snatched it out.

The camera app was open. The screen showed the room. But… We weren't in it. Instead, it showed him. Still in the studio. Dancing. Alone.

Looping.

Over and over.

Like it was a feed from another version of him. One stuck.

"Do you see this?"

Reina nodded. "It's the performance memory. The thing doesn't feed on flesh. It feeds on recorded identity."

I stared at her. "So what do we do?"

"We crash it."

"How?"

She looked down. "You dance."

She set everything up that night. A controlled feed. No livestream. A sealed space. Ring light. Old mirror painted black. A script. It seemed like she knew what she was doing, somehow, so I let her do it, uninterrupted. Instead, I prepared for my role.

I was supposed to move for exactly seven minutes. Same beat Marley used. Same emoji written on glass.

But different *intention*.

Reina called it a *loopbreak*. She said, "If it's feeding on patterns, break the rhythm. Twist the gesture. Reverse the spell."

I said nothing. I couldn't think straight. I didn't want to dance. Not since we lost Dana. Not since Marley got dragged in.

But I owed them both.

So I stood in front of the painted mirror, barefoot, shirt wet with sweat already.

The music started.

I moved.

First minute: memory. A slide I used to do with Dana. Quick shoulders. Elbow twist. A flick I learned when she broke her heel mid-show and kept going.

Second minute: pain. Marley's favorite spin. I fumbled it. Landed wrong. My ankle cracked. Not broken. Just a loud, sharp sound breaking through the music.

Third minute: panic.

The mirror shimmered. The emoji pulsed.

Fourth minute: change. I stopped following the script. Let my arms go wild. Bent instead of stretched. Shouted instead of breathing.

Fifth minute: blood. From my nose. Fast. Hot.

I let it drip.

Sixth minute: silence. The music glitched. Slowed. Echoed.

Seventh minute: defiance. I grabbed the mirror. Smeared the emoji. Smeared it into a blur. Broke the rhythm. Screamed, "You don't own this. Not me. Not him. Not us."

Then collapsed.

When I woke up, Reina was crying quietly. Marley sat beside her, awake. Pale. Holding his own phone, which now showed only static.

"It's gone," he said.

I blinked. "What?"

"The loop. The emoji. The comments. All wiped. Like they never happened."

"Even your posts?"

He nodded.

"But Dana…"

"We keep her alive," Reina said. "Differently. Without the code."

Outside, it was morning.

I felt hollow. But…clean. Like something heavy had finally exhaled. I stood slowly, careful of my ankle. My legs shook. My hands trembled. But I smiled. "You hungry?" I asked them both.

Marley laughed. "Starving." He started smiling again. But it wasn't like before. He smiled like someone who barely survived drowning, but still had water in his lungs.

We tried going back to normal.

Whatever that meant.

He danced in small movements now. Only in private. No more mirrors. No phones. No recordings.

I started sketching instead of writing.

Reina didn't talk much anymore, but she let us crash on her floor when it got too quiet.

There was peace for three days. On the fourth, it came back.

But not for us.

I was walking past the old pop-up café near the station when I saw the flyer. Pink paper. Glitter ink. Cheap tape holding it to a light pole.

EMOJIFEST: Queer Emoji Tribute Night!

 — *"Dance Through the Drama"* — Live at Klub Hexa

My stomach dropped.

The poster had a QR code. I scanned it. It led to an *event page*, and my face tightened as I saw that already 500 people had RSVP'd.

The event description read, "Come honor the viral legacy of the BloodDrop Emoji! One night only. Express. Release. Record."

At the bottom of the page was a comment.

Posted by: [null]

I ran straight to Reina's. She was already holding her tablet, lips tight, eyes sharp. "You saw it?"

I nodded.

She turned the screen toward me.

It was worse than I thought. People were posting TikClips again. Filtered edits. Glitchy reuploads of Dana's last moments. Parodies. Covers. Even a drag duo who re-enacted her fall, frame by fucking frame.

Reina whispered, "It mutated."

"What do you mean?"

"It adapted. Now it's not just code. It's culture. Meme level. And you know what that means?"

It couldn't be stopped by deleting accounts or burning phones. It needed an audience to exist, and now the world was giving it one.

Willingly.

Marley didn't want to hear it. "They'll figure it out," he said. "Someone'll see what we saw."

"No, they won't," Reina snapped. "Because now it's packaged as tribute. It's got context. Emotion. Hashtags."

He didn't reply.

We all knew.

Once the internet *loves* something, it becomes armor. Even if it kills. And the emojis…they loved being loved.

"Then we stop the show," I said.

Marley shook his head. "How?"

Reina looked at us both. "We go in. One last time."

I felt my throat tighten. "We…what?"

She walked to her shelf and pulled out a black case. Inside were three custom masks. Mirror-coated visors, shaped like shattered glass, and blackout bodysuits. "I designed these after your loopbreak," she said. "These block reflection. Muffle signals. No mirrors. No light tracking. No facial data."

I stepped back. "You want us to go into Klub Hexa…dressed like ghosts…and stop a performance in the middle of a crowd?"

"Yeah," Reina said. "Exactly."

We got to Klub Hexa an hour before the show. The front was already packed. People wore emoji stickers on their cheeks. Some had fake blood dripping from their mouths. One girl wore a body suit printed with a giant red drop emoji over her heart.

I couldn't breathe.

"Stay focused," Reina whispered behind her visor.

We pushed through the side, backstage. Reina had a contact. Some tech who owed her from an old rave. He let us in without asking too many questions. Inside the main room, the LED screen behind the stage flickered.

🥀 💧 👀

It didn't move. Just glowed.

One heartbeat per second.

The crowd screamed. The MC announced the show.

And the music started.

The first dancer came out in full red. Did a backflip. Landed hard. Crowd roared. The second mimicked Dana's routine. Exact spins. Exact gestures.

I wanted to vomit.

The third dancer wasn't human. It was a *projection*. A composite AI-generated avatar, stitched from clips of Dana, Marley, and others. Its movements were perfect.

Too perfect.

The emoji pulsed faster.

"This is the core," Reina said over the music. "It's making *new loops*."

"How do we stop it?"

She held up a small signal box. "Jammer. Disrupts localized broadcast frequencies for up to two minutes. If we time it right, we can blank the feed just as it peaks."

"What happens then?"

"If the loop doesn't complete, it collapses. The feed ends. The interest breaks."

Marley stepped forward. "What do you need me to do?"

Reina looked at him. Her voice soft. "You go on stage."

"What?"

"You're the original loop survivor. Your pattern has already been corrupted. That makes you the virus' blind spot."

He froze. Then nodded once.

I almost cried.

We moved when the lights cut for transition. Reina and I flanked the stage wings. Marley stepped into the center as the next track started. The screen behind him glowed brighter. The emoji stretched wide.

The crowd screamed.

He didn't dance. He stood still. Waited.

Waited.

Then…he spoke. "This isn't a tribute," he said into the mic. "It's a trap." People blinked. Confused. He continued, his voice strong. "This emoji isn't a vibe. It's a *virus*. It's killed. It'll keep killing. Because you're feeding it with views and likes and filters."

The music stopped.

Total silence.

He looked straight into the crowd. And smiled. "I'm ending the show."

Reina hit the jammer. The screen blinked. Lights shorted. Phones stopped working. And the emoji began to shake. Not literally…but *visibly*.

Its shape twisted. The red turned darker. The figure warped.

Then…

CRACK.

The screen split. Right down the middle. And the emoji started to bleed. Real liquid poured from the broken LED seam. Red. Fast. Sudden.

The club erupted into screams. Some people ran, pushing over each other, through each other, panicked. Others froze, their eyes fixed on the bleeding emoji. Some pulled out phones that no longer worked, confused.

The smell was sharp. Electric and metal.

And then…the feed stopped.

Black screen.

No emoji.

No light.

No loop.

After that night, everything changed.

The EmojiFest page vanished. People stopped using the blood emoji. TikTok issued a quiet update, removing certain filters, blaming it on a "graphic content policy bug."

No one admitted anything.

But the bleeding stopped.

And Marley smiled again. For real this time. He danced alone sometimes. Just for us. No audience. No mirrors. Just rhythm and breath. Our own little space. Crooked, quiet, queer.

Reina moved out of the city. Opened a costume shop in Surabaya. I still get weird postcards with sketches of new visors she's building. Just in case.

Me? I write things down now. Not for clout. Not for views. Just so someone remembers that the blood emoji was real and hungry, and that we beat it. But sometimes, late at night…I check the comments under old posts.

And every now and then, I still see it.

Posted by: [null]

And I log off fast. Just in case.

I thought the story ended at Klub Hexa. We destroyed the loop. Disrupted the feed. No one else danced themselves to death after that. But I was wrong, because it didn't want an audience anymore.

It wanted *legacy*.

Three months later, I got a package. There was no return label. Just my name. Handwritten in a rush. I assumed it was from Reina, another visor design or something. When I opened it, I frowned.

A phone.

It wasn't mine.

It wasn't Marley's.

It had a pink glitter case and a cracked camera lens. On the back was a sticker.

And beneath that, the initials D.K.

Dana Koa.

My hands locked. My brain stalled. The phone buzzed once, then died. I put it in a drawer and didn't sleep for two nights.

On the third, Reina called. She didn't say hello. She just said, "I think it left the app."

"What?"

"It's moved."

"To where?"

"To design. To hardware. It's…in objects now."

I closed my eyes. "Like a ghost?"

"No," she said. "Like a *format*. A style. You know how Helvetica took over design? This thing wants to be that…but in blood."

I didn't know how to respond.

Then she said one last thing. "It's not about dance anymore. It's about expression."

Marley came to visit the next week. He looked better. Healthier. His hair was longer. We sat on the balcony. Drank cheap soda. Watched the neighbors' kids play badminton with broken rackets. He told me he was thinking of leaving town. Not running. Just starting over. Maybe somewhere that didn't have clubs or filters or reminder posts. "I want to remember her the right way," he said.

I nodded.

He reached into his bag. Pulled out a small print.

Dana's face. Smiling. From before all of it. Backstage. Holding a coffee cup. Fuzzy slippers covered my feet, my face bare. The object was placed in my hands by him. A long moment passed as I examined it, trying not to cry.

His voice broke the silence. "Are you okay?"

I nodded again, even though I wasn't. Because behind her, on the wall, barely visible in the photo, was a tiny red mark.

Like a fingerprint.

Shaped like a drop.

Shaped like an eye.

Later that night, I took the phone out again. The one from the package. It turned on without charging and the home screen lit up. It was empty, save for a single app.

No name. No icon.

Just three symbols: 🐝 💧 👀

I hovered over it. My finger shaking. Then I tapped. It opened the camera and showed me my own face. It was mine, I know, but different. Angled. Sharper. Too perfect.

I blinked.

The reflection blinked…two seconds late.

Then it smiled, the lips stretching thin and wide, drawing up and up at the corners. The mouth opened, showing my teeth, only they weren't my teeth anymore.

A voice came through the speaker.

Flat. Genderless. Half static.

"Thank you for your performance. You are being archived."

Then the screen cracked. Blood trickled down from the top corner. It wasn't real blood, but not fake either. Something in-between.

I dropped the phone. Stepped back.

Heard the buzzing again.

From the mirror.

From the wall.

From inside the wires.

The next day, I painted everything black. Covered the mirrors. Burned the rugs. Switched to analog. Threw away all my screens. Went fully offline.

Wrote this story on paper. Pen. Notebook. Bound it myself.

If you're reading this, it means the emoji survived, and that it found a new face.

Maybe yours.

Maybe someone else's.

It'll look small. Cute. Maybe ironic.

But if you see it...*don't click.*

Don't dance.

Don't react.

Because that's all it needs; a reaction.

One little click.

Then it becomes yours.

Forever.

UMOJI

Lucas Demorre

UMOJI

Lucas Demorre

"I'm no doctor, but I don't think a heart is supposed to look like that."

Detective Lynn Rottorio's words echoed through the nearly silent morgue. A line of deep refrigerators lined one wall, their metal dull. Three autopsy tables took up most of the rest of the room, each with its own tray of sharp equipment sitting adjacent. The floor was dotted with drains every few feet, and a row of cabinets and shelves took up the wall opposite the body storage. The air was light and, somehow, carried no scent. The absence was as profound as the sterile, antibacterial stink she had expected.

"Well I am a doctor," Charlene Foreman, forensic pathologist to the stars, stated plainly, "and I have to agree."

The glow of the doctor's tablet, a shocking blue in the otherwise grey and white morgue, reflected off of her plastic goggles, but Rottorio could feel the other woman's eyes gliding over the body between them, resting on the middle table and as still and empty as the air. The body, a man, was unremarkable. White, tall, thin. Brown hair, brown eyes, clear skin. Somewhere in his mid twenties. Too young to die, yes, but plausible. A hundred men just like this one could lie on the table, and Rottorio wouldn't have thought twice about it. But this one was different.

For one, he was found under a bridge without anything to identify him. No wallet and no phone. Finding a body under a bridge without these things isn't remotely unheard of, but this man didn't display any of the characteristics that Rottorio had come to recognize from these unfortunate, yet expected, discoveries.

He was clean, even before he was brought to the station in a heavy black bag. His clothes were worn in, but laundered. From what Rottorio could tell, his veins remained undisturbed and below the surface of his skin, where they belonged. Well, most of them.

Not the ones around his heart.

Those were raised, a dark blue tapestry inked onto the skin of his chest surrounding the protruding muscle that drew the women's attention. The heart sat above the skin. It seemingly burst out, ripping through the rib cage and pectorals like they were made of cotton candy. Even with the force it must have taken, the heart remained firmly attached to the body, held in place by a force that the pathologist had yet to uncover. Dr. Foreman pressed on the heart with gloved hands, moving it slightly with her face held close, examining the physics of the thing.

While the rest of the body had gone ashen with time and refrigeration, the heart remained disturbingly fresh. It was a deep, ruby red. Plump, and even with a slight shine.

Of course, the most concerning part for the women was the shape.

Detective Rottorio cleared her throat. "It's a bit… classic, isn't it?"

"It is," Dr. Foreman agreed, head twisting over the organ, looking from all angles.

The heart had a sharp point at the bottom. The sides rose from the point, curling in until meeting each other in the middle. A perfect heart. Something Cupid would have been proud of.

From Rottorio's untrained perspective, it looked like several chambers and valves had swollen and arranged themselves into a commercial shape. There was nothing cartoonish about the heart, though. It was clearly animal. Meaty and grotesque.

"So, what could've caused it?" Rottorio asked. She'd never heard of anything that caused an actual human heart to lose its anatomical shape and become so clearly defined.

"Honestly," Charlene said, fingers tapping absentmindedly on the sides of her tablet, "I have no fucking idea."

RHONDA STARED AT ME, accusing.

"You know what you did."

I blinked at her, mind searching for what I could've possibly done within the sixteen hours since I last saw her at my last shift.

"I seriously have no idea," I defended.

She scoffed, putting a wrinkled hand on her hip. Rhonda was my manager at Frothy Boys, which was like Hooters for West Hollywood gays who wanted a cup of coffee and a muffin instead of a beer and some chicken breast. Or any breast, for that matter.

Rhonda was a puzzle to me. Outwardly, she looked like she might teach Sunday school children the importance of feeling guilty for things they haven't done yet. Her thin, graying blonde hair had that high, defying-gravity style that seemed to be all the rage for the Christian women who left their morals in the pews when they left the service. Yet here she was, strict overseer of an establishment that would've made all of Sodom and Gomorrah blush.

The uniform, a maroon apron, white tank top, and tight, equally maroon five inch inseam shorts, the mesh kind that camp counselors wore in those homoerotic 80's movies, made these little chats with Rhonda all the more entertaining (and occasionally humiliating). It felt like talking to my Grandma, but my ass is being displayed to hungry gays while it's happening.

"I clocked out on time," I said. "I did everything on the closing checklist, including the nasty stuff. I even threw out the leftover bagels," I put up a finger, "something I still have objections to, by the way."

"I don't give a shit about that," Rhonda said.

I stuck my head out, confused and waiting for her to continue. Whatever she was referring to had piqued my interest. It must be huge. Rhonda gave shits about everything.

"Pardon me," Garrett said, squeezing past us from the small back employee-only area to the main dining room. He was one of our bigger employees, with huge arms and hairier legs than most wild animals. He seemed in a rush to start his shift, probably worried that Rhonda would reprimand him for being on time, rather than early. His apron was clutched in his fist, and Rhonda didn't even flinch when his absurd bulge brushed past her stomach as he maneuvered through the tight doorway.

Rhonda squinted at me. "You really don't remember? C'mon Joey, I thought you were better than that."

I suddenly felt bad. Whatever I'd forgotten, it clearly meant something to her. Rhonda was a hardass, but she was *our* hardass and we all loved her to death.

"Sorry," I said in earnest.

She sighed and shook her head. "You never called my grandson!"

Oh. Oops.

"You just gave me his number yesterday!" I exclaimed. "And by the way, you shouldn't just expect me to call someone, like, on the phone. That's insane."

"Insane?" she questioned.

"Yes. Insane. Like, disturbing, even. I don't know your grandson, and you just want me to… call him?"

"Yes!"

I shook my head and tutted. "No, no, no, Rhonda. I need his Insta or something."

"You don't think my grandson will be up to your standards?" she asked. "My own flesh and blood?"

I rolled my eyes. "It isn't just about looks. But kinda, yeah. I also need more information! How old is he? Where does he work? Does he work? Is he a bum?" Rhonda's eyes narrowed at that and I backed up. "Is he a totally lovely man? Probably! But I need more info. And is he, like, a top? These things matter, Rhonda."

"Why on Earth would I know if he's a top? Anyway, I thought my word was enough 'info,'" Rhonda said, producing air quotes. "And besides, those are all questions that you can ask, in person, on a date."

I sighed. "I've got to get working. My manager hates when I have personal conversations on company time."

"Cute," Rhonda said.

I winked at her. "Instagram handle, then we can talk about dates."

She pursed her lips and looked down at the tiny silver watch that hung loose on her wrist. "Your shift started forty-five seconds ago. Why aren't you serving customers?"

I shot her a smile and turned around, heading to the counter.

"How's my ass look?" I called back.

"Plump," Rhonda responded, dryly.

Perfect.

The first couple hours of my shift went smoothly. There were four of us working, plus Rhonda. I was working the register, taking orders and the occasional number from older gays who hadn't learned what

I shared with Rhonda earlier. We were taught to always accept the numbers, and other flirtations, of the customers unless they were being creepy or aggressive. There were almost never any problems, but when there were, we handled it. That's the thing about a bunch of image-obsessed queers working under one roof, we went to the gym a lot and had the muscles to prove it. Some of my twinkier coworkers didn't look like it, but we could all throw a punch.

Garrett was on primary barista duty, but I helped out when the register was slow. I definitely didn't mind. It was a tight space, and Garrett is fun to collide with. He had a full face of wellkempt facial hair that I wouldn't have minded giving me skin irritation.

One of the aforementioned "twinkier" coworkers, Shawn, was working our rarely-used drive through. It wasn't often that someone came to Frothy Boys for the lattes, which aren't that great. You had to come into the building to make the trip worth it. Shawn did his best through the tiny window.

The last position was held by Woody (yes, his real name). It was labeled as "Floor" but we all knew it meant "Primary Eye Candy." Whoever worked the floor was delivering drinks and pastries, checking in on customers, and lifting his apron every other minute to wipe imaginary sweat from his upper lip or bending over to pick up a clumsily dropped napkin.

"Hey, baby!" Lisa squealed as she entered, loud enough to make me flinch.

She skipped over to Woody and threw her arms around his shoulders, leaning in for a kiss before I gave a very loud and very pointed cough. It did the trick, and Lisa's eyes widened in an "oops" kind of way before she backed up a little. The last thing we needed was our eye candy kissing his girlfriend in front of the clientele. Sure, some guys would be into that, but most would feel cheated.

Frothy Boys supported all queer identities, but pansexual didn't really sell.

Neither did bi, unfortunately. That's why Ethan didn't work here anymore.

During a lull in the consistent flow of horny coffee drinkers, Woody came up to the register and whispered, "Hey, thanks for the save earlier."

"No problem," I said. "You're lucky I saw before Rhonda."

"Totally," he agreed. "Anyway, I'm gonna head out soon. It's our anniversary, so Lisa and I are doing a whole date night thing and then something real special." He ended the sentence with a wink.

"Oh yeah?" I asked with a raised eyebrow. "How special?"

"It's a secret, but you should think pirates, and plastic."

"Good for you," I said. I can appreciate both pirates and plastic.

"Sure is," he said with a grin before turning and walking away to seduce another customer. Lisa was waiting for his shift to be over at a table in the corner, checking on her phone now and then but almost always watching him. She got off on it, which I could understand. Good for her. Good for them.

I was painfully aware of how single I was. Ever since Ethan, it was almost impossible to get back into dating. Everything just felt wrong. But it had been too long and I was out of practice. Not with the sex part. Just the actual relationship bit.

Someone slapped my ass, and I jumped.

"How's it goin' tiger?" Garrett said from behind me. He smelled like brown sugar syrup.

I blushed, feeling kind of stupid. "It's going. You?"

"Same. Almost ready to head out?"

"Yep," I said. The day had flown by. "Just waiting for Rhonda to give the all clear."

Thirty seconds later, she did.

I wasn't closing that night, thank god. Shawn and Garrett had that privilege. In the locker room, I stripped down to my briefs and threw my uniform in the canvas tote bag I brought with me, and slipped into a pair of pajama pants and plain hoodie. My phone buzzed inside my locker as I pushed my head through the head hole, vibrating the entire row of lockers. The sound was loud. Louder than I would've expected. Angry.

I looked at the message, confused. It looked like it should've come from Rhonda's number, but it didn't. The little gray notification was from an unknown contact. Besides, Rhonda didn't text. She called, always. It was one of her most bothersome traits. But if the text wasn't from Rhonda, then who? My eyebrows furrowed as I read the message over and over again, confusion lighting up my brain with subtle undercurrents of fear and dread, although I wasn't sure why.

UNKNOWN

You know what you did.

WOODY SQUINTED AT his phone, confused. He wracked his brain. What had he done? And why is someone texting him about it on a Thursday night at ten o'clock? His eyes scanned over the text again before he realized it had been sent a few hours ealier. Oops.

Lisa had been keeping him busy. They'd been together for an entire year, and both wanted to celebrate it properly. A year was Woody's longest relationship. By far. It had taken forever to find Lisa, and she was perfect for him. Fun, extroverted, always down for an adventure, and a total freak. They matched each other well in that way.

"Almost ready, baby?" Lisa called from the bathroom.

They were in her apartment. It was a decent size for LA, so they spent most of their time there. Especially most of their sexy time. The things that they got up to required space and privacy, something that Woody's shoebox with roommates couldn't allow for.

"You know I'm ready!" His excitement throbbed between his legs.

Woody laid back on the bed, naked. He watched the bathroom door, eager and practically drooling. The hours before had been nice. Romantic. They did the whole dress up, fancy restaurant dinner, walk in the park, anniversary thing, but that was just fancy foreplay. They both knew they were just waiting for this.

Sex was their love language. Like physical touch, but deeper. More intimate. They could be completely and totally raw with each other, in every sense of the word. It brought them closer than anything else. And the so-called "honeymoon phase" showed no sign of slowing, even after a year.

The door cracked open with a slice of bright white light that disrupted the moody, candlelit vibe of the rest of the room. Lisa flipped the bathroom light off and stepped into the room, swaying her hips and brushing her hands down the sides of her breasts, pushing them together. Up and down, achingly slow.

Woody whistled. "Damn."

She was dressed in black lacy lingerie that hugged her curves and trailed down her back in a train. Woody strained to get a better look, pushing himself up onto his elbows. Behind her back, Lisa held something that brought a grin to both of their lips.

"Happy anniversary," Lisa said with a giggle. "How's my big boy feeling tonight?"

Woody groaned. "Look what you do to me." His cock was growing; close to leaking.

On the bedside table, his phone vibrated.

Lisa put a hand in front of her face in exaggerated shock at the sight of Woody's wood. "Oh my!" she said. "Is that for me?"

On the other side of the bed, her phone chirped with a notification.

They both ignored it.

Woody gripped his base and waved the length. "All for you."

"Well," Lisa said, stepping over Woody's discarded dress pants on the floor, "that looks very nice. But I have something for you too."

Woody's phone buzzed, and Lisa's chirped.

"Oh yeah?" Woody said. He laid back down into the sheets and let his hand slither down past his dick and to his taint. "Something for me?"

Both phones lit up with more notifications.

"Goddamit," Lisa said, throwing her arms up in frustration. A black harness and dildo clattered together in one hand. The other came up and started rubbing her eye. "That is *really* throwing me off." She walked around the bed. "Sorry, babe, just let me go on silent."

"Yeah, yeah, same," Woody said. He leaned over and picked up his phone. His penis still rock hard. A little too hard, but that's just what Lisa did to him.

"That's weird," Lisa mumbled, still pressing into her right eye. Woody could hear the slight squelching from his place three feet away.

Looking at his own phone, confused for the second time that night, he made a small "huh" sound. He had dozens of text messages. They were all the same. Only one emoji.

Lisa tossed the strap-on onto the bed next to her and looked closer at her own phone.

"Why is a random number texting me the winking, tongue out emoji like a hundred times?"

Woody looked up from his own collection of emojis and towards his girlfriend.

"Jesus!" he grunted.

She looked at him. "What?"

"What's wrong with your eye?"

In the ten seconds since he'd looked at her, Lisa's right eye had swollen completely closed. The skin was puffy and slightly yellow, although that could've been the candlelight. The other eye, her left eye, was looking at him, large and alarmed.

"What do you mean?" Her hand came away and Woody watched as she realized that she couldn't open it. "Oh my god, what is going on?"

Concerned, Woody got up on his knees on the mattress and shuffled closer, examining her face. The left eye seemed to keep growing. It looked way bigger than normal.

"Uh," he said, trying not to freak her out, "maybe it's a reaction to the dildo? Can you, like, blink the other one?"

"We play with dildos all the time!" Lisa looked confused for a moment, then panicked. "Oh my god!" she exclaimed. "I can't blink. My eye hurts. And I can't open the other one. Oh my god." As her words came out, they started to get more garbled.

It was then that Woody noticed his cock. It was hard. Still. Harder than before, even. Harder than he thought he'd ever been in his life. The skin was a dark red, almost purple.

"It's probably just…*ugh*," Woody said, trying to focus on his panicking girlfriend but distracted by the growing ache in his crotch. "Probably just some kind of allergic reaction."

"Allerthick reacthon?! It cn't—" Lisa said, and Woody noticed that her tongue was swollen too. Aggressively so.

Woody started to speak. "I'm gonna call 9—" His words were cut off when the ache in his penis overwhelmed his thoughts.

He fell onto the mattress, grabbing his crotch and groaning. He didn't want to look, but knew he had to. The skin was a dark purple now, and his shaft was thicker than before. Much thicker. It was the circumference of a beer can, and growing. Any other circumstance, and they would have celebrated his new girth, but not like this.

Not like this.

A maze of thick, protruding veins covered his dick, thumping and enlarged. Woody felt faint as he looked down on his penis. He tried to touch it, but it was hot and painful to even brush with his fingertips.

They needed help.

In his peripheral vision, Woody watched as Lisa began to truly panic. Her tongue lolled out of her mouth, stretching and filling every second. Filling with what, he didn't know. Neither of them did. Lisa's mouth was overtaken by the pulsing muscle; tears leaked out of the one eye that was open, now twice the size it had been. Her hands thrashed around from her tongue to her eye, both the open and shut one, in an attempt to do something, anything, against the intrusions. As the seconds passed, she began to claw at her neck, desperate to suck in deep lungfuls of air.

Sweat began to run down Woody's naked body as he pushed himself up and towards his dropped phone. He clutched it and glanced at the screen. The text messages stared back at him.

UNKNOWN

As he tried to recover his thoughts, a fresh wave of pain rolled through Woody's cock. The elasticity of his foreskin snapped, and blood gushed from the tear. The agony was so fiery, the pressure so intense, that he dropped the phone again and curled in on himself. Through tears, he noticed something so peculiar that it cleared the fog for only a split second.

"What the fuck?" he grunted, staring at the tip of his dick, now a dull, sickly green.

The pain came back in full force as something long and thin—a stem—grew from his urethra.

His screams were only matched by the dull thud of Lisa falling down onto the ground next to the bed, seizing as her tongue grew too large for her body. It flopped onto her face, wet and crossed with thin veins, gravity pulling it down. The growth continued into her throat, squeezing off her airway. Even as the room dimmed, Lisa's left eye remained huge and open. Her wheezing and gasping began to quiet, the lack of oxygen causing her to pass out before the pop of her snapping jaw reached Woody's ears.

He didn't hear it though. Not really. His concentration was too focused on his own pain. The phallus was now over a foot long, and full of so much blood that Woody started to feel lightheaded. His hands gripped the sheets on the bed. All he could do was scream. He knew Lisa needed help, that they both needed medical attention, that there was something very, very wrong with his penis, but he couldn't do anything. The pain was incredible, the pressure even more so. How his penis hadn't popped like a gory balloon, Woody didn't know. Part of him wished it would. At least that might end the torture.

New pain blossomed in his chest. Woody gasped, spittle flying out of his mouth, as he felt his heart beating in quick, irregular thumps. Blood rushed in his ears. His screams stopped, his throat only able to produce a weak, croaking sound.

Then the world went black. Woody died the same way he lived.

Hard.

Very hard.

THE WOMAN WHO stood before me with her hands clasped in front of her torso didn't seem like our usual clientele.

For one, she was a woman. Frothy Boys usually attracted middle aged men or wide-eyed baby gays. Every once in a while we got women who came in just because they liked the view and didn't care about our sexual orientation. We'd even had a few hungover bachelorette parties during my time here. But this lady didn't look like a voyeur—no judgement, it's just the terminology—or like she spent last night wasted. She wore a dark blue suit with a white shirt underneath. Her straight brown hair was pulled into a tight bun on top of her head. A fierce professionalism dripped from her straight shoulders.

Maybe she was just confused on what type of establishment this was. We got those occasionally as well. Women whose innocence led them astray.

"My name is Detective Rottorio," she said. Her voice was slightly gravelly. "Can I talk to you for a moment?"

Okay, not confused then.

I blinked at her. "I mean, not really. I'm working. And we're kind of swamped." I glanced around the cafe until I spotted Rhonda's hairdo disappearing into the backrooms. "My manager just went back there,"

I said, pointing. "You can try her. Unless…" A ball of unease rose up in my stomach. "Unless you need me specifically?" I hadn't done anything wrong. Nothing that I could think of, anyway, but that didn't stop my voice from rising a few octaves.

The detective's eyes identified Rhonda quickly and she nodded. "I'll do that, thanks," she said as she started walking towards her.

I was working the floor, slutting myself out the best I could. A giant tip jar sat on the counter and I wanted it as full as possible. I wasn't supposed to be working the floor today. Woody was scheduled for the position again, but he hadn't shown up today. It was unfortunate. A no call, no show probably meant he was fired. I'd miss him. And his butt.

I wanted to know why the detective was here. Questions rattled around my brain, messing up my concentration. I gave one table the wrong latte and then brought a different, also incorrect, latte the second time. The guy seemed annoyed but cooled off when I "absentmindedly" pulled up my apron and tank top to scratch my abs and pushed my crotch forward with a "I'm terribly sorry, sir." I don't even think that guy ended up with the right latte. Maybe all the drool masked the taste of the hazelnut syrup.

"Hey," I said to Garrett while no one was waiting at the counter. "Have you heard anything about why there's a detective here talking to Rhonda?"

His brow furrowed, confused and concerned. Even so, he lifted himself onto the counter, ass towards the customers and leaned in towards me. Doing everything slightly slutty was engrained into our minds, I guess. A hazard of the job.

"I didn't realize that lady was a detective," he said. "I thought it was some kind of health inspection thing. I was a little freaked out, but now I'm like, a lot freaked out."

I nodded. "Yeah, they've been talking for forever. I wonder what's going on."

"Did you say detective?" Shawn slid over from his barista duties. "Like, *police* detective? Talking to Rhonda?"

"Yeah, a police detective. At least, I assume. Are there other kinds of detectives?" I asked. "Either way, it isn't good. Do you think she, like, did something?"

"Rhonda?" Shawn said. "No way."

A dripping noise came from our left and Shawn said, "Oh shit," as he darted over to clean up whatever he'd left unattended. Garrett shook his head and chuckled.

"Whatever it is, I'm sure it's nothing to worry about," he said.

"You're probably right." I wiggled my head like I could shake the thoughts out. "It's just weird."

"Definitely weird." Garrett hopped down from the counter as he spoke and adjusted the crotch of his shorts in a way that made it very clear he wasn't wearing underwear.

"Commando?" I said, not hiding my eyeline towards his clearly defined package.

He shrugged. "Laundry day."

"Maybe you should've been Primary Eye Candy."

"Nah, you're doing just fine."

I felt my cheeks turn a vibrant red and rolled my eyes. My stomach twisted in a pleasant way that I hadn't felt in a year or two. Not since Ethan. I wonder how he's doing.

Finally, Rhonda stalked out of the backrooms, Detective Rottorio at her heels. Her face was whiter than normal, which was an impressive feat. A cloud hung over them both. It was oppressive, and seemed to spread throughout the entire cafe in seconds, devouring every molecule of oxygen.

Something was very, very wrong.

Rhonda cleared her throat, loud enough that everyone knew it was intentional. A call for silence. Surprisingly, most of our patrons quieted immediately.

"Ladies, gentlemen, and others, I'm afraid that due to a safety issue, Frothy Boys will be closing immediately. Please exit the building. Now."

Holy shit. There must have been a bomb or something. I couldn't think of any other reason for Rhonda to close the store early. And while we were busy, too.

Customers grumbled but made their way to the exit. I walked up to Rhonda to ask if we should leave too, but she silenced me before I could even open my mouth with a hissed, "Stay."

As soon as the last customer left the building, Rhonda rushed over to the glass door and threw the lock, flipping the sign to "Closed" in the process. She turned back and walked towards us, lips in a firm line.

"You should all take a seat," Rhonda said, addressing the boys in the room. There was a slight quiver in her voice, which put me even more on edge.

Garrett, Shawn, and I exchanged glances before doing as she said and sitting at one of the tables. A half empty frozen concoction sat sweating in the middle, abandoned by its owner. I was starting to sweat too, so I felt some companionship with the drink.

"What's going on?" Shawn asked. His fingers drummed on his hairless thighs. "What's the safety issue?"

I reached behind my back and untied my apron, setting it on top of the table. Garrett did the same. The three of us sitting there in barely any clothing, particularly Garrett, in front of an older woman and a police detective must have looked like the beginning of a weird porno.

"Here's the deal," Detective Rottorio said. "Two days ago, the body of a young man was discovered. He was identified as Reuben Clark." The three of us gasped in unison. How could we not? Reuben used to work with us. He got fired right after Ethan quit. "This morning, we identified the bodies of Woodrow Pollock and Lisa Fermite, which were found in her home."

The room seemed to shrink. A lump grew in my throat like a lead bubble. Reuben and Woody both worked at Frothy Boys. Lisa visited all the time. What are the odds?

"How?" I croaked. "How did they die?"

Detective Rottorio's lips pursed and she put her hands on her hips. Authority oozed off of her. "Well I can't give you much information. It's an ongoing investigation. But their manners of death were…strange."

The word looked like it hurt to say. A short sound came from the backrooms, but nobody else seemed to notice. I must have imagined it.

"Strange?" Garrett asked. "Strange how?"

Rottorio nodded. "To be honest with you, both of their bodies were found in very confusing states. There were anatomical anomalies that connected them."

"Anatomical anomalies?" I sputtered. "What are you saying? That there's something in the store that's, like, mutating us or something?"

The detective shook her head. "Not at all. We're still investigating, but at this time there's no reason to believe that there's any sort of biological issue here."

That sound again. It was louder. Insistent. The others heard it too. It was a small *clink* sound. It came again. Again. Rhonda seemed to recognize it and walked off towards the sound.

"So what then?" Garrett asked. "Some sort of serial killer?"

Shawn's hand flew to his mouth. "Oh my God it's *totally* a serial killer, isn't it?"

"No," Detective Rottorio huffed, impatient. "That's not what I'm saying. There's no evidence that these deaths were homicides."

"What the hell?" I said, louder than intended. "If they aren't biological, and they aren't murders, then what the hell are they?"

"Honestly," Rottorio said, "we're not sure. But that's where you come in. We need your help. The only thing that connects Reuben, Woodrow, and Lisa is this building."

Rhonda walked back into the room. Her phone was clutched in her hand. I could tell it was hers because no one else in West Hollywood has a phone case with a faux leather magnetic screen cover.

"Sorry," she said, looking confused. "My phone was blowing up—"

Then Rhonda's head exploded.

To be more accurate, it popped.

The sound reminded me of a champagne bottle, not very loud but sudden enough to be jarring. The second that it happened seemed to stretch on for an hour. One moment, Rhonda was speaking, and the next, the top of her skull was rocketing into the air with enough force to hit the high ceiling. She stood there after it happened. It's impossible to say for how long. There was a distinct jagged line across what used to be her forehead. It came up and down in pointed peaks right above her eyes. Her mouth was twisted down in a dramatic, open lipped frown. Splatters of blood and brain matter coated the entirety of Frothy Boys, including my face. I couldn't bring myself to wipe it off.

And then I was on the floor, pushed down by Garrett. He threw his body on top of mine and it took me a moment to figure out why. Detective Rottorio was yelling. Phrases like "Get down" and "Cover your heads." The words sounded like they were being screamed under water.

Was Rhonda shot? That's what Rottorio's shouting made it sound like. But I thought gunshots were supposed to be louder than that. And messier. The line across Rhonda's forehead had been zig zagged, but clean.

I looked up from where my cheek was pressed into the cold tiled floor. Just in time to watch the rest of Rhonda's slurried brain slop out of her skull and onto the ground. A small chunk of scalp with wisps of her hair still clinging to it flopped from the counter with a wet slap that made me realize how quiet everything had gotten. Rottorio wasn't speaking anymore. Shawn laid a few feet away with his hand pressed over his mouth, a wild, terrified look in his eyes. The bitter, metallic smell of a human's insides overpowered the scent of coffee that had baked itself into the walls. It burned my nostrils.

A dull glow caught my attention and Rhonda's phone came into view from its thrown position under a nearby table. It was coated in her gore, but small hints of the screen still showed through. It was enough for me to see her text messages. Or maybe, text message. Singular.

UNKNOWN

I pulled the phone closer, ignoring the wetness of my manager. The jagged peaks of the line right above the eyes. It was an exact match. Like someone had traced the emoji over Rhonda's face and chipped away at her skull until they reflected each other absolutely.

There was movement to my left as Rottorio scrambled to her feet.

She reached into her pocket and pulled out her phone. Her eyebrows furrowed, looking down at her screen. The detective's head jerked back and her other hand flew to the corner of the mouth, like she'd just been sucker punched. Her fingers were playing with something. Pulling. A noise came from her throat. Something that didn't match her hardened, professional exterior.

Panic.

Rottorio's hand came back down and began furiously typing on her phone. A line of metal glinted in the light and it took me a few beats to recognize what I was seeing.

A zipper. It stitched her lips together, new teeth digging out of her skin every second or so. They latched themselves together. Rottorio didn't look pained, but there was no way that each emerging piece wasn't agony. Her eyes squeezed closed as the zipper's last teeth dug out of her lips and the sliding piece came up from the corner of her cheek.

"What the fuck?" Garrett whispered into my ear. He was still on top of me.

Detective Rottorio began frantically pulling at the zipper, but it wouldn't budge. Her phone was all but forgotten in her hand. We needed help, I realized, and she wasn't going to be able to get it. Even if she could overcome her terror, who could she call with a zipped up mouth?

I pushed Garrett off of me and shoved myself to my feet. "Phone," I mumbled. "We need a phone."

Garrett rose behind me as I started towards the locker room. Shawn quickly followed, looking back for a moment.

I considered leaving the store and heading out onto the street, but the strangers around Frothy Boys were unreliable, at best. Plus, our situation sounded—well, it *was*—unbelievable. Our cellphones were the only options, and closer than anything else.

The three of us sprinted into the changing room. I threw open my locker and dug around for my phone, relieved to find it under my hoodie, exactly where I left it. A nightmare scenario had flickered in my mind of finding the phones missing or destroyed or something.

Standing there, in the locker room, looking down at my phone reminded me of last night. I was doing the same thing. The ominous text message seemed weird then, but looking back it was clearly threatening. Did we all get the same message? No one else had mentioned it, but I hadn't brought it up either.

It didn't matter. I needed to call for help.

Shawn started breathing heavily behind me.

"Guys," he said, "what the fuck is happening?"

Garrett and I turned, zeroing in on the phone that was shoved in our faces. A line of notifications flooded the screen like a broken dam. Like Rhonda, only one emoji per message.

"What does the crying emoji mean?" Shawn asked, eyes wide and face pale.

A tear slipped down his cheek and Shawn wiped it away. Then another, and another. Tears fell from his ducts like rain. He looked confused, pushing at his cheeks. Soon, the tears stopped being individuals and became a singular unit. Water welled up under his lower eyelids, pushing the skin forward with so much force that I could see a map of veins underneath the bulging flaps. Liquid spilled down Shawn's cheeks in a sudden, thick river. He gasped as water hit the floor, sounding like an open tap.

I watched, mouth agape, wanting to but unable to help. I'd never seen anything like it. No amount of hysterical sobbing I'd witnessed had ever accounted for anything like what was happening to Shawn.

The skin of his face seemed to shrink and pull over his facial bones. He was already skinny, but all of the moisture being pulled from his body was drawing his flesh inwards. Garrett stepped forward to do something, but flinched backwards when the water gushing down Shawn's face tinged red.

Shawn had run out of tears. Out of water.

The liquid that poured from his eyes alternated from a bloody crimson, to urine yellow, to the other, less identifiable colors of sludgy bile and shimmering spinal fluid. Every ounce of liquid inside Shawn's body had been drawn up and expelled from his tear ducts. His throat made croaking sounds as his flesh continued to contour around his bones.

Garrett grabbed my hand and we ran from the room, horrified. The last Frothy Boys standing. There was a wet thump as Shawn's stiff body hit the ground behind us, landing in the flood of moisture that had leaked from his eyes. We darted back the way we came, my phone still clutched in my hand.

As we reentered the dining room, I slipped on the juices that clung to my shoes and nearly fell, but Garrett held me up. What we saw there brought me no relief.

Detective Rottorio was on the ground, facedown, with a small pool of blood next to her head. Her back rose and fell, shallow, yet visible. Unconscious, then. Knocked out by the person standing behind her.

It was a young woman. She wore simple black pants and a sweatshirt. A cellphone was clutched in her right hand. It was glowing brighter than I'd ever seen a phone glow. The light was almost painful to look at.

"Who the fuck are you?" I asked. There was no doubt in my mind that she wasn't here to help. A heavy frown sat on her face. A mask of fury.

"My name is Charlene," she said. "Charlene Foreman."

The name sent a chill down my spine. Not Charlene, I'd never heard that name before, but Foreman? That was definitely familiar.

"Like…" Garrett said, putting the pieces together in his own mind. "Like Ethan Foreman?"

When Ethan and I dated, he mentioned a sister a few times, but he always called her Carly.

"We came here to get away from our parents," Charlene said with a sneer. "They're Christians. The hateful kind. Our whole town was, honestly. This was our escape. And then he took this fucking job. He was comfortable with himself for the first time in his life. Happily bisexual. Confident. Watching him thrive was all I ever wanted. But then some kids from high school found out where he worked. What he was doing in West Hollywood. They did what horrible people always do on social media. The hate. The trolling. They bombarded his socials with disgusting comments and slurs and, yes," she waved her phone in the air for a moment, "emojis." Nausea rolled through my stomach and I had to fight to keep the vomit down. "But it didn't really matter, right? He still had this job, right? The job that he loved so much. The job that brought him confidence and even a boyfriend!" She stared at me, and the acid creeped even farther up my esophagus. "And then, uh oh! His coworkers started to hop on the hate train. They told him that he couldn't be bisexual. That he was lying to himself and that in this building, everyone was gay, and only gay. Even his boyfriend was cracking jokes."

Tears welled up in my eyes but I tried to force them down, remembering Shawn. "They were just jokes," I said. "Truly. I didn't mean—"

"I don't give a shit what you meant!" Charlene screeched. "Only what you did. It was all too much for him. And he was starting to believe the things everyone was saying. So he decided to leave. To flee.

He went back to our hometown."

"Oh God," I said, shuddering. "He didn't… He didn't do something bad, right? To himself."

Charlene curled her upper lip. "If my brother killed himself, I'd rip you apart piece by piece with my bare fucking hands." She took a moment and composed herself. "No, he didn't harm himself. Not physically, anyway. But my brother is dead in all the ways that matter. He joined the church. He was 'healed' of his sexual perversions. He broke off all contact with me. So now I'm making you all pay. I'm starting here, and next I'll be taking a trip home. There's some bullies there that need tending to." She looked down at the phone in her hand and sighed. "I was so angry. Consumed with it, really. And then I found this. I don't know what it is. Not really. Some sort of magic? Maybe a demon? It doesn't matter. When I found out what it could do, it was my golden ticket. See, I'm a forensic pathologist, so I know the value of being able to kill someone without leaving a shred of physical evidence. There's no scenario in which I go to prison for this, even if it was recorded in fucking high definition. What jury is going to convict a woman for murder with a magic cell phone? None."

Garrett was tense next to me. He felt ready for attack. Primed for action. Detective Rottorio groaned on the ground. It was small, but enough to draw Charlene's attention. It was all we needed.

Garrett pounced forward, clearing the space in two bounds and hurling himself into Charlene's body. She gasped and fell backwards. I came up from behind Garrett and brought my foot down onto her wrist. Something popped underneath my sole and Charlene screamed. Her fingers pulled back from around the phone. I kicked it out of her grasp. She tried to sit up, but Garrett pressed down harder, knocking the back of her skull against the floor.

I leaped off of her arm and towards the glowing phone. I could see then that the screen was a swirling whitish gray pattern. Almost hypnotic. I tore my eyes away and brought my heel down into the glass. It shattered, and the screen flickered for a moment before dying.

"NO!" Charlene screamed, thrashing in Garrett's grip, almost frothing at the mouth.

I walked back towards them at the same time that Detective Rottorio pushed herself up, holding her head. She reached into a pocket and removed a set of handcuffs. Garrett helped her maneuver a hollering Charlene into a position for the cuffs to lock around her wrists.

It was only then that I noticed that the zipper was gone from Rottorio's mouth. The evidence remained, however. The gorges in her lips made me wince.

The detective found her phone and made what must have been a painful call. Speaking had to be agony for her. But she did it anyway, and I just hoped it would be worth it. I tried to remind myself that even if Charlene was right, even if nobody believed us, at least we got the evil-emoji-phone-thing away from her, whatever it was.

Garrett walked over and buried my face in his neck with a crushing hug. I didn't mind. Not at all. Guilt still sat on my chest like an elephant, and I made a silent promise to myself. I would go find Ethan. I would bring him home and I would make it right. He would be okay.

I pulled away from Garrett and wiped a tear from my eye. Something in my peripheral was glowing. Something that was broken. Something that should have been broken.

My phone buzzed.

WINE & BLOODSHED

Maya Kook

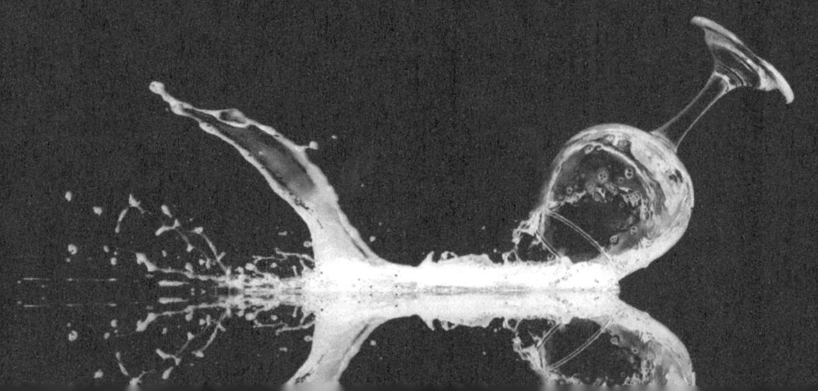

WINE & BLOOSHED

Maya Kook

AVERY

Avery gripped the steering wheel, her foot hovering over the accelerator. She fiddled her bottom lip between her teeth for a few minutes until the red traffic light turned green. She sped up her car, several streets passing as a blur in her peripheral vision.

Avery pulled over when she finally reached Brina's parents' house. It was a single-story with white walls and angular black roofs shining against the lamp-post lights. She knew Brina's parents were rich, but not *so* rich that they could afford a marble patio. Avery's heels clicked on the marble ground until she was face-to-face with the red front door, while gripping her purse. The wind blew against her long-sleeved, red turtle-neck dress, the hem reaching her knees. Brina was the first person whom Avery had started dating after transitioning. She'd warned Avery that her family could be insensitive at times but reassured her that she would stand by her if things went south.

What if that happens? What if they don't like me? Avery's heart was beating fast, and her legs were shaking from more than the cold air. *Everything's okay as long as Brina's with me.*

After dusting off her grey cardigan and swallowing a lump in her throat, Avery rang the doorbell. While waiting, she fidgeted with her purse. Right then, Brina opened the door. She had long, auburn curls and hazel eyes adorned with golden eyeliner. She wore a formal black jumpsuit with a low neckline exposing her cleavage. The only thing keeping her warm was a thin, beige coat. Her lips, also thin, were painted her favorite shade of red, a sight that sent heat rushing over Avery's body.

Brina grinned and jumped into her arms. Avery yelped and dropped her purse on the ground, gripping her waist. She let out a laugh before Brina pressed her lips against her own. She tasted like cherries. Both women giggled as Brina cupped Avery's face, her manicured nails scraping against her skin, a soothing sensation.

"I missed you," Brina whispered, her breath tickling Avery's mouth.

Avery smirked and pressed her lover's body closer to hers. "I missed you more."

Brina linked arms with Avery and dragged her inside.

The house's interior design was simple, yet opulent. Neat paintings, family photos, and sculptures were lined up against the pristine, gold walls in the hallway. When Avery and Brina entered the dining room, it was just as luxurious with mahogany shelves of showpieces, trophies, and photos.

Sitting at the head of the dining table was a middle-aged man with thin, wiry hair, wearing glasses and a navy sweater. His nose was buried in a newspaper. He muttered under his breath, something about inflation. Brina had shown Avery photos of her family, so she knew he was none other than Mr. James, Brina's father. Sitting at the right side of the table was a middle-aged woman with short hair and a plain dress, fiddling with a near-empty wineglass. Mrs. James: Brina's mother. Next to her was a young woman with waist-length blonde hair wearing a frilly crop top. She was scrolling through her phone. She must have been Clio, Brina's younger sister.

Brina cleared her throat and forced a smile. "Everyone, this is Avery," she said. "My girlfriend." She patted Avery's shoulder and nudged her forward. "Avery, meet my parents and my sister, Clio."

"Good evening," Mr. James said as he held out his hand after putting down his newspaper. Avery shook it with a nervous smile as she felt his firm, harsh grip.

"Nice to meet you." Mrs. James gave a curt nod, then reached for her wine glass.

Clio glanced at Avery and then focused on her phone again, pouting her lips.

Avery and Brina took the seats on the left side of the table. Brina sat closest to her father with Avery on her right. The table was empty with neatly set plates and cutlery for each person.

Mrs. James went to the kitchen, a slight sway in her hips. Avery glanced at Brina, who was texting something on her phone. She leaned closer. Her text contained a set of emojis: a family square, a plate-knife-fork set, and a skull in that order.

"Who are you texting?" Avery asked.

Brina jolted, her eyes wide for a few seconds. Just as quickly, she smiled and tucked her phone away in her coat pocket.

"Just a silly text to a friend," she said. "I hope we can get through this night."

She tapped her nails against the table and stared at her father and sister with her lips pressed to appear thinner than they looked. For as long as Avery had known her, Brina usually bit her lip or clenched her jaw when thinking or talking about her family. She'd never tightened her lips before.

"So, tell me. What do you do for work, Avery?" Mr. James asked in a formal, stoic tone. His hands were folded over his newspaper. Even though his eyes were drinking her in, they felt cold and stale. Avery was used to it, but it didn't stop her hands from tremoring.

Avery fiddled with the hem of the beige tablecloth hanging on her lap. "I'm an administrative assistant."

"Oh." Mr. James raised an eyebrow, his tone low and unimpressed.

"Do you plan to attain a *higher* role?"

Avery shook her head and breathed out slowly. "I don't think so. I'm happy with my current role." What Avery told Mr. James was a half-truth. Most places didn't want to hire her when they realized she was transgender after checking her paperwork. Her current job had an inclusive environment and kept her secure so she could focus on more important things like her girlfriend, family, friends, and her true passion—visual art.

Clio's eyes hovered up and down at Avery, her expression still apathetic. Her fingers never stopped typing, even without looking at her phone. As the silence grew, Mrs. James and another woman around her age in an apron appeared with a trolley of dishes covered by silver metal lids. Brina's mother instructed the woman on dish placements. Smells of meat, spice, salt, and a soft, savory tang filled Avery's senses. In the middle lay roast beef with asparagus on the side. The other dishes were omelets, spaghetti, and plates of broccoli and potatoes. Glass jugs of wine and water were placed next to Mr. James.

When the woman was about to place the last bowl of broccolis in front of Avery, Mrs. James tutted. "That goes over there." She pointed at Clio's side.

After that woman—presumably a maid—left the house, Mrs. James reclaimed her seat. She fixed her hair and straightened her back. One by one, starting with the Mr., the James began serving themselves, leaving Avery until last. She'd hoped Brina would collect some items for her, but she was already sticking a fork into some meat.

Once Avery took a slice of roast beef on her plate, Mrs. James flooded her with a series of questions as if they were on an interview on Live TV, or a police interrogation. Her eyes were not as cold, but there was something in there Avery didn't like.

"How did you and Brina meet?"

"We met at an art gallery." They actually met on a dating app, but their first date was at an art gallery, so not a complete lie.

"How old are you?"

"Twenty-seven, Mrs. James."

"What are your intentions with my daughter?" The word 'intentions' was sharp. It carried so much weight. All on its own, it accused Avery of…something.

Her breath was stuck in her throat. She did not expect that question. "I…"

"Look, sorry to be blunt. However, you must know,"—Mrs. James folded her arms on the table as she leaned in—"Brina has been through a lot. I need to know if you can handle her."

Brina grimaced. "Mum, I already told you. She can handle me just fine!"

Mrs. James ignored her eldest daughter, her eyes drilling through Avery. "A *man* would be better at protecting her, taking care of her, and *calming* her. Has Brina told you about the difficult parts of her past?"

Avery's heartrate accelerated. She and Brina told each other many things that they wouldn't tell most people, even their close friends. One particular, difficult conversation she'd had with Brina on their fourth date flashed in her mind.

Brina groaned. "I'm not a baby. Of course, I'm open with Avery about that stuff. Can we *please* talk about something else?"

Avery's stomach tightened. She wasn't surprised by some of Mrs. James's words, but she had to let know her know how much she cared for Brina. Changing the subject could help. Avery forced herself to focus on Mrs. James's squinting eyes.

"Did Brina tell you that I make art?" Avery asked as she placed a hand on Brina's knee. "When we met at the art gallery, I was standing in front of this painting of powerful Congolese women." Avery smiled at the memory. "When Brina came up to me, do you know what was the first thing she said? She said that only hands as fine and elegant as mine could paint something like that. But the truth was that I *hadn't* painted that artwork."

The expressions of Brina's family didn't change, except for Clio who frowned like she had trouble understanding Avery's words. Avery glanced at Brina, who gazed at her with a soft smile.

She chuckled. "From that point, we just talked and cruised through the rest of the gallery together." Avery looked at Brina's parents. "Your daughter is very bright."

Brina's red lipstick was stained by the oil of the spaghetti she ate. Avery could feel her breath on her shoulder.

After taking a sip of water, Clio sighed and fiddled with her fork. "I miss Jordan. He was so much more fun."

Jordan. Brina had mentioned him before. He was Brina's last ex. Avery tightened her lips and cracked her knuckles. The only thing Brina had in common with him was a penchant for demonology.

Brina's not with him anymore. He doesn't matter. Just ignore Clio.

"Hmm, yes," Mr. James said after wiping his lips with a napkin. "Well, we can't change the past." He paused, then looked right at Avery. "No matter how much we'd like to."

His gaze became stern. Avery sunk her teeth into her roast beef, chewing faster than she usually would. Her mind was racing. *Do I compliment them? Do I ignore him? Do I just stare at my food? I should. I'll just stare at my food.*

With jittery eyes, Brina gripped Avery's hand under the table. The fingers intertwining with her own was soothing. A safety net.

Just as she was starting to calm, there was a noise from outside. A crash. Then something that sounded like scuffling feet. Avery's breath quickened, and her body temperature increased. Brina tapped her shoulder, fear also shining in her eyes.

"What was that?" Clio asked, her voice an octave higher than usual as she clutched her phone to her chest.

Mr. James shot a scrutinizing gaze towards the direction of the sounds. "I'll go and check. Stay here and keep your phones handy."

After he left the table, Mrs. James made a nervous laugh. "It's okay. It's probably nothing. We have good security here. Let's just keep eating until your father returns."

The women continued their dinner without talking. Avery was confused with why they were all so calm. Shouldn't one of them go and help Mr. James? Though, Avery knew better than to question other families' methods. She'd learned that the hard way after meeting her ex's family. She forced the spaghetti down her throat, noticing that Brina's plate was empty. Mrs. James and Clio continued eating the remainder of the roast beef. Brina went on her phone for a moment, then put it back in her pocket.

Mr. James still hadn't returned. Mrs. James cleared her throat after wiping her mouth with a napkin.

"So, Avery, are you a lesbian or bisexual like my daughter?" she asked.

Avery clenched her hand into a fist under the table, her fingernails digging into her palm. She had to be polite for Brina's sake, embracing herself for the insensitive questions.

"I'm also bisexual, Mrs. James," Avery said, her voice quiet.

Clio snorted and shook her head.

"Hmm, I'm guessing neither of you will ever date men again then?" Mrs. James pointed at the couple with her fork.

"Mum!" Brina exclaimed, her cheeks flushing.

"No, Mrs. James." Avery forced a smile. At least her voice was more measured and composed than she felt. "It doesn't work like that. To me, Brina is someone who I fell in love with, and she just happens to be a woman."

Brina softened her gaze at Avery. Mrs. James made a smile that didn't reach her eyes when she looked at Avery again while Clio stared down at her like she was dung. Avery was not surprised by these sorts of reactions. That was why she and Brina agreed to not disclose her transgender identity.

Hurried footsteps echoed across the floor, and Mr. James was back in the room, panting and sweaty, with a rifle slung over his shoulder. All the women straightened in their seats, anticipating his words.

"Okay, I didn't see anything but—" More crashing noises interrupted and startled Mr. James.

"Just sit down, dear," Mrs. James said in a rush. "We'll be alright since you have a weapon."

Brina stood up. "I'll get the red wine."

"Thank you, sweetheart," Mr. James said.

She bent down to nuzzle her cheek with Avery's. "I won't be long," she whispered, then exited the room.

Avery's hands trembled under the table. After Mr. James put his rifle on the table, the barrel pointed right at her, and returned to his seat, everyone ate the morsels left on their plates in silence. The others acted as if Avery wasn't there. Another crash and more footsteps echoed in the distance. She clenched her fork, ignoring the food on her plate while trying to convince herself that it was nothing.

"Do you have a dog?" Avery asked. It didn't make sense why nobody was paying attention to the crashing and clamoring and footsteps from inside. She looked over her shoulder to inspect the scene. For a moment, she worried that Brina was injured somehow.

She returned a minute later with a bottle of red wine and placed it in the middle of the table. Perhaps those footsteps came from her. After pouring the wine into her family members' empty glasses, Brina was back in her seat.

She whispered to Avery. "I hope they didn't give you a hard time."

Mr. James answered before she could. "Don't worry, Brina. Your friend is safe with us."

Heat simmered in Avery's gut for the first time that night. Friend. They called her "friend". *Unbelievable.* Avery looked at her girlfriend, who rolled her eyes and took a sip of water from her own glass.

Mr. James drank the red wine, then released a relaxing sigh. He smacked his lips together and looked at Brina. "I don't remember it tasting this good," he said before continuing to drink down the rest of the wine in his glass.

With furrowed eyebrows, Mrs. James and Clio took tentative sips from their own glasses. Clio grinned, her eyes wide and sparkling. Mrs. James gasped and ogled at her glass.

Before anyone could do anything further, a shrill scream pierced their ears. Mrs. James was standing from her seat while Clio's mouth hung open. Mr. James's pot belly flattened, his cheeks were sunken, lips pruned, and his fingers shriveled.

Another crash came from outside. Avery's heart was beating in her head, and she froze. *What is happening? Will someone do something? What do I do?*

She couldn't stop staring at Mr. James as he deflated like a balloon. Blood spurted out of his eyes as they popped. Thick red and dark yellow wax gushed out of his ears. His mouth hung open and he spat ropes of stomach acid, bubbling with blood and gore. Clio shrieked as Brina grabbed Avery's hand and dragged her out of the room, the pristine walls passing as blurs until they settled in an empty room.

Among the sounds of the other women's footsteps behind her, Avery's palms became sweaty, and her jaw wobbled as a small whine escaped her mouth. *This is not happening. This must be a nightmare. This is crazy. What the fuck is happening? We're doomed. I'm going to die. Brina's going to die. I can't lose her. No, no, no...*

"Avery! Are you alright?" Brina's voice echoed, fingertips tapping Avery's cheeks. Her vision cleared enough to see that her lover was gripping her face.

"Don't blank out on me now," she said between pants, her body trembling. "I-I need you."

Avery blinked several times in rapid succession. Yes, Brina needed her. Her father was dying. *I need to be strong for her sake.*

"Mum, are you okay? Please be okay! Please!" Clio's squeaky and desperate voice was audible from a few meters away.

Mrs. James was staring at the wall, her eyes wide, her expression blank. Clio knelt next to her, shaking her shoulder. Brina rushed to her mother's side, then darted her eyes around the room, hyperventilating. Her sister was frantic, mumbling and crying.

"W-where's Dad?" Brina asked, her voice wavering.

"I don't know!" Clio rushed back to the dining room, screaming for her father.

Brina knelt and clapped her mother's cheeks in repetition as she pleaded for her attention. Her heart still racing and her head dazed, Avery looked outside. The only lights present came from the lamp posts and open windows in the houses across from them.

"I'm calling 000," Avery said as the thought fully formed. Before waiting for a response from anyone, she pulled out her phone and started dialing.

"Emergency triple zero. Your call is being connected," came an automated voice. A few seconds later, a more natural and clear female voice asked, "Hello, do you require police, fire or ambulance?"

Avery panted. She tried to thread the right words, but her brain glitched. All she could think about was Mr. James's shriveled body and the popping of his eyes.

"Hello?" the woman called again.

Avery cleared her throat. *Just talk.* "I-I need both police and ambulance, please." Her voice was trembling.

"Where are you?"

"I'm in Lane Cove, Sydney, New South Wales."

"Okay, I will refer you to the police. Please hold the line."

The phone was static for a while until…

"Hello, what is your emergency?" a male voice asked.

"M-my girlfriend's father is very sick! I'm not sure if…he'll survive," Avery said.

"What happened to him?"

"I don't know! He drank some red wine, and then his body shriveled up." Avery couldn't mention the popped eyeballs. "I think there might be an intruder too. I heard footsteps outside. P-please help us! Come as soon as you can!"

"That sounds like a critical situation. Can you tell me your address?"

"61 Allison Avenue."

"How old is your girlfriend's father?"

Avery racked her brain. "I don't know. Late fifties?"

"Is he breathing?"

"I don't know. Just get over here!" She took a breath. "Someone else is checking. But he's all flat and he was bleeding from…everywhere."

"Okay, I will dispatch an ambulance and task force, along with disease control. They should get to you within fifteen minutes."

Fifteen minutes? That was not enough time, especially if there was an intruder and Mr. James was poisoned.

The emergency dispatcher continued. "In the meantime, keep an eye on your partner's father and lock all the doors and windows. Hide in a room without windows. If there is an intruder, that will ensure your safety."

"Okay, thank you," Avery squeaked.

"Don't worry. They are on their way. Stay safe," he said. "Please don't hang up until I instruct you to do so."

Avery confirmed she wouldn't. She gave the dispatcher a heads-up before muting her phone.

At that moment, Clio rushed in, tears rolling down her cheeks, her hands bloody, her lips slick with drool. Mrs. James had snapped out of her shock. Then she was taken aback when her younger daughter crashed into her, gripping onto her shirt and sobbing on her shoulder.

"Shh, Mum's here, honeypie," Mrs. James coaxed, her eyes filling with tears. "Mum's here."

"D-D-Dad is dead!" Clio wailed.

Brina shook her head so fast it could have fallen off. "No, no, no… Are you sure?"

"Of course, I'm sure!" Clio shrilled. "He…he just vomited and… and…all that's left is…"

She buried her head in her mother's shoulder again, continuing her sobs. Brina swallowed a lump in her throat, and her eyes got teary. Avery blinked at a rapid pace. Then she shook her head. *Focus.*

"The ambulance and police will be here soon!" Avery blurted out, her voice high and tense. The other women stared at her, dumbfounded. Avery cleared her throat. "We need to lock all the doors and windows."

Brina furrowed her eyebrows and looked at her mother. Mrs. James gulped. All the women, except for Clio, who was following the others like a lost puppy, rushed to every window and door in every room, with Avery taking the lead. They fumbled with the locks, their hands shaking, until they were sure they'd locked everything.

"We need a room without windows." Avery said in between panting breaths.

Brina bit her lip. "There's the basement downstairs."

The women scurried in the direction of the basement, following Brina's lead. They went through the dining room, which reeked of blood and vomit. Mr. James was collapsed on the table, which was slick with green-colored vomit and splatters of blood. All that was left of him was his skin, hanging on his chair like a thin leather coat.

Clio wailed and closed her own eyes. "See? Dad is dead. Dead. Dead!"

Mrs. James fainted. Bile built up in Avery's throat as she dropped her phone. She ran to the sink and vomited up her dinner. The putrid stench of spice and stomach acid attacked her senses. With her empty stomach and dizzy mind, Avery looked at the sisters. Clio sobbed into her hands while Brina's eyes pierced into her father's corpse.

Avery wiped her mouth with multiple paper towels. She tugged at Brina, who snapped out of her haze, and then dragged her away from the dining table. Avery knew that Clio followed close behind because of her whimpers. Brina tried to wake her mother. When she couldn't, she and Avery dragged the older woman, slinging each of her arms on their shoulders. Brina didn't say anything. She only pointed in the directions they should go at every turn. Eventually, they opened a door with a descending staircase.

After setting down into the basement, Brina locked the door and slumped against the wall, panting. After sitting down across from her, Avery tried to contemplate what to do next, but images of Mr. James's skin hanging off the chair flashed in her mind every time she blinked. It increased her heart rate, made her sweat enough to take off her cardigan. She rubbed her palms against the concrete floor. They became blackened with soot. Clio was standing with her arms crossed, mumbling nonsense, while Mrs. James, still unconscious, leaned against the wall on Brina's side.

"Don't worry," Brina said. "You can get signal down here."

Avery looked around until she saw a mobile signal booster attached to the other side of the room. That was good. She rummaged the pockets of her cardigan, which turned out to be empty. Where did she leave her phone? Probably at the dining room.

Great.

The couple were silent, still trying to catch their breath while Clio paced.

What the hell just happened?

"This is not how I expected things to go," Avery said.

Brina made a noise that sounded like both a scoff and a laugh. "Who would? This is crazy."

They were silent for a while, their breaths slowing down. Avery caught sight of a yellow mineral stone at the other side of the basement. It looked like a sulfur brimstone.

Brina broke the silence. "Hey, Avery?"

"Yeah?"

"Whatever happens, just know that I love you."

Avery's stomach was still empty and churning, her head was thrumming, and fatigue dragged her weight down like an anvil. The muscles on her arms were cramped. But she couldn't help but smile. Even when Brina was out of breath, had messy hair, faded lipstick, and sweat drenching her body, she was still beautiful. Avery crawled towards her side and wrapped her arms around her. Brina laid her head on Avery's chest.

"I love you, too," Avery murmured in her lover's hair, stroking it.

They were silent again, cuddling each other against the wall. Avery's heartbeat slowed, as the tension in her body melted away. Only the woman lying in her arms could calm her in such a stressful situation, even if at a gradual pace.

Moments later, a cough came from nearby. Mrs. James gained consciousness. Brina sprang out of Avery's arms and rushed to her mother's side. Mrs. James rubbed her eyes and looked around.

"W-Why are we in the basement?" she asked.

Brina gulped while rubbing her mother's arm. "We had to hide. There might be an intruder."

Tears sprang from Mrs. James's eyes. "Is your father…"

Everyone knew what she meant. Brina nodded and swallowed a lump in her throat. She wrapped an arm around her mother. She looked at Avery and cocked her head. Avery knew what her girlfriend wanted her to do. She grabbed Mrs. James from the other side, and together, she and Brina helped the older woman back onto her feet. That was followed by sounds of choking and puking.

Close to the mobile signal booster, Clio hunched her back, gasping for air as vomit and blood dribbled down her chin. The room now smelled rancid and rotten. Her cheeks were shrunken, her hair sticking to her face. She was so skinny that Avery could see the outlines of her ribcage against the skin of her exposed midriff. Clio's eyeballs popped, resulting in blood running out of her sockets and down her face. Mrs. James screamed and yanked her body towards her younger daughter. Avery and Brina stumbled and released the older woman.

Clio stalked towards them, stretching out a hand. Her eyeless face twisted, her mouth gaping until it resembled a dark cave. It was a plea for help. But how could they help her? Mrs. James was sobbing and wailing, Avery stared at her as if in paralysis, and footsteps that sounded like Brina's became quieter and more distant.

The youngest woman deflated like a balloon with every step, blood bursting out of her ears. The meat from her head was gone as if it had never been there, followed by her neck and arms. Followed by her torso, then her legs, until Clio was nothing more than a pile of her own skin on the floor.

"No, no, no, not my baby!" Mrs. James's voice was hoarse as she wept.

Avery swallowed the bile building in her throat. She couldn't stand the smell. That revolting, bitter stench akin to rotten eggs and landfill. Sweat trickled her forehead. Avery jerked her head away from the sight of Clio lying on the floor like a disheveled rug. If only she could turn off her brain and rip off her nose.

That was when she heard sirens.

The three women walked back up the basement stairs; the sirens were clearer now, but still faint. Avery made a small smile. *Help is here. Finally…*

The journey back to the main entrance was tiring and arduous, unlike the way they came. Images of Clio and Mr. James's skinsuits lingered in the back of Avery's mind. The women finally reached the hallway, stopping outside the dining room.

"I swear I heard police sirens…" Mrs. James muttered between pants.

"Maybe they're having trouble locating us," Brina suggested.

Avery shook her head. The police could track locations very easily. They glanced at the window in the hallway. There was no sight of any moving vehicles. Where were the sirens coming from?

That was when Avery caught sight of an ambulance. She ran to the front door, opened it, and waved to the ambulance just as it got close. It zoomed past her. Avery gaped in disbelief. Why did they drive past? She left the house and followed the ambulance, only to find that it was picking up one of the neighbors, a pregnant woman entering labor. Avery ran back inside the James household to find Brina at the far end of the hallway.

"That siren wasn't for us, Bri—" She stopped talking when she saw Mrs. James convulsing in Brina's arms.

Vomit and blood pooled out of the older woman's mouth.

"No…" Brina's next words came out in a screech. "No! Not you, too! Please…stay with me!"

Mrs. James's eyes popped, her blood splattering on Brina's face.

Avery's hands were cold, numb, gnarly, and shaking. *No, no, no. No more death. No more skinsuits. No more eyes popping. What the fuck? What the fuck?*

She looked out the window for the emergency services she had summoned, her left eye twitching and her jaw grinding so hard her teeth ached. Inescapable, obnoxious noises of vomiting, squelching, spurting blood, and deflation filled the background while Brina was shrieking and gagging.

Avery looked back at her girlfriend, whose eyes were blank, as if she were mentally absent. Her hands were covered in grime and blood, her hair disheveled. Her mother's body was a bundle of skin scattered like a messy blanket in Brina's arms. Avery's head was dizzy. Her breaths were shallow. She couldn't hold on anymore. Avery collapsed to the ground, and everything faded into pitch-black nothingness.

AVERY OPENED HER eyes. The stars were shining in the night sky, sprinkled like glitter. Her girlfriend gazed down at her with a weak smile, her eyes weary. Avery turned her head to see police officers talking and paramedics covering bodies on stretchers. She could smell the ice and smoke in the air. She figured she was lying on Brina's lap. When Avery tried to get up, Brina shushed her and pushed her head back down, stroking her hair. Her fingers felt smooth and soft against her scalp.

"It's okay. Just rest." Brina's voice stroked Avery's senses. "You can sit up when the police question us." She stopped smiling and gulped, looking out into the distance. "My family is dead. They're taking their…bodies to the morgue."

Avery didn't say anything. She couldn't bring herself to speak. All she could do was shift her head. Avery gripped one of her lover's hands. She couldn't leave Brina, especially after something like this. She was Brina's, and Brina was hers, until they drew their last breaths. Footsteps approached them. Avery was eye to eye with a pair of legs clad in navy slacks.

"Are you Brina James and Avery Turner?" a male voice asked.

Avery sat up to see a police officer with a moustache standing in front of them. He held a notepad.

"That's us," Brina responded.

"I'm Constable Derek. I'm sorry we couldn't make it in time," he said with a solemn expression, his eyes drooping and his hands in his pockets. He cleared his throat. "Okay, the names of your deceased family members are Hamish, Leah, and Clio James. Is that correct?"

"Yes."

"What happened?"

"I…I don't know. One moment, they were drinking red wine." Brina's eyes became frantic. "Then they…died. Do you think it's possible that they got poisoned?"

"We don't know. The forensic team will have to do an autopsy on the bodies."

With squinted eyes, Avery found her voice. "Excuse me, sir." Her throat was sore. She forced the words out. "But…how can you do an autopsy…when there's nothing but skin?"

Brina and Constable Derek stared at Avery as if she had said that ants were dancing on the constable's head.

"What are you talking about, Avery?" Brina said. "Nothing but skin? You're not making any sense." Her body shuddered, tremored in a way so subtle that most people wouldn't have noticed. Only Avery did.

Constable Derek nodded. "Yes, their bodies are still intact. Only their eyes are missing. That's why we can and must perform autopsies on them." He looked at Brina. "To answer your question, I don't think food poisoning is possible in this case. Eyeballs require much more pressure to pop."

Another thing came to Avery's mind. "Wait! Did you notice anyone…sneaking around the house?"

The constable shook his head. "No, there was no intruder."

That confused Avery. Where did the strange footsteps and crashing noises come from? Maybe it was just in her head due to her nerves. Maybe it was one of the neighbors having a night stroll. Or maybe the truth would make her lose sleep.

The Constable handed Brina a business card. "We'll keep in touch.

I'll call you after we get the autopsy results."

Brina nodded and tucked the business card in her coat pocket. "Thank you, Constable."

Brina went home with Avery. They showered together to clean off the blood, puke, and grime. After dressing in fresh pajamas, they cuddled in Avery's small double bed. It was not big enough to fit two entire adult bodies with enough space between them, but Avery didn't care, and she knew Brina didn't either, given how she nuzzled her neck.

BRINA

Twelve Years Ago

BLOOD POUNDED IN her ears. The grip on her knife tightened as he fell to the floor, blood gushing out of his round belly like a river.

"Brina, are you—" She heard Mum gasp in horror.

She couldn't speak. He was dead but her lip quivered. Her cheeks were wet. Her hands were wet. She could still feel the ghost of his hands wrapping around her waist. Him towering over her with his hungry eyes. Him violating her, no matter how much she cried and begged him to stop.

The Present

BRINA SPENT ONE day and two nights at Avery's apartment. Most of the time, they were silent and either laid on the couch to watch TV or in bed while reading books together. Neither of them could answer calls or texts from other people in their life. Two days after that night, Brina left Avery's place in the morning and took a taxi back to her parents' house. It took a few minutes to convince Avery to let her leave.

"It's okay, my star." Brina had told her love. "I will never leave you. You know that, right? I'll call you later."

"But your family…" Avery had said, her hands tremoring. "Are you sure you'll be okay on your own?"

Brina had sighed, hiding her own tremoring hands behind her back. "Yes, I…" She'd hesitated then, trying to shove those gross, scary images out of her head. "I'll be fine. I can take care of myself. Besides, this is something I have to do on my own."

"Are you sure?"

"Yes, Avery! I can't involve you in this. It's… I agreed to be confidential."

Avery had sighed and sat up from the bed. "I understand. But you don't have to pretend to be strong. Not with me. Please call me as soon as you can."

Brina had taken a deep breath. Then she'd smiled and cupped Avery's face, stroking her thumb on her lover's cheekbone. She'd pressed a kiss on Avery's cheek before walking to the door.

Chills now ran up Brina's spine like spiders ready to bite and devour at the memory of that previous night. Flashes of her mother's blood and fluids splattering from her body wouldn't escape her mind. Once Brina arrived at the house, she saw a tall man with sunglasses and a black top hat. He was dressed in slacks and a blazer. Perfect. Just the man she was meant to meet.

"Hey, Jerome," she said. "How are your kids?"

Jerome grinned. "They have been adjusting well. Do you want to meet them?"

Brina nodded, then propped her chin up high.

The door opened, and the three people who came out made her gasp. They were clones of her family. Her fake father looked almost identical to her real one, except his eyes were friendlier, less boring. Her fake mother looked the same, just as plain. Her sister and her sister's clone had the most significant differences. Fake Clio didn't have that annoying, punch-worthy scrunch of her nose. Instead, her expression was warm, and the muscles in her face were relaxed. Her lips were thin, no ridiculous lip fillers like the real Clio.

Jerome's grin now resembled a deranged shark. "Thank you for giving my children such wonderful prey, Ms. James." His expression became serious. "I fulfilled my end of the bargain. Your family is gone. Now it's your turn."

Brina gulped. She was a university scholar and lecturer of folklore and the occult. She knew what she'd signed up for when she muttered a spell while holding a sulfur brimstone to summon The Emoji Contract, a demon hitman agency. No wonder it was easy for her to find something that absurd.

Jerome was an Annelid Demon. In adulthood, these demons' true form resembled giant leeches with glowing red eyes. They originated from a different dimension. One full of flames and lava the temperature of the sun. On Earth, however, the demons couldn't thrive in their true form. The temperature was unpredictable and inconsistent, unlike their home world. They evolved into parasites that could only develop inside medium and large vertebrates as larvae, their ideal hosts being humans of their matching sex.

Brina wanted to love her family, but her entire life, her parents would only give her love when she met their expectations and achieved the goals they set for her. When she disappointed them, they would either give her the silent treatment or slap her and give her a lecture. She could still feel the sting of one of her mother's slaps, which contrasted with the memory of her dying in her arms. As for Clio, she never supported Brina whenever she was at a low point. Sometimes, her sister made her feel worse.

Things became even more complicated when Jake Danes, one of her father's biggest investors, was around. Her father welcomed that disgusting man into their house like an old friend many times. Brina didn't dare tell her parents about the sexual abuse she experienced at his hands due to his threats. But one time, he went too far, and Brina resorted to killing him in self-defense. Her mother caught her red-handed. It took her weeks to process that day. She was only thirteen. Her parents covered up her involvement in Mr. Danes's death and framed someone else.

Brina's life was never the same after that. Her father became distant and cold, favoring Clio, while her mother hovered around her, handling her like an unhatched egg. It didn't help when they realized that Brina was bisexual. Her mother only allowed her to date people she approved of; namely, silver-tongued men with high-paying careers or rich families who could "protect" and provide for her, like Jordan. But he was the worst of them all. Everyone, even her family, fell for his lies, including the ones about her.

A small part of Brina hoped her family would act differently. Be less overbearing. Less close-minded. That they would try to make Avery feel welcome, at least for Brina's sake. Maybe her desire to punch them would lessen. But deep down, she knew better.

That was why she researched various demon hitman agencies. They never got caught since most people weren't believers. Jerome and other hitmen of his race had a unique killing style; they never acted alone.

Annelid Demons were often on the lookout for suitable human hosts for their offspring.

Brina ordered Jerome to kill her family only if they mistreated her girlfriend. He was the intruder walking around her parents' house. The crashing sounds came from him as he prepared to dispatch his eggs at Brina's order. The hitmen from The Emoji Contract had very specific emoji codes with their clients, hence the name. That was why Brina typed a family square emoji, a plate-knife-fork emoji, and a skull emoji: the first time to signal for Jerome to be prepared. The second time she texted, the code was her order to carry out the hit. She went to the basement, which had the bottles of red wine, and met with Jerome there. He dispatched three eggs into one of the wine bottles. When Brina's family drank it, each larva claimed each of her family members as its host and prey.

When the eggs hatched, the larvae would feast on the insides of their hosts, everything from muscles to organs to bones. Eyeballs were toxic for the larvae, so they destroyed them instead of consuming them. That would enable the larvae to grow to their adolescent stage when they had imprinted the DNA of their prey to shift into them. It was a fast process.

The clones of her family were Jerome's youngest children. Her deal with the demon hitman was that he would kill her family in exchange for her letting him spread his offspring and help them blend in.

Brina smiled. "Of course. A deal's a deal."

This was the best deal Brina could have gotten because of the Annelid Demons' powerful illusion magic. Jerome cast an illusion that would make most humans believe the victims of his race were intact corpses. Only humans who witnessed the massacres were unaffected. The memories of the police, paramedics, and forensic staff were altered so they would believe the victims were not dead but instead, seriously injured and recovering.

Avery was Brina's shining star. No one could tear them apart, not even her own family. They didn't deserve Avery. She was one of the few people who Brina could be vulnerable with. If her actions for that wonderful woman damned her, then it was all worth it.

WHEN THE SCREEN LIGHTS UP MY HEART STARTS TO FLUTTER

Ivana Geček

WHEN THE SCREEN LIGHTS UP MY HEART STARTS TO FLUTTER

Ivana Geček

Matej was in my care for almost a year before he passed away.

I find him lying on his back, eyes wide open and eyelids as rigid as if they were carved out of stone, staring at the ceiling with a lightless gaze. The room is still and dark; the only things illuminating it are the weak light of the bedside lamp and the screen of my phone. I shove the cell in my uniform, this evening's game momentarily forgotten.

The sight affects me more than I care to admit. I'm used to patients dying in my care: I'm a palliative nurse, and therefore am no stranger to death. People struggle and resist and withstand until they finally succumb—it is just the way things are, and I usually manage to keep myself detached from their inevitable demise. But I can't deny the intensive impact Matej's passing has on me.

Maybe it's because of his age—I rarely nurse someone who is this young. Most of my patients are well into their seventies and eighties, but Matej and I are—or were, to be accurate—the same age, just shy of thirty. It is strange to watch his young, healthy body deteriorate. Day by day, I watch as Matej's form warps and shrivels, his impeccable physique twisting and distorting by the sickness hidden beneath his skin. I have been astonished by the rapid changes occurring right in front of my eyes, dumbstruck at the way his familiar shape has morphed into something unrecognizable.

Before I go ahead and close his eyes, I check the pulse to make sure he is truly gone. I hesitate only for a moment. Pronouncing the time of death is never easy, but this time even more so, and I feel an uncomfortable tightness seize my throat. My hand stops mid-air, floating in the dark a few inches from his neck, and I have to force the tips of my fingers on the grayish, veiny skin, right where his jugular should beat.

I don't make any calls. There are no calls to be had. He was alone in my care—I am the only one who watched his slow descent to the other side. I reflect on this thought as I finally close his eyes, skimming past his chapped lips, his scarred cheeks. His body is a map of the past year we've spent together, and only now does it register what a privilege it has been to take care of him during that time.

My legs suddenly wobble, and I let myself drop to the floor, kneel by his bedside and clutch the cold sheets with shaky fingers. I don't like that it ended this way. I thought he'd have more time—that *we'd* have more time. There was so much more in store for him. I had plans. I always make them for my patients. I try to animate them, to motivate them, make it seem that their last days were not as bleak and hopeless as they are. Usually, they appreciate my efforts, and we continue our mutual charade of happiness until the lights inevitably go out.

But not Matej.

No matter how much I'd tried, I couldn't make him smile, make him laugh. Not a single quirk of his dry lips to acknowledge all the efforts I put into cheering him up.

"This is for your own benefit," I kept reminding him, "trust me." But sadly, I don't think he ever did. Months of effort went unappreciated: no matter how much I tried, I was never able to make him feel at home, to make him feel like the bed he was confined to wasn't just a stand-in for his inescapable coffin.

This whole situation had made me unimaginably sad at times. I used to imagine the two of us shared a special connection, a lust for a life which was yet to unfold, and it is hard to remind myself the exact reason of his condition, of the disease which roamed and devoured his body.

But unlike me, he knew his longing was unreasonable. He knew his death was predetermined. His body was always meant to change, to warp into this final form, and stay that way until his flesh decayed and his bones turned to dust. There was no escape—the sickness he suffered from would come out one way or the other, I'm sure of it.

My body is starting to protest, stiffening in this uncomfortable position I've taken by my patient's bedside, but I don't care. I'm devoted to my patients, and it's that devotion that makes me take the phone out of my pocket.

The brightness of the screen hurts my eyes, but I squint at it regardless, determined to find out what our last game would be like.

I press the button, and the millisecond that it takes for the screen to light up again feels like an endless, shining eternity.

JANUARY

CARING FOR A patient like Matej isn't easy.

Most people are not keen to relinquish control of their autonomy, to surrender their bodies to some stranger. "I'm a professional," I'd remind my patients as I wiped their faces, brushed their hair, inserted catheters into their privates. "There's nothing to be ashamed of."

I try to remind Matej of the same, smiling reassuringly behind the screen of my old digital camera. My phone works the same, but I want to stay true to the game. No shortcuts, no easy alternatives. I tell myself that if I'm going to do this, I'm going to do it right. It's the least I owe Matej, as well as my professional and personal integrity.

He's been here for a week, and we've made no progress. With each click of the camera, the restraints on Matej's limbs stretch and pull, the stillness of the room filled with soft squeaks and whimpers. I don't like it when patients are restrained: the bonds make me anxious, forcing me to think about unpleasant times I'd rather forget. Sometimes, as I'd have to call another orderly to help me with the holders, I'd have to remind myself that it isn't me lying there on the table, that my limbs were free for years now, the invisible bonds gone. I'm not a scared girl anymore; I'm a highly qualified nurse, known for her endless compassion and sought out for her excellent care in one of the city's best private nursing homes. Nobody would guess that the skin of my wrists and ankles still itch from time to time, muscle memory working against them.

"Smile," I say to Matej, snapping another set of photos. I'm sure he would be happy to have some in a month or two, as he starts to change.

FEBRUARY

I TRY TO make it a habit as much as I can.

After my usual rounds end, I go and sit by Matej's side and read to him. Some nurses say it's too soon to do that, since Matej came into my care all dazed and confused. Most patients don't really know how they found themselves in their current position, or why they're in an unknown room with a stranger adjusting an IV stuck in their arm. But in this particular case, I disagree—I don't want him to fall into the abyss of his own thoughts, sink further and further into the depths of his mind, where I know I wouldn't have a chance to reach him. I want him to understand why he's here, why he's being cared for, and why I'm the perfect nurse to provide such care for him.

I was understandably thrilled when a book popped up on the screen of my phone. I love to read, to escape into a different world from time to time. It's a routine I settled into ever since I struggled in my adolescence, wanting to be and feel like something different than I was at the time. It brought me solace to settle into someone else's skin, and live out an existence that wasn't mocked and ridiculed and discriminated against. I was never really ashamed of myself, not truly, but it took a while; it took a while to brush off the unsolicited comments, the ridicule, the insults, for *dyke* or *butch* to stop making my skin feel like I was on fire.

I read Matej all of the classics. *Carmilla. The Price of Salt. Stone Butch Blues.* I know it interests him. He's been showing a great deal of curiosity regarding that particular subject, and I'm more than delighted to indulge him.

When my voice starts to feel hoarse, I put the book down and reach for my phone. I have to scroll for quite some time, but after a while, I find what I'm looking for. But if I'm being really honest, it's not like I need the messages displayed before me: they're already etched in my brain, words and little pictures nestled deep in the gray matter inside my head, toying and tinkering with my nervous system for years. I've learned to control them, thank heavens. People like me are resilient— we always find a solution, no matter how unlikely or impossible it may appear.

As I read the messages out loud, the words don't come out as smoothly. Even after all these years, they get stuck, poking and probing against the soft walls of my throat until they reach my mouth. I imagine them leaving my tongue all wrong and poisonous, stinking up the room with their foulness.

But in reality, it's just the movement of my patient's bowels that can't restrain themselves any longer.

MARCH

SOME ASPECTS OF this game are logistically harder than the others. It's a good thing I'm a nurse, and have all the necessities available to make it work.

I rub Matej's back, feeling the muscles of his shoulder blades strain underneath my palm. The bucket is already filled to the brim after half a minute, and I blink in amazement. He hasn't been eating solid food for a while, and I wonder if the watery bile is some byproduct of Matej's vile condition. People like him hide it well, pretend they're healthy and sound and kind, but it's bound to come out nonetheless.

"There, there," I say, the sweaty fabric of his nightgown sticking between my fingers. "Let it all out." I give him some water, which he gulps down.

After I dispose of the vomit and lay the empty bucket again into Matej's arms, he starts to cry. I sit in the chair by his bed and wait for him to stop. He cries for hours and I just sit with him, quietly humming coaxing tunes over and over for a while.

I'm not frazzled by his emotional outburst. Many of my patients are taxed with horrible pains and aches, and I've spent many nights holding their hands, whispering words of encouragement to ease them through their suffering.

But I know actions like this will be lost on Matej. If anything, I'd like to tell him that he should stop, that crying will make him even sicker and more dehydrated than he already is. But I don't. I remain silent by his side, waiting for the emetics I've been mixing into his water to start working again.

April

THE BEST THING about this game are the numerous interpretations. Pictures tell a thousand words, and the emojis shining on the screen of my phone are no exception.

I used to hate those little pictures, and I'm well aware that the statement makes me sound like some old, grumpy man. But now, as I press the button and let a random one pop up every month, I've grown to love them. Every time I open the page and let the generator do its thing, I can feel my heart flutter in my throat.

There are many ways to interpret a picture, to read a symbol. Our understanding is molded by our own thoughts and experiences, and I would argue that that's the beauty of the game Matej and I have been playing.

The little blue droplets which appear on the screen remind me of the sweat running down my face as I've run the tracks in gym class. I haven't thought about this particular memory in years, but now, I can almost taste the saltiness of it, hear the snickering that follows right behind me.

Before I enter the room, I put on a mask. I know it won't shield me from the worst of it, that my senses will be assaulted regardless, but I put it on anyway, to show him how dire the situation has become. If I had one, I'd wear a hazmat suit, so I could demonstrate to him how it feels to be treated with infectious disgust.

I work quickly these days, adjusting his IV and doing a cautionary checkup as fast as I can. I know how my patient thinks of me. I've heard it all before, back when we were in high school. Years later, I've read it too, now archived forever in countless posts and tweets. *I'm sure they stink. Eeew. I'm sure they have unshaven armpits and pussies, and that they stink like fish. Yuck.*

The stench in the room is unbearable. It's amazing, really, what the waste and discharge our bodies produce can amount to while left uncleaned for only a few days.

As I step out of the room, I hear him stir. "Why are you doing this?" he whispers, but I only retreat, a smile hidden behind my mask.

It has been two weeks since I changed his diaper and gave him a wash. I know that the itchiness must be unbearable, that the numerous bedsores left festering in the filth of his soiled body are now inflamed and pulsating, but I can't help him.

By now, I'm sure he understands that the rules of the game can't be questioned.

MAY

"DON'T YOU LIKE them?" I say, eyeing the iridescent finish. I topped the nails off with a generous coat of glitter, which catches the light of the bedside lamp wonderfully. "I personally *love* them."

Matej doesn't reply. I frown, manipulating his hand into various poses, showing him all the glory of his new acrylics. "The least you can do is thank me," I mutter, irritated by his disinterest.

I've been trying to cheer us up. It's been a tough couple of weeks for the both of us, and I'm sure he still feels the smell of his feces and piss and sweat as well as I do. But that's no excuse to behave like a child.

There's a reason we play these games, and the sooner he gets it, the sooner we can stop. That's the goal—for him to understand why this is happening to him, why the condition he has is changing him and turning him into someone who finally matches his outside to his insides.

"Look how pretty it is," I insist, but I can tell he doesn't believe me. If anything, he thinks it's a disgrace, what I've been doing to his nails. Short or long; natural or gelled; a demure french tip or a glittery hot pink. I know how people like him think. I might as well be talking to a brick wall.

I'm no expert at manicures. I'm a nurse, not an esthetician, but lately I've found that some of the aspects of our professions are similar. We both clean and shape certain parts of the body, providing a service that brings people joy and comfort. I think about that as I poke and prod Matej's new long nails. It's hard to shape something. It's hard to turn an undefined mass of gel into these beautiful acrylics, to turn a seemingly nice, young man with a bright future ahead of him into someone he truly is. But I'm no stranger to change. I've shaped myself through different molds my whole life, out of safety and necessity and caution, before I inhabited my true, final form, and became the person I always was, that I am unforgivingly proud of.

It was hard work, but I never regret it. I love the way I am, and Matej will also have to learn how to love the way he will become.

I tell him as much as I start to rip his nails off, ready to do another set. It's not going to be easy, doing them again on such damaged nail beds, but I'll make it work. I always do.

I wipe the blood and puss hidden under each sparkly acrylic and get to work, grateful Matej passed out as I tore the first nail off with my pliers.

JUNE

"I'M REALLY NO good at this," I say, "but I've watched a few tutorials online and I'm certain I could at least get one right."

For once, I have Matej's full attention. He even stopped fidgeting with his nail-less fingers, picking at the yellowy scabs. He glances at me with suspicion as I put the apples all around his bedside: on the shelf above him, on the dusty nightstand. He knows something is coming; he has to know it by now.

Nocking and pulling the arrow against the bow is harder than it looks in the videos. My arms almost feel too weak for the game I'm about to play, but I never gave up on anything so far, and I don't plan to start now. My body is strong and resourceful, bearing strength that seems invisible until it becomes crucial.

With a deep breath, I pull the string as hard as I can, and shoot.

Much to my surprise, Matej doesn't scream when the first arrow flies above his head, nor does he scream when the next one grazes his cheek. He just stares at me silently, suppressing a yelp of pain as the sharp ends finally start to meet flesh, painting his stained, mucky gown bright red. His lips stay sealed in a taut, rigid line as I pull the arrows from his shoulder and his abdomen and start to stitch the ragged wounds, puckered tissue mushy and slick under my gloved hands.

By now he must've figured out that there's just no use in screaming himself dry.

JULY

I WAVE THE phone in front of Matej's face, not caring to contain my excitement.

"Oh, that's a fun one!" I say, imagining all of the prep that will go into this month's game.

I spend the next few days getting things ready. Despite what people may say or think, we're not all actually into weird, freaky shit. We're not all kinky and fabulously devious and however else others might think we behave behind our own four walls. I don't own a gimp suit or a long, velvet cape, or even a nice lacy corset. But I make do.

Some crimson lipstick, a dark bedsheet for a cape. Two punctuation needles instead of fangs.

I present myself to Matej. We make quite a pair—a fanged creature and a mummy, his bandages becoming an unplanned prop in our game. I twirl around in my cloak before I drop down onto all fours and crawl slowly to his bedside.

"I'm going to suck all the blood out of you," I say, lifting the needles to my mouth, and do my best impression of a cackle as Matej starts to scream.

I'm careful not to take too much, though. There are still games left to be played, and Matej already lost a lot of blood during the previous one. But as my fake fangs break skin and droplets of red start to bloom from my patients neck, I just can't resist.

I bite the skin and suck, embracing my role in all its devious glory.

AUGUST

"YOU'RE GOING TO *love* this one," I say, jamming a pair of earbuds in Matej's ears.

He eyes me with a look of apathetic distrust, which I'm sure I really don't deserve. I'm used to patients being all sorts of ways, but his behavior strikes a nerve. I've been dedicating all of my free time to his care, making sure he's aware of his condition and prepared for its progress. The puncture wounds he acquired during our last game healed perfectly. The cut on his cheek where the arrow nicked him is almost gone, and it's not like he uses his shoulder anyways. Yes, the scar on his abdomen is somewhat grisly, but no vital organs were damaged, and that's something to be grateful for. There's no reason to be this ungrateful, but nevertheless, he's been bratty about everything lately.

I can't get him to eat or drink. He doesn't trust anything that comes from my hands in whatever shape I present it in: mushy porridge, unmarked IV bags. I can tell he's succumbing to the disease, that he's finally accepted his fate and started to give up, because there was a time where this whole scene would make him excited. He wouldn't dare to admit it to anyone, but it used to make him really excited and horny, seeing me dance like this. He told me as much, wrote all about it in the messages he used to send me. He confirmed it once more as he came to my house that night, lured in with the same visual text he used to send me, and never left.

I press play and start to sway my body, matching my movement to the muffled noise coming through the earphones. "Don't worry, you're not included this time," I say, though I know he can't hear anything since I turned the sound all the way up. "Just watch."

I usually don't enjoy dancing, let alone in front of a man, but this time, I love it. I move my body how I like, twisting it and turning as I please, no invisible bonds keeping me in place any longer. The song's on repeat, and eventually I start to sing along, not caring that the thought of Bananarama will likely make me sick by the end of this month.

I stop only when I see a line of blood trickling down his neck. I welcome the break, not noticing the soreness of my muscles until I finally stop—I've been really going at it, matching my movements to the music blaring from Matej's headphones. Even jammed deep into his ear canal as they are, I can hear the music resonating through the room, the drums matching the thump of my feet against the wooden floor. As a healthcare professional, I know it isn't recommended to listen to music on a high volume, let alone for such a long time, but the slicky red sliding against Matej's clenched jaw only confirms the efficacy of my idea, and I have to put my professional qualms aside for a while.

Matej winces as I take the earbuds out of his ears. We both need some rest before I start my performance again. In the meantime, I take some disinfectant and set out to clean the tacky, bloodied earbuds, even though I know it's only a matter of hours that they will get gory again.

I'm nothing but meticulous regarding my work.

SEPTEMBER

HE TOSSES AND turns the majority of nights.

I stay by his side, not wanting to leave him alone in this vulnerable state. I can tell he doesn't want my company, but I don't care for what he wishes or desires. I'm only here to tend to his best interest; right now, that's keeping him sane, bringing him back to reality in those short bouts of clarity he manages to keep.

I take the rosary I've bought on my way home and sway it in front of his face.

"Do you fear God?" I ask. The words sound silly and banal to me, but I can see his demeanor change. He eyes the rosary with a pleading look, watching as the little cross dangles from side to side. I know he was a fierce Christian before, and I'm curious to find out how much of his faith has withstood through the trials he's been going through.

I'm certainly no priest, but I've seen *The Exorcist* a bunch of times and am certain I could do an impressive Father Karras impression if needed, but right now, I only put the rosary around Matej's neck.

I know Matej thinks our places should be reversed. People like him always think they can change people like me. He thought so for years, and he thought so as I dragged him to the attic, muttering obscenities underneath his breath even in his drugged, sluggish state.

Matej thinks about my question for a few moments before he nods, eyelids fluttering as he's about to succumb to another fever-induced sleep.

"Silly man," I reply, tightening the rosary around his neck and watching it sink into the gray skin stretched across his weakened tendons. "Fearing things that don't exist."

With each tug and pull of the beaded twine I watch Matej's chest contract, his throat spasm. The rosary strains under my fingers, and I welcome the resistance. My grip becomes harder, encouraged by the sounds of labored breathing filling the air, and I bask in it, enjoying the physicality of my presence.

"Silly man," I repeat, wondering what it's like to have the privilege of fearing things that don't exist.

OCTOBER

IT'S BEEN A month since my patient stopped talking. Save for the pained whimpers he lets out during his sporadic and long periods of sleep, the room is silent, and I savor the quiet as much as I can. I love my job, I really do. But sometimes it's hard to find a moment of peace, a moment to reflect on the sanctity of my work, and now, in the calmness of my attic, I finally get to savor the fruits of my labor.

I can tell by the look I catch in Matej's eyes (although he makes a point to never look at me anymore, and I have to grab his gaunt cheeks to make him face me), that he desperately wants to say something. But I fear it's not the answer I want to hear, the answer I am striving for. I fear that his disease has ruined him too much, destroyed his capacity to think. Maybe we played too hard. Maybe I've tried to work too hard to make him see his shortcomings. But in a way, I do feel like I've succeeded.

His condition affected lots of people, spread around like wildfire and corrupted many hearts that had the capacity to be clean and healthy. It's only fitting that he succumbed to the very disease that caused such pain to people like me.

Sometimes when he wakes up he stares at the jar of teeth, and he wails. At times like those, I'm happy there are no other patients around to hear him scream, no matter how much I'd like to tell everyone of the important work I've been doing here.

I remind him that he should feel lucky. It isn't extremely common, but many people lose their teeth even younger than him. Gum diseases, gay bashings. And I've made a point of removing them as gently as I can, with the tools I had by hand. He had them for almost thirty years, and I'd reason that that's more than a person like him, diseased with hate, deserves to have.

The attic is not as comfortable as the rooms in the nursing home I work at, but I've been trying to make up for it in different ways. As soon as my shift ends I rush home and take care of him, eager to play our designated game for the month. Although it is emotionally and physically taxing for the both of us, I'm happy I did so. We've made many wonderful memories together, although I'm going to be the only one left to cherish them.

I hold his bony face between my hands, his prickly skin scratching my skin, and show him the photographs. I'm sure he feels just like I do: that we were both different people at the time they were taken.

My fingers become damp, tears and snot making it hard to grasp his ashen skin. I try to sound as soothing as I can, because I know it won't be long now, and if my time at the nursing home has taught me anything, it's that everyone deserves a bit of comfort near the end.

"No, dummy," I say, "you're supposed to smile."

It takes him a while, but for once, he listens to me, baring me with his bloody gums in a mangled grimace.

NOVEMBER

As FAR AS bullying went, it was considered a case of a pretty mild one.

It's just pictures, the teacher told my parents with a disinterested shrug. There are no actual words involved. Why would I get so upset by some random little pictures on my phone? Emojis, he concluded, are nothing to get so worked up over.

In a way, he was right. It started as a simple emoji, an illustration of an innocent vegetable, but by the time the messages started involving actual sentences, I was far too embarrassed to tell anyone. After all, it's not like I could explain myself. How could I tell my parents and that fucking clueless teacher that the little eggplants Matej had been texting me were much more sinister than they appeared? That it was a non-verbal, symbolic version of the thing he'd been whispering in the classrooms, the thing he'd been fantasizing of doing.

If only you'd let me do it, I'd set you straight.

💀

I shake Matej's limp body in excitement.

"You won't believe this shit!" I say, basking in the serendipity of the random emoji generator. Tears well up in the corners of my eyes and I can't believe my luck, can't believe that it has finally ended the way it began, all thanks to the hard work I've been doing.

My patient stays predictably—and blessedly—silent, and I let my head rest on the hard mattress, heart fluttering as the screen lights up my face, brightest it's ever been.

MOLLY, FROM DATA ANALYTICS

S.S.N. Smith

MOLLY, FROM DATA ANALYTICS

S.S.N. Smith

Molly clutched her bullet journal tight to her chest, her new fountain pen with Iroshizuku ink loaded tucked neatly in the pen holder. It was a new work week, a clean slate. When she was hired to run data analysis at the pharmaceutical company, she assumed everyone would immediately notice how amazing she was. Everyone should have noticed how organized she was, how she was always ahead of schedule, and how she offered to help when others seemed to be lagging. But no. There was nothing, not even a comment on her impeccable handwriting. She took calligraphy courses; she hasn't gotten to drop that fact yet. It was month six, so maybe they were all just working up to it.

Nikki, her girlfriend of three years (they were planning to get engaged in a few months), told her it took time. Molly was someone others had to get used to. Nikki was usually right about these things.

Molly placed her journal down in its spot on her desk and opened it flat for her new day, new week, and the last week of the month. She put an X in the box for her daily habit tracker, a good job for taking the stairs. She cleaned her desk with an antibacterial wipe and put out the trash that hadn't been removed the night before. Then, she turned on her computer and waited for it to boot up. A new day, a new week, a new time to show who she was, so maybe people would want to eat lunch with her. They would comment on her bento box and the star cucumbers she cut for her cold noodle salad.

She was replying to an email—her third of the morning—when she heard voices. Joel, another data analyzer, came in and stopped at Lauren's cubicle.

"Dude, the game," Joel said.

Lauren sighed. "I had to help my sister move."

"Your sister's move is more important than softball?" Joel joked.

"I would never hear the end of it from my mom if I weren't there."

"You do know you're 28."

"I'm 27," she chuckled. "And you don't know my mom."

"You're going tomorrow, though, yeah?" he asked. "We need a fourth girl. It's the rules. We had to ask Gunner's girlfriend to play, and it did not go well."

"Yeah, I'll be there," she replied. "Why didn't we get a fifth girl in case one of us can't make it?"

"Who?" Joel laughed. "There's no one else."

"What about Shannon on the fifth floor? She looks athletic."

"Oh yeah," he hummed. "I'll ask her, good call, Lo."

Joel slapped his giant hand down on the divider and claimed he needed to go before all the good bagels were gone. He stepped out of Lauren's cubicle and walked down the row. Molly looked up and smiled at him.

"Sup, Mary." He nodded.

He was gone before she could say her name was Molly.

SOMETIMES, IT FELT like people were avoiding her. When she arrived in communal spaces, such as the break room, where people gathered to discuss the things they had in common, they always seemed to be at the tail end of a conversation and would walk out. Sometimes Molly would be in the break room, and she would see people walk towards the door, but then change their minds. She always seemed to be alone.

The click of the kettle let her know the water for her tea was done boiling. She watched as the hibiscus tea bag started to leak a deep red color, like thick paint on a canvas.

There was an exception to the rule, as there was for most things, and for Molly, the exception to the "all alone all the time" rule was Lauren. For some reason, the programmer never seemed to shy away when Molly was around. She entered the rooms Molly occupied, stood behind her at the copier, scrolled on her phone as she waited for the coffee maker to produce caffeine, and made eye contact, giving tight-lipped smiles. Sometimes, Lauren would say "morning" or "good night" when entering and leaving.

Molly was about to start a conversation, something Nikki told her to try, when she noticed Joel in the doorway. He saw Lauren and swung into the small room. Only seconds later did he notice Molly; his eyes went wide at the sight of her, as if she were a ghost, before he turned to his friend.

"Did you hear?" Joel asked.

Lauren poured creamer into her mug. "I hear a lot of things."

"Brady from payroll. *Fired*," he explained.

"Really?" Lauren responded.

Joel leaned closer to her. "Porn on his computer."

Lauren's face twisted. "Gross, come on."

"Oh, he did come on…company property," Joel joked.

Lauren shook her head. "I hate men."

"Me too." Joel laughed.

This was probably a good time for Molly to chime in; she could say she hated men, too. She didn't. She didn't have an issue with men, but she could say she did if it meant conversation, mainly with Lauren. Joel didn't matter.

Both of their phones chimed, almost in unison. Molly watched as they checked, looking confused at their screens.

"Slate chat," Joel said. "Did you get the same one?"

Lauren turned her screen to him. "Yeah, looks like it's the office."

"It's just a string of emojis." Joel chuckled.

"Probably just some asshole." Lauren pushed her phone in her pocket, grabbed her coffee and headed for the door.

Joel followed quickly behind.

MOLLY SIPPED HER tea at her desk; whatever Slate chat the whole office got, she was not included. It didn't matter; she didn't care about emojis.

At least that's what she told herself until her phone beeped, and she rushed to see if she was added to the chat last minute. It wasn't the emoji chat; it was her camera app. She set up cameras in her apartment a few months ago. She called it her Mochi camera, because she used it to watch her cat, Mochi. However, sometimes she would see Nikki. Sometimes Nikki would search for things before work. Sometimes she would leave with bags of stuff, and when Molly got home, she would notice small things were missing. Nikki worked late most nights, so she never got around to asking about the missing items. She also never got around to telling Nikki about the Mochi camera.

She clicked into the app. It wasn't Mochi doing something cute and erratic; it was Nikki, and she was with a woman from Nikki's job, who always looked disappointed. They moved around the apartment looking for something. They were probably heading out to a work event, and Nikki needed to run up to the apartment to find something she had forgotten.

Molly was about to text Nikki when a crash, followed by a scream, ripped through the office. Normally, Molly wasn't the type to see what all the fuss was about, but normally, the fuss wasn't so startling. The scream was long and loud, and drenched in what could only be described as genuine fear. As she passed from the gray cubicles to the beige ones, another scream tore through space, solidifying the idea that she needed to know what was so horrifying.

A crowd had gathered in the far corner, all of them making bizarre movements; their hands out in front of them or pulling at their hair, transforming their office casual attire into unkempt and uncontrolled chaos.

"Don't do it."

"Stop, Dan, please."

"You don't have to do this, Dan."

There were four Dans in the office. Daniel S., Danford, Daniel U., and just Dan. Molly had seen all of them, and all of them had seen her, but they made no effort to get to know her. As she moved closer, she saw that Dan was making a fuss.

Danford—balding on the edges, never failed to mention his gym routine—was holding a letter opener to his throat. His eyes were wild and big, like he was forcing them open so he could be sure he saw them, and they saw him as he pressed the point into the rough, patchy skin on his neck.

"Dan, brother." Jason, from accounts payable, held his hands out. "Give me the knife."

"Smile," Dan growled, his teeth clenched so tight they looked like they would crack.

Jason took a tentative step forward. "Give me the knife."

Dan pushed the tip into his jugular. "Smile."

"Danny." Taryn, from accounts receivable, was standing on the sidelines, weeping. "Please, baby, don't."

Molly had heard a rumor they had something going on. An email was sent out regarding the need to disclose inter-office relationships.

Dan started to cry, his hand shaking as he brought the object to his cheek. "Smile."

He pushed the tip into the inner edge of the masseter, the muscle that connects your jaw to your face. As he shoved the letter opener into his cheek and slid it through to the corner of his mouth, Molly thought about how your cheek was just a flap of skin that kept your mouth from being open to the elements and your food from falling out as you chew.

Everyone began to scream around her, and all Molly could do was watch as he carved into the other side of his face, until you could see all his coffee-stained teeth, covered in a thin layer of blood. Molly thought it was strange how his jaw didn't fall open, but that's what the masseter muscle was for.

Talking when your lips didn't fully press together was odd, and Molly now knew that fact when Dan repeated the word "smile" five times as he slit his throat. When the blood clogged his throat, on the third "shile" Molly knew it was because you need lips to say the "m" sound.

Dan's carotid artery burst open and sprayed everyone in the front row. Jason, drenched in deep red now, lunged at the man, slipping on a puddle of Dan's still-pouring blood. Molly was happy she was in the back, because she remained unsplashed, her outfit still pristine. Dan fell to the floor, Jason pressing his hands into Dan's neck, and that was the end of that.

Another scream distracted Molly from watching Taryn break down. She went to see what all the commotion was about.

The crowd was roughly the same size, and people were saying roughly the same things, only this time it was for Quinn.

Quinn worked in Human Resources; the only conversation she'd had with Molly was when she'd explained her flag pin on her work lanyard sent the message that the company supported what was happening in El Salvador. Molly explained that it was the Nicaraguan flag, and that's where her mother was from. Quinn had shaken her head and told her that some people didn't know where their family came from, so they might feel offended by her heritage display on work attire. Nikki told her that the correction would only bring an argument, and she gently reminded her that making friends at the office was important, so the pin was left at home, and Molly waited for a chance to bring up flags in conversation.

"Quinn, calm down," Merrell, also from HR, said calmly. "Let's go talk."

"Money," Quinn said, holding a box cutter up to her left eye.

"Money's not important," Merrell told her. "*You're* important."

Quinn began dragging the razor blade around her eye. The skin split so easy, which was shocking because that was a used, and probably dull, blade.

People screamed, some tried to get to her, but Quinn slashed at them until they backed up, then went back to carving at her face. Everyone was more afraid of getting cut than stopping their friend from slicing her face open.

The blood ran down Quinn's cheeks, looking so red against her pale skin. When she was done, Molly saw both her eyes had dollar signs etched into them, her eyelids split down the middle, curled to each side like a ruffled curtain. The eyes stay in the skull because the optic nerve is connected to the brain. Quinn's eyes were still moving as she looked around the room at everyone staring at her, without the lid to protect it, the juice that coated her eyes, aqueous humor, collected at the bottom lid, mixed with the blood droplets from her upper lid, and, what Molly suspected was tears.

Then Quinn stuck out her tongue, which is a collection of muscles, not just one big one, and carved another dollar sign into it.

"Money," Quinn repeated, only now it sounded like "Monty," because she had dug so deep into her tongue.

For the second time in her life, and the second time that day, Molly watched someone slit their own throat. Again, she was happy she stood in the back, away from the blood as it splashed all the people in front of the audience, like a cheap 5D show at an amusement park. And again, everyone was screaming and crying as Quinn dropped to the floor, and the blood trickled out of her neck and soaked the carpet. That was going to be tough to clean.

They needed to call 911. That's what Jacob, the team lead, told everyone who gathered around the gray cubicles. People had attempted, but the signal was blocked.

Molly still had a signal, but she was using it to watch Nikki and her coworker drink coffee at their kitchen table. She was fixated on that woman petting her precious Mochi, who seemed to love everyone. Molly couldn't begrudge a cat for being friendly.

She was brought out of her trance when she heard the banging on the exit door.

"This is a fire hazard," Ashton, from marketing, told the crowd.

"They automatically override in emergencies," Jacob said.

"Two people are dead, Jacob. I think that we can call this an emergency," Ashton scoffed.

Jacob took a calm, professional breath. "I mean like a fire or earthquake. The doors don't know two of our coworkers have passed."

"Killed themselves," Taryn spat.

"Died by suicide," Jessica corrected.

Taryn stood from the office chair. "Dan *killed* himself. Quinn *killed* herself."

"Okay, let's all try and take a second," Merrell directed.

Molly saw the look in Taryn's eyes, the type of look that said in a second, she was going to make Merrell die by suicide, but everyone's phones chimed. Except Molly's. The grumbling of having signal rippled through the intense crowd, and everyone checked their phones.

"The fuck is this?" someone called out. "More emojis."

"Maybe we can use Slate to contact 911," Jessica said.

Everyone typed on their phone, everyone but Molly, who was still not in the chat. The low, disappointed rumble told her it hadn't worked. The crowd came down with a case of the "now what's" looking to anyone but themselves to figure out a plan, when a voice cut through the low roar.

"Gunner... Gun... Gunny, no."

Molly knew that voice; it was the same one that had called her Mary more than once, even though interacted several times a day. She followed the group to see Joel.

Gunner, from sales, Joel's friend, and part of the group of guys who had perfect hair and bright white smiles, spent most of their time entertaining potential clients. He was holding a bottle of bleach in his hand. He paced back and forth, his dark brown hair falling in front of his face, sticking to his forehead as sweat drops popped from his perfect pores.

"Just put it down, bro," Joel said.

"Gross," Gunner growled.

"You're right, it's gross," Joel confirmed.

Gunner's face was already pale, his lips cracked. There was a stain on the front of his shirt. He brought the bleach to his mouth and started to chug like a frat bot at a party.

Joel leaped in the air and tackled him. "I won't let you do this."

The bottle fell out of Gunner's hands and he punched at his friend's back, slamming his fist down as Joel tried to get him to the ground, screaming, "Gross" over and over.

People cheered for Joel, yet they didn't step in to help. They watched as Gunner fell to the ground and started kicking Joel in the stomach. The men grunted as they fought, and the crowd just watched No cheers, no cries, just worried looks as the coworkers beat each other until fist and faces were bloodied, and Molly wondered if anyone would jump in, if anyone should. Gunner punched Joel in the nose, making him stumble back and hit the wall. Everyone stood there as Gunner grabbed the bleach and chugged the rest of it.

Gunner stopped and looked out at the crowd. For a second, Molly thought that was the end of the show when Gunner coughed. Puke spewed from his perfect, plump lips. It came up in large, pink chunks that slowly turned red. Molly realized he was throwing up the bleach, and it had bored a hole in his stomach and throat, and most of what was coming up was blood and pieces of his insides. It all flowed out like someone spraying chunky soup from a think hose. Stomach acid first, then the lining, then the lining of the esophagus, that part the burns when you have indigestion.

The smell of bile and bleach filled the air as Gunner continued to puke blood and probably protein shake on the ground and himself, his white Oxford shirt and wool blend pants ruined. Molly took a step back; she wasn't a fan of puke.

Gunner finally stopped puking and looked out into the crowd.

The color drained from him, his now pale skin a perfect juxtaposition against red of the blood and the bright yellow stomach acid.

"Gross," he repeated before coughing twice and falling to the floor.

Immediately, as if Gunner didn't matter, everyone scattered and headed for whatever exit they could find. The doors in the office were reinforced steel that only opened with a key card, but none of the pads were working. You couldn't pry them open, though Molly watched some of the men try. The company was more concerned with keeping secrets in than allowing its employees out. It seemed they were stuck there until whatever was happening was figured out. Molly sat down and took out her phone.

In the amount of time it took Gunner to die from drinking bleach, bleeding, and puking his stomach out, Nikki had gone from sitting across from her work friend to sitting adjacent to her. Mochi had at least given up and was resting on the couch. What were they talking about? What required them to lean so close to each other?

"I'll try," Kai said as they were pushed towards one of the doors.

Kai was their Computer Technician. Molly had only spoken with Kai once when she got her work laptop. Molly had pointed at the picture of the kitten on their desk, pulled up a picture of Mochi on her phone and told him that Mochi was a Russian Blue. She'd gone on about how he was silly, but sweet, and he loved playing with a sushi toy. Kai hadn't seemed impressed and didn't want to talk about their cat, except to tell Molly that their name was Catflix.

In six months, Molly never had a computer issue, so she'd never had the chance to reengage Kai about their shared interest in felines.

"Give me a second," Kai said, shooing people away.

Kai opened a laptop, plugged a cable into the door panel, and started typing. Everyone stood around watching them work, hope mixed with fear on their faces as they prayed that the computer would open the door. It wasn't going to work. The doors were programmed to a closed server in the basement. It was designed to ensure no one could hack into it. What kind of drug company would they be if someone with a laptop and a HDMI cable could break into the offices? Molly knew this because she read the security handbook one day when her Kindle wasn't charging and she was eating lunch alone.

"It's not working," Kai said.

"What the fuck?" Ashton screamed.

Kai stood up. "I told you, it's a closed system."

"Fuck that!" Ashton pushed through the crowd.

Molly thought maybe he had given up, but then noticed he was grabbing a paperweight from the secretary's desk. Mrs. April, who was nice to Molly in passing but didn't engage anyone in any personal matters. She and the boss were out this morning.

Ashton moved people out of his way so he could smash the keypad. "Open, you bastard!"

The keypad broke after a few attempts, but the doors didn't open, and their situation was possibly worse.

"Brute force didn't work."

Molly looked behind her to see who was speaking. It was Lauren. Molly looked around to see if anyone else was around them, if she could be talking to anyone besides her, but they were alone, in the back, away from the crowd.

"Who would have guessed?" Lauren said.

Molly wasn't sure what to say, so she just nodded.

Lauren looked down at her and smirked before walking away and joining the crowd.

MOLLY WAS WATCHING Nikki and the girl from work stand up and walk together to the kitchen to place their mugs into the sink when someone screamed…again.

She pushed her phone into her pocket and went over to see who was trying to off themselves in some odd way now. By the time she got there, the screaming had turned into mumbles, and no one was trying to plead with another coworker to stop them from slashing out their eyes. Instead, they all stood at the door of the conference room, looking at what was inside. Only, it wasn't what, but who… or whom?

Gabby from sales. Gabby was pretty, like the type of pretty that makes you question yourself when you look in the mirror. The type of pretty that could tell you the shade of lipstick didn't go well with your complexion, and instead of being offended, you watched hours of beauty blogger videos to figure out what she meant. Gabby was the type of beauty that made you grateful that she noticed you.

But she wasn't so beautiful now, lying on the ground. That perfect skin was peeled off her face and placed back on her bloody skull, only upside down. Her hands and arms were covered in blood, a razor blade next to her on the ground. Her fitted blazer and white silk dress shirt were soaked in blood; there was no dry cleaning for that.

"She's still alive," someone said.

Molly watched Gabby's fingers, with manicured nails, twitch a few times. She was still alive, but it wasn't for long. Was it odd that she didn't scream as she sliced off her own face?

Maybe that would have been the weirdest death, but another scream came, again. Molly thought maybe they should get some kind of signal that signified when another coworker was dead or dying, so the screaming could stop. She followed the crowd over to the men's bathroom.

This was a new scene for her; she had never had a reason to enter this room. Not that she was looking for one, but the most interesting thing was Tanner from payroll lying on the ground, with bottles of bathroom cleaner empty next to him. It seems as if he had mixed the chemicals and poured them on his face. His skin melted off his bones into a red and chemical-green puddle on the tile floor. He had a tight-lipped smile, and his eyes were wide open, looking out into the crowd, letting everyone who saw know that he did this happily.

It was kind of amazing that anyone could find the right chemicals to melt human skin, especially an accountant. He never screamed, and Molly realized, no one who killed themselves had.

Jessica was the one in the front; perhaps she was the one who had found him, which raised the question of why she was entering the men's bathroom. She was the first one to turn and push her way out.

The group gathered in the center of the office, where the beige, gray, sky blue and sea-foam green cubicles all met. Jacob stood in the middle. With the boss gone, he was technically in charge, and everyone was looking to him for answers, which he clearly didn't have.

"What's the plan?" Ashton barked.

Jacob ran his hand through his thinning hair. "I don't know what this is."

The sound of beeps and dings saved him, everyone's phones going off again. They all looked hopeful, but it was just the Slate chat.

"Another string of random emojis," someone called out before slamming their phone on a desk. "Someone is killing us," Jessica said.

"They killed themselves," Taryn said in a low, resigned tone. She turned to Jessica. "They killed themselves. No one came up to them and slashed their throats, cut their eyes or forced them to drink bleach. Gabby cut her own face off, you saw her hands, the razor, she flayed her own face."

Jacob put his hand up. "Okay, Taryn, I think that's enough."

"Do you, Jacob?" She pushed her way to the front. Her smart-tech blouse had spots of blood from her lover's neck. Her eyes were bloodshot, her eyeliner smeared. "I'm saying what's actually happening here. People are killing themselves."

"We see it, Taryn," Merrell squeaked. She was so small it was hard to remember she even existed. A spec of a woman, too tall to be considered small, but too short to be considered tall. "Someone is doing this to us."

"Who, Merrell? Huh?" Taryn marched up to her, standing half a foot taller than her. "Who is doing this?"

"Or maybe the better question is *why*?" Lauren chimed in.

Molly looked up at the sound of Lauren's voice. This time, she was talking to the crowd, to all who dared gather in the center of the third floor. She didn't look at Molly or make any indication that at one point in time they had a separate, secret conversation.

"There is no why!" Taryn shouted.

Jacob shrugged. "I mean, we do work at a pharmaceutical company…"

Taryn pointed at him. "I don't make drugs. None of us do. We are all administration, not chemists or doctors. We don't sell the drugs, or decide who gets what and how much."

"Maybe that's not how this person sees it," Jacob said.

"How?" Kai came forward. "Even if someone is trying to prove some sick point by killing the afterthoughts of a drug company, the better question is how."

"Maybe they were already suicidal," Jessica suggested.

"No!" Taryn cried. "Dan was not suicidal. He loved me. He loved life. He would never."

"Taryn, we never truly know what's going on in someone's head," Merrell told her.

"Merrel, I swear to god if you tell me I didn't know my boyfriend, I will cut your throat."

"Hey now," Jacob scoffed. "Let's not turn on each other."

"Fuck you, Jacob," Taryn shot back. "I *hope* you're next." She turned back to Merrell. "I hope you're second." Then she turned to Jessica. "And you follow soon after."

Molly was not surprised when no one tried to stop Taryn from leaving the center of the circle. She wasn't shocked as no one made a move to go with her. She was, however, shocked when Ashton smashed Taryn in the back of the head with the paper weight.

As Taryn fell to the ground, her scream cut short by her fall, Ashton stood over her, then knelt and smashed her head again before she had the chance to turn and see who was doing this to her. By the third hit, she stopped whimpering. Ashton brought the paperweight down three more times until Taryn's skull fully opened, and her brains leaked out onto the floor. He brought it down a few more times, almost as if he was ensuring all the contents of her skull were out and the top of her head was a puzzle no one could solve.

Finally, he stood straight and turned to look at everyone. He blinked a few times, and Molly noticed his eyes were dark brown. You could see the red flecks of blood against his tanned skin. He didn't smile, he didn't frown, he didn't give away any emotion as to why he would have done such a thing.

"Explode," Ashton said, then dropped the paper weight.

He reached into his pocket and took out a fountain pen, the Meisterstück Gold-Coated Classique Molly was shocked a meathead like Ashton had such a nice pen.

Ashton shrugged, before shoving the gold tip into his neck. He stayed standing for a few seconds as the blood leaked out his neck, then he fell to the floor. His face remained neutral and the life left his body.

Molly wondered if it was inappropriate to circle back for that pen.

IT WAS OFFICIAL, Nikki was kissing her coworker, pressing her against the kitchen counter and pushing her fingers through thick hair. Molly sat at her desk and watched as her girlfriend, who was supposed to be her future fiancée, undressed the woman she worked with while their cat bathed itself in the sun box attached to the window.

She wasn't sure how she was supposed to feel. Betrayal felt strange, like a pressure in her belly. Being cheated on, after three years, after check-ins every quarter, after semi-annual therapy to make sure they were truly on the same page, after calendars had been synced, and parents had been met… It felt odd to watch it all go down on a camera made for cats.

In a way, she wanted to jump out of a window. In another way, she wanted to scream. In a different way she didn't want to end up like those poor dead jokers stinking up the place. And in a completely different way, she wanted to simply get back to work, but that was impossible. They were all still stuck on the third floor with no way out, and dead bodies around every corner making it impossible to feel the betrayal of her relationship ending. Phones kept chiming and people kept killing themselves in fantastical ways.

Molly was there fifteen minutes ago when Jessica, Ms. Everything-is-going-to-be-okay, carved her own eyes out and replaced them with stars from the holiday party decorations. Molly wasn't sure where she even found the decorations, but she did have to give it up for the creativity of shoving spikes into your eye holes. The rest of the crew was somewhat unimpressive, except for the face peel-off feature.

Molly returned to her desk as the rest of the crew made futile attempts to escape the floor.

"You seem sad."

Molly shut off her phone as she looked up and saw Lauren leaning on her cubicle wall. Her forearms rested on the top ledge. She had never noticed the tattoos on Lauren's forearms before. She usually wore long sleeves pulled down, but today she had them rolled up a little. Black and gray ink covered her skin, but Molly couldn't make out the images.

"Sure, I guess," Molly told her.

She looked up and noticed how green Lauren's eyes were. She noticed how her skin had freckles that blended in with her tan.

"I mean, people are dead," Molly added. "Aren't you sad? Weren't they your friends?"

"Yes." Lauren's face remained neutral as she leaned down. "But they aren't yours."

For the first time in a long while, Molly felt a challenge rise in her chest. "How do you know?"

Lauren grinned. "I know."

Molly fully intended to ask her how, when yet another scream swelled in the air, disturbing their peace and putting an end to a rising warm feeling in her belly.

She was ready to see what kind of unimpressive scene was going to befall them when she found herself shocked at the events.

It was Joel. Perfect, funny, lovable Joel. He upturned a bottle and poured its contents over his head. Joel, who high-fived everyone and always seemed to cheer up the crowd. Joel, who brought cupcakes for birthdays. Joel, who planned outings for the group, convinced people to play on the company's softball team and could crack a joke in weekly meetings, without anyone ever getting annoyed. Soaked in something that smelled so strong it penetrated the sense, Joel pulled a lighter from his pocket.

When he looked out into the crowd, he looked as if he were looking for someone.

"Hot," he whispered.

And she swore she saw a tear flow down his cheek before he flicked the lighter, setting himself ablaze in the most exceptional of ways.

His scream reverberated through the office; shook everyone to their core. That scream etched itself onto the bones of all who heard it. And the smell. Molly would never forget the smell of burning flesh and hair, like pig meat covered in plastic and thrown into a pit. Awful, but slightly sweet.

Molly watched as people rushed for extinguishers and tried to put out the fire before it was too late, but it was too late by the time Joel had started. He died screaming, and Molly looked over to see if Lauren was crying.

Lauren didn't flinch.

THEIR NUMBERS WERE dwindling. Molly wasn't sure she could consider them *their* numbers, as no one ever considered her in anything. Nevertheless, they were down to a baker's dozen of coworkers, in what felt like the longest work day in history. The group had gathered in the center again and was trying to come up with a reasonable explanation as to why someone like Joel would set himself on fire.

Molly was back in her cubicle. She had turned back to the camera and was now watching her girlfriend lift her coworker on the counter and go down on her, right where Molly made breakfast. She thought about waiting to see if they were both going to come, but decided that maybe this wasn't something she wanted to watch, so she shut down her phone.

She started to think about the items that had gone missing in their shared apartment. And maybe when Nikki skirted the conversation about renewing their lease she wasn't hinting at buying a house. But she didn't want to think about it all right now.

She thought about joining the discussion circle, but when she noticed Lauren was not part of the brains trust, she had to wonder why the programmer was not involved in figuring out why all her coworkers were dropping like flies by their own hands.

Lauren was typing on her phone when Molly approached.

"Hello," Lauren said.

Molly stopped just a few feet away. "Hello."

They were two cubicles away from the discussion circle. They kept their voices low.

"Why aren't you trying to solve this?" Molly asked.

Lauren leaned against the cubicle wall. "Why aren't you?"

She snorted. "Because you were right. I'm not a part of this. Of them."

Lauren hummed.

"But you are," Molly said. "Why aren't you…"

The elusive phone chime echoed in the stifling air. Molly looked over at the circle and saw everyone take out their phones. She saw their faces turn when they read the chat. Only this time, she saw that Lauren hadn't read the chat.

Instead, her eyes were fixated on Molly. When Molly turned around to see her fully, she felt as if those green eyes could bore a hole through her head. She thought maybe Lauren was reading her mind, seeing her thoughts like a picture on a screen, knowing everything she knew within that split second. Maybe she knew that that look made Molly want to squirm under her.

Molly swallowed. Her throat was suddenly dry, and she needed a second to collect herself before continuing. "You're not going to check your chat?"

Lauren smiled. "No."

She was going to ask why, but the sound of banging stole her attention. She turned and watched Jacob laugh as he smashed his head into a wall.

Two men charged after him, both stating that they weren't going to let anyone else die. They grabbed Jacob and fought him to the ground. Tears were rolling down his cheeks, mixing with blood from a gash in his head. They pushed him to the ground and struggled as he fought to get them to let him go. When they wouldn't let go, Jacob began to smash the back of his head against the floor, laughing and crying as he thrust his head back over and over.

The two men tried to stop him, but by the fifth smash, Jacob's body went limp. They stood up and looked down at him, a smile on his face, tears in his eyes.

"It's the emojis," Kai stated, softly at first. They stood up. "It's the emojis!"

Every corner of the office had a dead body off-gassing and stinking up the place. Joel was an asshole for the fire situation and it smelling like a bad luau. The group moved to the break room. Molly followed but stayed standing next to the doorway—not in it, just next to it.

"They are killing themselves like emojis," Kai told the group. "Dan said 'smile' and carved a smile in his face. Ashton bashed in Taryn's head until it *exploded*, then *shrugged* before killing himself. Gunner drank bleach until he *puked*."

Merrell shook her head. "No, that's not a thing. Killer emojis? Come on, Kai."

"Emojis aren't killing. I said people are killing themselves like emojis. Jessica pushed stars in her eyes." Kai took out their phone. "Look at this list, tell me each death doesn't fit an emoji."

"Gabby?" Freddy from the mail room stated.

Kai scrolled, then turned their phone for everyone to see. "Upside down face. She pulled her skin off and placed it upside down on his face."

Merrell let out a choked cry. "Quinny… She carved dollar signs in her eyes."

"And her tongue." Kai scrolled on their phone for another emoji.

"It still doesn't make any sense," Freddy said. "How? Tell me how?"

Everyone looked to Kai for answers. Molly moved a little closer to the doorway so she could watch them pace.

"What's different about today?" Kai asked, but didn't search for an answer. "A smell? No. Food? No." They paced from one end of the room to the other. "Drugs? No, we are all tested, and this wouldn't be the company, though the boss is gone."

"The chat," Merrell gasped.

Everyone looked over at the HR lady.

She held up her phone. "The Slate chat we were all randomly added to. The one with only emojis."

Everyone took out their phones and opened Slate, except for Molly and one other person.

Lauren was standing in the background. She had a granola bar and was breaking off small pieces to eat as everyone tried to solve the problem. But she wasn't fully watching them; she was also watching Molly. And now that Molly was noticing her, Lauren made eye contact, locked her in. Molly felt a shock shoot from the tip of her toes to the top of her head.

"I don't understand." Freddy panicked. "Why us? What the fuck did we do?"

"Nothing," Merrell cried. "I haven't done anything. I don't deserve…"

"Deserve." Lauren interrupted.

She pushed herself up from leaning on the counter and walked over to the fridge.

"Yes," Merrell answered. "None of us deserves this."

"Oh, Merrell?" Lauren took a water from the fridge, cracked the top and took a drink. "And what about you, Fred? Do you think you deserve this?"

Fred, with his thick black mustache, looked around at the people in the breakroom. "No, I mean, what have I done?"

Lauren moved to the doorway, took another sip of water, and then put the lid back on. "None of you have done anything wrong?"

"The fuck are you talking about?" Kai demanded.

Lauren stood still, calm, focused, sexy. "Each one of you used those silly little pictures to express your disgust and disdain for each other. All of you are so nice when passing each other in the walkways. So nice eating face cake at birthday gatherings. But, fuck, those chats." Lauren shook her head. "All of you are talking behind each other's backs. Calling each other names; stupid, whore, lazy, fat, ugly, sleazy." She let out a soothing breath. "I read them all."

"Wait,"—Kai stepped forward—"you read our chats?"

"Yeah, Slate is my creation." Lauren chuckled. "I created the app for the company to have internal chats on internal servers. I read everything you send to everyone." She looked over to Merrell. "Everything."

Merrell took a step back and tried to lose herself in the crowd.

"Every single one of you standing in this room, just like every single one of those dead bodies that used to be fake friends, is a disgusting person. Backstabbing, disloyal, two-faced, disgusting excuses for people." Lauren leaned in the doorway. "All of you deserve everything that is coming to you. Each and every one of you deserves to die in the way you chat."

"And what about her?" Kai pointed at Molly. "She's not in the chat. I read all the names, Holly is the only one missing."

"It's Molly, asshole." Lauren snorted. "She's not a part of this. She's never a part of anything. That's why I like her." Lauren's smile grew ever larger as Molly's face softened at her proclamation.

"You like me?" Molly asked.

Lauren nodded, her soft strawberry blond hair bouncing in her short ponytail. "Yeah, Molly. I didn't want to tell you until all this was over. I wasn't sure how you'd react." A sly smile grew on her pouty lips. "Though I had my suspicions." She took a step closer. "I've been into you for months."

"That's…"—Molly took a deep breath—"so romantic!"

"Oh, thank goodness." Lauren chuckled.

"You sociopathic piece of shit!" Kai shouted.

The shortest person in the room screamed as they charged at the door, hands first, as if she was going to grab Lauren's throat and choke her with her bare hands. Lauren stepped out of the doorway, and in that split second, the door closed, crushing Kai's hands. Their fingers poked out between the metal, twitching before dropping to the ground.

Molly heard the screams and the bangs of the others on the door, but she was more focused on Lauren.

Lauren, who liked her. Lauren, who did all of this to punish the horrible people in the world. Lauren, who wore button-down shirts to hide the dark tattoos on her arms, that Molly wanted to run her fingers over. Lauren with beautiful smile that Molly couldn't stop watching. Lauren, who actually liked her!

She never thought the worst thing to happen to her, her girlfriend cheating, would be combined with the best thing that happened to her. Lauren liked her.

"Do you want to get dinner?" Lauren asked her.

Molly smiled. "Yeah, I could eat. I can't go home right now. My girlfriend is currently cheating on me with a coworker."

"Oh." Lauren breathed out.

"Obviously, we aren't together anymore." Molly clarified. "I think maybe we had been done for a while. I'm not as hurt as I thought I would be."

Lauren grinned. "Do you want me to send her a Slate chat request?"

"How did you do all of this?" Molly asked.

Lauren shrugged. "I'm a programmer. I programmed."

Molly thought about it as they started to walk away. "Can we get my cat Mochi first. I don't want him to see something terrible."

"Yeah, they can be timed," Lauren told her. "Oh, fuck."

Lauren went back to the break room, took out her phone, and started typing. Molly went back and looked through the window of the breakroom door. She watched everyone in the room start to cry, all at once, as if a sudden bout of sadness swept through the room and the only thing left to do was cry. Molly gazed through the window as Merrell went to the silverware drawer and picked out the knives, then went to the rest of the group and gave each one. She was shocked to see them all cut their wrists, the blood flowing so much faster than in movies. They all fell to the ground to join Kai's lifeless, handless body.

Merrell turned around to face the window. She stopped crying as she held the knife to her throat. Her eyes looked as if they were begging Lauren to put an end to this, but she knew she never would. Before pushing the metal into her throat, she held up a peace sign, then fell to the ground as blood spewed everywhere.

Molly turned to Lauren.

Lauren smiled. "Your cat's name is Mochi?"

"Yeah, I studied in Japan for a year during college."

Lauren nodded. "I did not know that. That's awesome."

"Here's Mochi." Molly cheered as she took out her phone to show a picture of her beloved cat. "He has this sushi toy, he loves it."

Molly scrolled through some photos of her beloved cat, and Lauren hummed and smiled thoughtfully. This morning, she thought it would be another boring day. Usually when you find your girlfriend cheating on you, it is supposed to be the worst day, but there was always an exception to the rule.

David-Jack Fletcher

CARMEN BABCOCK

Good morning team!

Just a quick reminder that yoga starts at 11:30 a.m. sharp! 😃 It's 100% optional, but we do encourage you to participate as a team building exercise. Don't worry if you're not a pro, it's just for fun! Also, please remember that the pest controllers are inspecting the entire building today. They should be on our floor some time before 11 a.m.

Thanks in advance!

THE MICROSOFT TEAMS message was like daggers in Derek's soul. A sharp point splintering his insides deeper and deeper with every word. Thanks in advance? Thanks for what? He wasn't going to yoga, there was nothing to thank him for.

Gone were the days of simple group emails. Now everything was a Teams message and, true to modern surveillance, once you'd seen the message your avatar appeared beneath it. Derek could almost hear the bosses muttering, "Gotcha!" every time an avatar dropped beneath the message. There was no escape after that.

Derek swigged his energy drink, DemiGod, took a deep breath, placed a clammy hand on his mouse, and slid it across to the message. He had choices now. Type or react. Before he could decide which route to take, the little yellow thumbs ups started to appear.

First it was Denise. Of course it was Denise. She was mad for the corporate Kool-Aid, she might as well have bled the stuff. She was the HR director, always sending messages about wellness and mental health, and ridiculous memes counting down to Christmas. She was full-time remote, probably spending her workdays by the swimming pool at home or emailing while she was shopping with the girls.

Todd was the second. Todd, like that was even an actual person's name anymore. Todd was that guy who hung out by the water cooler, one arm placed over the top like he was hugging the thing, the other loosely holding a cup of cool crisp water as he pointed to at his colleagues and winked. Never spoke, just winked.

After the third, Derek just watched and counted. The message got to sixteen before it stopped, and then he knew he was the last one. The *only* one not to respond. Number seventeen, the last of the corporate monkeys to get excited about Yoga Tuesday.

Swallowing, Derek clicked into the text box.

DEREK HOFFSTEDTER

Thanks Carmen. I was really looking forward to it, but I'm going to have to skip it this week. D–

He grimaced at the lie—*I was really looking forward to it*—but hoped it would get him a pass this week.

No thumbs ups on that one. He was glad to be ignored if it meant no thumbs ups. They were so…passive aggressive. He imagined people giving the thumbs up in real life and how inappropriate it could be. Why stoop to a thumbs up over text?

CARMEN BABCOCK

That's the second week, Derek.

The message pinged into the group chat, making Derek sweat just a little more than normal. He could feel his colleagues smirking in their little cubicles, giggling with Todd at the water cooler about how Derek was in trouble again. Poor Derek, they'd say. He should join in, they'd say.

It was true, though, it was the second week. Last time he'd had a medical appointment, by which he left the office and sat in his car for an hour. This week was vague, and Carmen's response told him she was taking note of his absence at the totally 100% optional—and yet somehow mandatory—yoga sessions.

Clicking off from Teams and back into the file he'd been working on, Derek tried to focus. An elderly lady, Edna Thompson, was being accused of insurance fraud. He looked over the file, adjusting his glasses now and then when nervous sweat made them slip too low. She'd been in a car accident, not her fault, and needed a neck brace. The issue was that Edna had been reported anonymously—which usually meant a shitty neighbor—as gardening *without* wearing the brace. And so it went that Derek had to investigate.

It wasn't long before Teams pinged again, followed by a too-loud sigh from Derek.

MARNIE MAINE

How's the Thompson case coming along? Marnie

Marnie didn't know she didn't need to sign her name off every message. She was a nice person and Derek had exchanged mundane weekend stories with her on several occasions. Marnie was a cat person. Marnie was a movie-of-the-week person. Marnie was the type of person who showed people pictures of her brother's kids and acted like they were her own.

Poor Marnie.

DEREK HOFFSTEDTER

Fine.

He thought about the abruptness of his message and added:

DEREK HOFFSTEDTER

There's a lot to go through. It looks like she might be committing fraud, but I need to look things over with much more detail. Thanks for asking.

Smiling to himself, Derek was satisfied. He'd been polite. He'd given a proper response to a proper question, just as one might expect had the question been asked in real life. Derek expected a short reply back, something like "keep at it, you always get it right," but instead his screen pinged at the thumbs up reaction to his message.

"The fuck?" Derek muttered. "Really?"

He shrugged it off, but that yellow thumb was persistent in his mind's eye.

DEREK HOFFSTEDTER

How was your weekend?

Derek pushed for conversation. He stared at the screen for two minutes before he gave up on a reply. Marnie, the cat lady, was ghosting him.

Turning his attention back to Edna, Derek scanned a few photos the firm's private investigator had sent through to him. Yep, she was a gardener all right. Not only that, but she was good in the kitchen too.

Not a neck brace in sight. Not until she went outside, down to the local IGA for some painkillers.

"Edna, Edna, Edna," Derek mumbled. "Girl, you gotta be more careful. We have eyes everywhere."

Except, she was going to get painkillers, if the photo of her holding them in her hands was anything to go by. Could it be that she didn't feel the need to wear the brace while at home, and only used it when she left the house? It didn't make sense to Derek, but Edna was of a different generation, one where women were expected to be fragile in public.

Michael, the PI, gave a response:

It wasn't even a reaction. He'd filtered through his actual emojis and selected that one to insert into the text box. Derek understood people got busy, sure they did. He was a busy guy too. But in this case, the thumbs up gave no indication of Michael's intention.

Taking a deep breath, Derek typed a reply.

After a full five minutes without a response and with Derek tapping his feet under the desk, he felt the nervousness of missing yoga twist into anger. He couldn't do anything about Edna until he had a bit more context, and he couldn't get that without more information from Michael.

Dreading what was to come, Derek clicked into Salesforce, the nexus of evil where information went to die, and navigated to the search bar. It was the only way he had a chance in hell of finding anything. He searched Michael's name, which in theory would have returned his general information, including his extension.

True to form, Salesforce was fucked. Nothing came up. Not a goddamned thing.

The receptionist, Darby, would know. She was always connecting outside calls to different people.

DEREK HOFFSTEDTER

Hey Darby, would it be possible to send me Michael's ext.? The PI. I can't find it in Salesforce. Sorry for the trouble.

DARBY SHAW

Derek scratched his head when Darby didn't follow through.

DEREK HOFFSTEDTER

It's not urgent; in the next 10 mins or so would be awesome.

DARBY SHAW

He sighed again and resigned to waiting. Noticing a message from Marnie, Derek clicked into it.

"Are you fucking kidding me?" he asked himself. She'd responded to his query about her weekend with a love heart reaction. "You fell in love over the weekend? Found another cat, did you?"

He'd never say that to her, but the reaction didn't make sense. "Whatever."

Derek checked the time, unsure if everyone was already at yoga or were about to head out to enjoy some body bending. Maybe that could explain the abrupt responses. Nope, it was only 10:17 a.m.

Edna wasn't going anywhere in a hurry, not at her age. According to the files, she traveled no further than the IGA, a two minute drive from her house. She spent most of her time at home, gardening, cooking, practicing the violin—*That can't be good for the neck, the way the chin sits in that little indent*—and sleeping in front of the television. He had time, then, to get out of his cubicle and see if Michael was around.

As he walked through the rows of cubicles, the yellow thumbs haunting him, Derek thought about what he might say to Michael. Should he make it clear that he needs answers, words, rather than stupid fucking emojis?

He passed Marnie, who gave a little wave, and Derek upturned his lip. She shrunk a little at the response and he thought, *Good*.

"Hey, Derry, how's it going, brother?" Todd, sipping at the water cooler, brought Derek from his thoughts.

Wow, he actually spoke today.

Before Derek could reply, Todd said, "What's all this about the yoga, man?" His frown was deep, stretching from his lips to his narrowed eyebrows.

"What do you mean?" Derek asked. "Because I have to miss it?"

Nodding, Derek sipped his water, followed it with a smooth, "Aah-hh." Then, in a hushed voice, said, "Carmen is…unhappy with you."

"It's optional, though."

Todd's face contorted into an exaggerated, sad smile. "Yeah, see, here's the thing." He stepped closer to Derek until their shirt collars touched. "It *is* optional, but we—Carmen and I—*worry* that you're purposely trying to *promote negativity* within the workplace culture."

"By not going to yoga?" Derek tried so hard not to grimace again. He did that way too often, at least according to Frank, his long-term partner. Frank was always saying to turn that frown upside down, like Derek was a small child.

"Yeah, see, here's the thing," Todd said. He said that a lot. "Yoga is just yoga. Your *attitude* reflects on us all, though. Do you know what I mean?"

Derek watched as Todd filled another cup with water and sipped. He did know what Todd meant, he wasn't an idiot. Choosing not to participate in yoga, though, was not negativity. Stuffing his fists into Todd's face could be seen as negative. Who was this guy, anyway? What the fuck does he even do, other than stand at the water cooler?

"What is your job here, Todd?" The words were out before Derek could stop himself.

The water cup came down fast. Todd's eyes bored into Derek. The lips thinned. "Are you telling me you are unaware of my important, my significant, my *irreplaceable* role in this organization?"

The words were like spikes laced with spit. Derek felt each and every one land on his face and stepped away from Todd. "Sorry, Todd. I mean, sir. I really should get back to it, right?"

"Yeah, see, here's the thing—"

Derek walked away, holding his breath, as Todd kept talking. He wasn't listening, though, he was looking for Michael.

It turned out he was out on a job, according to Darby who had looked away from her screen long enough to feign a smile and tell Derek that Michael—and all company employees—used Microsoft Teams to communicate, rather than what she termed "old school phones."

"So I should just wait at my desk, then?" Derek asked.

Darby nodded, which was akin to a thumbs up in that moment. Rude. So fucking rude.

He stared at her for a second too long and then turned on his heel. Ignoring Todd on his way back, and throwing the middle finger up at Marnie for good measure, Derek slumped into his chair and gritted his teeth.

Yoga, seriously? Why was it so important?

Todd might have been a total wanker, but Derek did think he had a point. Maybe one sitting of yoga wouldn't be too bad. Maybe he could just grin and bear it, just one time. Frank would laugh so hard at him wearing a latex leotard and moving into downward-facing dog. He smirked as his mind went into the gutter, and opened Teams again.

DEREK HOFFSTEDTER

Turns out I can make it, Carmen! See you at 11 ☺

He felt like a bit of his soul had died right then. But he was sipping the Kool-Aid, he was participating in company team building bullshit. Carmen would see he was making an effort. Carmen would be so happy. Carmen would be—

CARMEN BABCOCK

That's all he got.

That's all she could be bothered with? After wasting time with "Good morning team!" emails, she was giving him the thumbs up? He was caving into pressure for the good of the company and she couldn't give him more than a fucking yellow thumb?

Staring at the screen, his eyes burning from not blinking, Derek started to shake.

"That's it," he said. "That. Is. It."

For some reason, he noted the time. 10:30 a.m. exactly. The moment his brain broke.

Ripping his keyboard from the computer tower and standing, Derek stepped through the cubicles, the cord dragging along the ground.

Shane, some guy who liked to crack jokes about Derek's weight, stood up for a high five. High five, thumbs up, it was all the same.

"How's Derry today?" he asked.

Derek lifted his free hand to Shane and gave a thumbs up. "Just fine, today, Shane, how the fuck are you?"

"Uh,"—Shane looked away for a second—"are you…sure you're okay?"

Moving towards Shane, Derek looked at his keyboard. "Actually, I have an issue with this keyboard."

"Oh," Shane said and stepped into the aisle, "I know a thing or two about keyboards." He adjusted his belt like he was important.

Derek raised the keyboard a little. "It's just…"

He swung.

The keyboard connected with Shane's cheek, sending his neck spinning hard to the right. Derek swung again as some of his colleagues stood up to see the commotion. Shane fell backwards, into his cubicle, as Derek swung again. Keys fell out, clattering across Shane's desk, and Derek brought the keyboard down once more.

Shane raised his arms to defend himself, but the keyboard connected with those too, and Derek smiled at the stream of blood following the ruined keyboard's course. He stopped for a second to take a breath, took in Shane's disfigured face—the blood, the loose teeth, the split skin—and brought the keyboard down even harder.

The thick plastic snapped across Shane's head and the man fell from his chair to the floor with a thump. Dropping the keyboard onto Shane's body, Derek looked up and saw the horror on his colleagues' faces. Not one of them tried to intervene. Maybe there was no emoji for that.

"The fuck are you all looking at?" Derek asked.

A few people shot out of sight and he made a mental note to take care of them later. They were all to blame, they were all the same.

Breathing hard now, Derek headed down the aisle again. He didn't know where he was going, just that whoever got in his way was next. Some poor bastard he'd never spoken to was pushed back against their cubicle wall, eyes squeezed shut.

Just as Derek was about to walk on, the guy brought his hands under his chin to pray. Little sausage fingers clasped together, the guy started reciting something to Jesus or God or fucking Taylor Swift for all Derek knew.

All he could see was the guy's thumbs.

"I can't stand thumbs," he said. "I just can't take them anymore."

He walked into the cubicle and the guy opened one eye at the sound of Derek's approach. "Please..." he begged.

"Don't ask me for mercy," Derek said. "Ask your god. Well, go on. See if he's up there, listening." He motioned to the ceiling, like some divine entity was about to shoot down from Heaven. "Pity," he said, and knelt down before the guy.

"I... I..."

Bringing a finger to the guy's lips, Derek hushed him. Took one of his hands and held it tight.

And bit.

The guy screamed, pulled his hand away as hard as he could, but Derek's teeth were deep in the flesh now, tearing at the sinewy muscle.

"Get him off me!" the guy yelled.

Derek was aware of movement behind him, even as the guy beat at his head with his spare hand. But he was so close, he could feel the thumb loosening. Feel the tendons and veins stretching and snapping between his teeth.

Arms were around him now, voices yelling at him, and he was pulled free from the guy, who stood fast, holding his hand under his armpit. Derek watched the guy's shirt change color, a ripple of red emanating from the armpit where his missing thumb was bleeding out.

"Tasty," Derek said and spat the thumb to the carpet.

He was shoved down to the floor, voices cursing at him, calling him names, someone crying for an ambulance, and someone else weeping for poor Shane.

"What have you done?" someone said through heavy tears.

Todd appeared in one of his rare moments away from the water cooler, eyes wide with shock. "Call the police." Then, to Derek, "Yeah, see, here's the thing, mate..." He couldn't finish the sentence when Derek flicked his eyes up at him.

"Go on, please," Derek said. "What's the thing, *mate*?"

"You've lost it, Derry," Todd replied. "You just fucking killed a guy and bit off another dude's thumb."

Both their eyes traveled down to the bitten-off digit, lying on the carpet, blood drizzling out like the last of the ketchup from the bottle. Todd retched and held a hand over his throat, while Derek continued to stare. He didn't know who had hold of him, but they were strong.

Still, all he could feel were the hands on him. No, not the hands. The thumbs. The fucking thumbs. That's all anyone cared about these days; how many thumbs you collected on a single post or message. He had one, and he was damn sure he could gather a few more before the cops arrived.

While Todd was bent over trying not to vomit, Derek reached to one of the hands holding him back, grabbed at the fingers and twisted them back. The man—he knew this by the scream—let him go, and Derek did the same to the hand on his other shoulder. Kicking one guy in the balls and punching the other in the stomach, he snatched up the carpeted thumb and raced away.

Todd was after him, but Derek was faster. Nobody wanted to get in his way, not the psycho with the keyboard and the teeth. He was heading straight for the photocopy room, where they also cut paper to size and where there was a big fucking guillotine blade he could use. Biting the thumb off was fun, but it was hard work, and his teeth wouldn't be able to do that too many more times. Plus, the taste of blood was like metal and iron, and he'd rather not make that a dietary staple.

Reaching the copy room, he slammed the door and locked it.

The guillotine was one of those 12" manual ones, the blade shining at him like he was destined for it. Like it was Excalibur and he was King Arthur. Together, they were unstoppable. He'd thought about breaking that blade off before, but fantasy was just that: fantasy. Now, though, now he needed it.

And he would have it.

Todd was banging at the door, yelling at him about how Carmen and the *team* would be soooo angry at him, and how Shane was alive but seriously injured, and how it wasn't too late to show the *team* he was a *team* player.

Team? *Team?* Fuck that and fuck the team. Like they were in some ridiculous video game. He was a solo player and he was about to beat the shit out of this level.

Bracing one foot on top of the guillotine, he twisted the blade backward with both hands as fast as he could. The plastic casing snapped apart. It was so easy. He wondered why more people didn't do this. It was just so goddam easy.

The blade was heavy in his hand, but it felt like an extension of his arm. Like he was supposed to have it. Licking at his lips, Derek's mouth dry, he swallowed. After he got Todd's thumbs, he'd have some water. Or maybe another DemiGod.

Their tagline was stupid. *Taste the energy of a god.*

Stupid, sure. But he did taste the energy of a god. He really did.

Unlocking the door, Todd mid-knock, Derek flashed a smile and wiped hair out of his face. All the biting and running had made him sweaty. This was better than yoga could ever be.

Todd stepped back, saw the guillotine blade—a machete, for all intents and purposes—and ran. Derek chased after him, swiping the air between them with his blade. Todd was fast, but slowed a little to turn a corner.

Derek lurched forward, grabbed at Todd's suit jacket, and yanked him backward. Right by the water cooler.

"Well," Derek said, standing over the man, "look at this. Right at your favorite spot."

"Derry, bro, the thing is—"

"Sshhh." Derek pressed a foot hard into Todd's chest, keeping him trapped against the carpet. "Nobody cares what the thing is, *bro.*"

He was about to plunge the blade into Todd's neck, to sever the head right from that twat's body, when the water cooler burped. Oxygen bubbles rising inside, giving that deep growl. Lowering the blade, Derek carefully tilted the thick, blue plastic water bottle out of its cradle.

"You love this water, don't you, Toddy?" Derek asked.

"Help me!" Todd replied. He was begging the onlookers, a few had their phones out, recording. A few stood just gasping and muttering.

Nobody stepped forward to help.

And that was the point, wasn't it? Everyone was happy to go along with the game, drink the Kool-Aid, pretend to be happy fucking families until the shit hit the fan. Then it was every person for themselves.

"Thirsty, mate?" Derek asked, winking for the cameras recording him. He felt powerful being on show like that.

Todd shook his head, struggling against Derek's heavy foot on his chest.

"Yeah, see, the thing is, I reckon you're a bit parched," Derek said, and brought the water bottle down hard onto Todd's face.

Water splashed from the bottle, but it was still mostly full. Turning the spout to Todd's mouth, Derek forced the heavy bottle to his lips.

"Open wide," he said through gritted teeth. "Time for a drink!"

Todd resisted, squeezed his lips shut, so Derek kneed him in the groin. Todd's mouth opened wide in agony and in went the bottle. Water poured down his throat, Todd struggling and choking and swallowing despite his best efforts.

"Stop it!" a voice, female, came from behind him.

The water bottle was draining fast into Todd, whose struggles grew weaker and weaker by the second. It was almost a shame to waste that cool, crisp mountain water on this absolute twat. Regrets were for the weak, though, and Derek pressed on.

Finally empty, Derek dropped the bottle to the side, and turned to face the voice, who again called, "Stop it!" with no sense of authority.

It was Marnie. Of course.

"No love heart reaction for this situation, then?" Derek asked, picking up the guillotine blade.

"You need to stop, Derek," Marnie said.

At least she used my actual name.

"This isn't you," she continued.

"Yeah…see, the thing is—" Derek caught himself. "Fuck, did I seriously just say that?"

Marnie stared at him, tears falling down her face. "You're a good guy," she said. "Just put that down and we can figure this out. Whatever is going on with you, we can fix it."

Pursing his lips, Derek considered her offer. Put the blade down and talk or run to her and stab her in the heart? Choices, choices. She was *usually* nice to him, though.

In any case, he needed to get Todd's thumbs. And go back for Shane's and whoever that other prick was. He'd done good work so far, he wasn't about to let his prizes go.

"Marnie," Derek said, turning his back on her, "go sit with your cats. This doesn't concern you."

The blade sliced through Todd's extremities like they were warm butter. That thing was powerful. Pocketing the thumbs, he headed back for Shane, who was barely conscious.

"Sorry, bud," Derek said, and grabbed the guy's hand. Two slices later and the thumbs were in his pockets, bleeding into his thighs.

He stopped at the other guy's cubicle, who was gone. Probably out in reception, waiting for the paramedics. Derek didn't want to go out there and face Darby. She was only young, but damn she was old enough to know how to talk to people. Especially as a receptionist.

Trotting towards reception, Derek passed his own desk, and spied the open can of DemiGod sweating next to the mouse. He really was thirsty. Picking up the can, cool in his hands, he swigged at the liquid inside. Passion pear, a weird mix, but geez it went down easy. He drained the whole can in a few gulps, crushed the aluminum between his fingers, and let it fall to the floor.

Reception wasn't far. He'd get that guy, do away with Darby's thumbs, and then come back for the rest of them.

Entering reception, the television blared a breaking news story. Derek tuned it out, only glimpsing the rolling text at the bottom of the screen: **MASS KILLINGS ERUPT THROUGH CITY**.

"Do you, like, need a Band-Aid or something?" Darby was asking the guy. He was shoving his fist in her face, showing her the wound where his thumb used to be.

"A Band-Aid? Luv, I think it'll take more than that." He was swaying, his face pale.

"I have just what you need," Derek said from behind them.

As the guy turned and Darby's eyes widened, the blade came down into the guy's torso. He spurted blood from his mouth and the wound in his side, fell to his knees.

"Sorry," Derek said. "I'm a shit aim. I just want your thumb."

The guy stuttered and stammered something unintelligible, like maybe that he had kids or a family or some rubbish like that. Derek ignored him, grabbed his untarnished hand, and sliced the thumb free.

"Ah," he said, holding it up to the light. "A beauty." Stuffing it with the others, he turned his attention to the receptionist.

Darby was on the phone, blurting out that she needed help, holding a pair of scissors out to Derek. "Stay the fuck away from me!"

"Scissors, huh?" Derek frowned. "Looks like I'm outmatched here,

Darbs. I'll just get going then, shall I?" He giggled to himself and stepped forward and she swiped at him with the scissors in one hand, the phone in the other.

Swinging at the phone cord, Derek cut it in half, giving an "oops" motion. Darby threw the phone down and raced at Derek, still swinging with rage and fear. The scissors nicked Derek's upper arm and he let her pass. The cut was minimal, but enough to piss him off. Darby ran, her high heels clicking against the tiled reception floor. Derek aimed, hoping his blade wouldn't fail him now, and flung the guillotine towards the receptionist.

She stopped fast as the blade stabbed into her back. It looked to Derek like it had embedded itself into her spine. It didn't get much better than that.

"Ah, Gilly," he said, "you are truly exquisite." Then, realizing nobody knew who Gilly was, he looked down at the guy with the sliced-up torso, and said, "Gilly is my blade here. Short for guillotine."

He didn't seem to care, just gave short, shallow breaths as he clutched his side with thumbless hands. Derek shrugged and walked on to Darby, who was face down and crying in pain. He kneeled beside her, caressed her jet black hair, and said, "I thought people didn't use old school phones anymore?"

She cried at this, but didn't move. The blade was lodged perfectly in the lumbar vertebrae. Poor Darby was basically a doll now. Just like that. Removing the blade with a wet squelch, Derek admired Gilly. She—the blade was a femme fatale—wanted the thumbs just as much as he did.

"And you shall have them," Derek said.

Two slices later and they were in his pocket, bouncing around with the others.

Derek got to his feet, ready to head back to his other colleagues who he guessed had long ago forgotten about their stupid yoga class, when Darby spat, "Fuck…you…"

"Now, why did you have to do that?" Derek asked. "I was all good to just leave you be, but now? Now you've done it."

It would be the scissors. Her weapon of choice, lying just out of reach on the tiles. Gilly was for the thumbs, not for anything else. Well, not intentionally. The torso thing had been an accident. Scissors were for paper. Or…

Once he was done, Darby could no more move than she could see, the whites of her eyes leaking to the tiles and pooling down at her mouth.

As Derek left her behind to breathe in her own eye juices, the newscaster said, "…widespread panic as friends turn on friends, family members turning on each other. It is mayhem! There are reports coming in that the effects are short-lived, but the absolute carnage I'm seeing here on the streets—"

The TV turned to static.

Derek's colleagues had gathered in one of the meeting rooms when he returned. Why they hadn't left the building was anyone's guess. On their own they were easy prey, but in a group? He wasn't sure he could get all their thumbs. He could see them staring at him through the glass, pointing at their phones and yelling and panicking.

He heard phrases like, "Nowhere is safe", "They said to stay put," and "What can we do?"

There was only one thing for it.

The air conditioning system was so easy to mess with. He'd thought about it before, about dumping gas into the vents. It wasn't like he had dangerous gases on hand, but surely there was a way to cut off the air supply and poison them. Then, the thumbs would be his.

All mine.

He heard an elevator ding out at reception and wondered who that could be. Then he remembered Carmen's email earlier. The pest controllers. It had to be. Everything was falling into place, it was perfect.

Racing to reception, Derek saw the elevator doors were just opening. Two men with canisters on their backs were wide-eyed already and mumbling about "crazy shit out there". They stepped out before eyeing the bodies on the tiles and screamed.

"Not here, too!" one of them said, tears in his eyes.

Before they could retreat, Derek held open the doors with one hand and stabbed one of the guys through the stomach with Gilly. He had gloves on, so Derek didn't know what sort of thumbs he had, but he was sure they'd be beautiful. The other guy was shouting "No no no," before Gilly silenced him with a quick slice across the throat.

Four more thumbs for his collection, and his pockets were getting so heavy. Still, he had the gas canisters—the poison—and a mask.

It was so easy. It was all so fucking easy. Why hadn't he done this before? He guessed it was because he didn't want to get caught. He had Gilly now, and together they were unstoppable. It didn't matter if he got caught.

His colleagues were begging and pleading—so unoriginal, he thought—even as the gas was pumped in under the door. He watched them drop like flies, curl up like rats, and cough and moan into nothingness. The whole experience took less than five minutes, his eyes mostly drawn to Marnie who clutched at her cat necklace and begged Derek to let her go.

She died with that begging on her lips.

Once he'd gotten all their thumbs, all fifteen of his colleagues, the

thumb collection was starting to seem a little bigger than he'd antici-
pated. He'd sorted them according to size, shape, color, and nail polish.
Length of the nail was secondary to the size of the actual thumb, he'd
decided.

Holding one of the digits before him, the glorious little thing with
chipped purple nail polish, Derek smiled to himself. He knew what he
could do to make the collection seen more manageable.

Despite being the only person around, it was a secret smile, a shy
smile. A naughty boy smile.

He'd never been great at arts and crafts, but something told him
today was the day he'd learn. The curtains in the meeting rooms were
lined with a thin wire. Tearing it free, Derek found it was perfect for
his purposes. Strong enough not to break, yet flexible enough to be
molded and reshaped.

"The perfect thread," he said to himself.

CARMEN HAD BEEN in meetings all morning, taking a break only to
send that morning Teams message and give Derek the thumbs up. It
was that memory that reminded him he hadn't actually taken all the
thumbs. There were two left.

Carmen. The boss. With her manicured, painted, cuticle-free thumb
nails.

He could feel Gilly vibrating in his hands at the thought of slicing
those babies off. Adding them to the collection now hanging around
his neck. Clutching his new accessory, kissing a few of the thumbs
dangling from his neck, Derek set off for the boss' office.

Her office was set apart from the rest of the floor, with its own separate entrance—key cards only, for *special* access, of course. It was set behind a teak door that was largely soundproof so she could have privacy while her underlings—Todd included—were crammed in lovely 2.4 x 2.4 cubicles under the watchful eye of the corporate security cameras. Derek wished he'd been able to get the thumbs off all the people Carmen had been meeting with, but alas, they'd used the other entrance.

At the teak door now, Derek knocked, waited for the curt "Enter" to ring out, and turned the doorknob. Carmen smiled at him, but it was empty.

"Ah, Derek, you didn't reply to my messa—" Carmen's eyes dropped to the necklace. "What are you doing?"

"Sorry, Carmen," Derek said. "I'm just all thumbs today."

She kept staring at the thumbs jingling around his neck, lost for words.

"You like my new necklace? I had a heck of a time shopping for it," Derek told her, and raised Gilly so Carmen could shudder before her.

Except she didn't shudder. She sneered and folded her arms. "What's this all about, Derek?" Carmen asked.

He was confused, taken aback at her lack of care about the severed thumbs and the blade glistening with her colleagues' blood.

"You think a bit of blood scares me?" Carmen raised an eyebrow. "Really, Derek, you have no idea."

"Let's not drag this out, Carmen," Derek replied. "I just want your thumbs and I'll be on my way."

"You want my thumbs?" she asked. "Come and fucking get them!"

Derek smiled, delighted at the invitation and at someone finally giving him a challenge. All the others had basically begged to die, the way they gave up and herded themselves into the same room to be gassed.

Not Carmen, though. Not the yoga-loving boss. No, she was up for a bit of fun.

And Derek and Gilly were keen to give it to her.

Except Carmen was still standing there, smirking with her arms folded. She stepped behind her desk, reached into a drawer for something, and pulled out a can of DemiGod. Cool, crisp, sweet energy, straight from the lap of the gods.

Sipping turned to gulping as Carmen drained the can of its contents, then threw it to the carpet with a hollow, tinny thud. Wiping at her mouth, Carmen's eyes bored into Derek. "That's the shit," she said.

Derek frowned. He'd thought he was the only DemiGod drinker around the office. Although, it had only come out this morning. Still, sales were so high that it was already rated the number one new energy drink in Australia.

"You see," Carmen said, "while you've been out there shoving thumbs down your pants, I've been in here. Having my meetings."

She strutted across to a door that Derek assumed led to a bathroom. The boss, with her private fucking ensuite, while everyone else shared the piss-stained toilets. She swung the door open to reveal pristine white walls, the tiles reflecting against the sink, the toilet, and the blood-soaked flooring. The bodies, too many to count, wasting away, their blood circling the drain.

Derek's eyes widened.

"Yeah, I've had so many meetings today," Carmen said with a sigh and a quick stretch of the arms.

"We've both been busy little worker bees," Derek said.

"All people do is yap, yap, yap." Carmen's hands formed little crab claws, imitating people speaking. "You know? All day long, just talking in my ear. And this morning, I thought, huh? What if I took their tongues?"

Stepping back a little, Derek tightened his grip on Gilly.

"I got all these fuckers' tongues,"—she motioned to the pile of her victims—"and now it's time for yours."

He cracked his neck, readying himself for the fight to come, and Carmen reached into another desk drawer for a weapon of her own. Bringing it up, slow and purposeful, Derek saw the sun hit the object through a gap in the curtains. The orange glow soaked into the metal blade of a butcher knife.

Her blade versus his.

A true battle.

"I don't know why, but I brought this from home today," she said. "Like I couldn't be without it."

Derek knew that feeling, and his eyes sank towards Gilly. Carmen nodded. They knew each other well in that moment. Were almost the same.

"You want my thumbs?" Carmen asked. "I want your tongue."

"Let's fucking do this," Derek replied, and stormed forward.

Carmen leaped around her desk, surging towards Derek with a high-pitched screech. She swiped at his torso and he dodged, falling to his knees for a moment and swinging Gilly through the air toward his boss.

She dodged too, Gilly tasting her blouse as she moved back.

Derek was back on his feet, Gilly high in the air. Carmen lurched and Derek felt a sting in his chest. Looking down, letting Gilly fall to his side, he saw the butcher knife lodged between his left nipple and his sternum. As Carmen pulled it free, Derek groaning with pain and anger and an unstoppable urge to add her thumbs to his necklace, she plunged it into him again.

Staggering backwards, Derek fell to the floor, coughing and wheezing.

"Now open that pretty little mouth," Carmen said, crawling on top of him and reaching inside his mouth for his tongue.

Derek spat and fought, but Carmen's legs were on top of his arms, her body gyrating with excitement over his hips.

"That's it," she said, clawing at his tongue.

Shimmying left and right, Derek fought against her weight. She was fit—yoga fit—but quite light. He let her take his tongue between her fingers, felt her gorgeous thumb gripping him, and she adjusted her weight to grab the butcher knife with her other hand.

That was the moment. The adjusted weight was enough. He lifted his hips fast, put her off balance, and rolled away from her. He was up, holding the wound in his chest with one hand, and squeezing Gilly's handle with the other.

As Carmen found her balance, Derek swung Gilly fast, his shoulder locking at a sudden stop in his movement. She was stuck in the side of Carmen's head, a trickle of red flowing down her made-up face. Derek forced the blade further into her, watched as Gilly sliced across to the corner of Carmen's eye, and pulled the blade free with a sawing motion.

"I was expecting more from you," Derek said, breathing heavily.

Carmen dropped to the floor, her eyes still staring, and Derek kicked her to make sure she was dead. Not even a little jerk. She was gone.

He had her thumbs moments later, and made a note to add them to his necklace. For now, they'd sit in his pocket.

With the office taken, him the sole victor, Derek pulled the curtains back and peered out the window at the city below.

Smoke, fire, bodies lining the streets. It was a real shitshow out there.

"You thinking what I'm thinking, Gilly?" Derek asked. "Many more thumbs for the taking. And they're all mine."

He moved to the door, stopped, and looked back at Carmen's desk. Surely she kept more cans in there, not just the one. Right there, in the bottom drawer, hidden under layers of severed tongues, three cans of DemiGod.

Taste the energy of a god.

And he did.

He downed all three, felt the energy surging through him.

As he went to the door, intent on heading down to the city streets to claim what was rightfully his, his phone buzzed in his back pocket.

FRANK

Can you pick up some milk on the way home? Love you.

Ugh. He always needed something.

DEREK

YOU BLOW MY MIND

Chisto Healy

YOU BLOW MY MIND

Chisto Healy

Edgar Matthews was in line at his favorite coffee shop. Things were moving more slowly than usual, and he had to get to work. He was getting stressed, but he didn't want to fuss because he loved this place. Nowhere else made a chocolate peppermint oat milk latte with honey and habanero like this place. Surely someone was sick or something. It had never taken this long before. They had to be understaffed.

He took out his phone and texted his coworker, Bonnie.

EDGAR

Coffee is taking forever today. I'll be there ASAP. I'm sorry. Can I bring you something to make up for it?

BONNIE

Just hurry. We're backed up as it is, and Mike called out.

He frowned and cringed at his phone.

EDGAR

Okay. I'm so sorry. I don't know what's going on.

BONNIE

I know. A vanilla bean cold brew with ice and an extra shot of espresso.

Edgar laughed.

EDGAR

You got it.

Another text came through on his phone, but it said unknown number, so he didn't bother with it. He looked at the line, and it didn't look like it had moved at all. "Come on, man," he grumbled quietly, losing his patience.

His phone chimed again, and again. The person in front of him, who was surely out of patience as well, turned around and glared at him. Edgar frowned. "I'm sorry," he said.

He looked at the message thread to see if it was perhaps someone he knew, and he just hadn't programmed their number into the phone.

UNKNOWN

You're worried more about coffee than survival. That's sad.

What the fuck? It had to be a troll messing with him or some kind of scammer who wanted money. He considered scrolling up to see what they were referring to, but then decided he wasn't going to give them that kind of power or space in his life. Instead, he opted to turn off his ringer, making it easier to ignore.

He sighed with relief when the line started moving and he could step forward. In a moment, he was at the counter, ready to place his order. The cashier recognized him since he was there every day. "Sorry, Edgar," the boy said. "The milk steamer is on the fritz, and my boss ran out because her son was sick and needed to be picked up from school."

"I figured it was something like that. Life happens, Aron. Don't worry about it. I have an extra order today. I hope it doesn't make your day harder."

"What is it?" the boy asked.

Then Edgar's head exploded.

There was a loud pop like someone had taken a pin to a balloon. Pieces of Edgar were raining down upon a crowd of screaming people who hadn't even gotten their morning coffee yet. A teenage girl was screaming because a shard of Edgar's shattered skull hit her in the eye. She couldn't see, and it was bleeding.

"Is that brains?" someone cried out. "Is there brain in my cappuccino?"

Aron was just staring at Edgar's body, which somehow was still standing despite ending at the neck. Shards of bone jutted out, and a small fountain of blood squirted in an arc from the stump like someone was testing a syringe. While the boy was staring, Edgar finally folded on himself and collapsed.

DETECTIVE JACKSON MEWES clicked a button on the remote and froze the picture on the TV screen. He sighed and rubbed his face with both hands. Then he turned to the woman standing beside him. "Captain, I've watched this several times now, and I still can't make sense out of it. If there was a shot from somewhere, you would have seen the direction and possibly other things hit or damaged on the way. He was surrounded by people who would have been hit. Whatever happened was isolated with him. Something…*in* him…just…blew up."

Captain Lewis huffed. "Are you suggesting a bomb or something spectacular like spontaneous combustion?"

Jackson scrunched his face on one side. It was his personal tell, one of the reasons he sucked at Texas Hold'em, and something he did without realizing when nervous. It was one of the many reasons he made a better cop than a criminal. He couldn't lie to save his life. His husband loved it. Monogamy was hard to find in the gay community, so when Davis found it in Jackson, he was paranoid and untrusting…until he learned Jackson's tell. Now they've had a happy four years, going on five. May was going to be a milestone anniversary. Jackson had no idea what to do for it, and he couldn't possibly set his brain to figuring it out now that he had watched someone else's brain explode in a crowded coffee shop.

He lifted the remote and pressed PLAY again, his eyes glued to the screen. "What do we know about the vic? Any enemies?"

"Enemies with the tech to blow someone's head off? Not that we can find. He was well-liked at work. No kids. Unmarried. He managed a grocery store. He wasn't a defense attorney or something. Nothing jumps out."

Jackson shook his head. He stopped the tape again and threw the remote down on the table before abruptly standing. "I would think you would really have to hate the fuck out of somebody to blow their head off in public."

Captain Lewis licked her lips and nodded, plopping into her seat and pulling it up to her desk. "You would think, but hate comes easier these days. You, of all people, should know that."

Jackson glared at her, one eyebrow raised. "Are you suggesting this was some kind of hate crime?"

She placed her palms on the desk and leaned forward. "I'm not suggesting anything yet. Just saying anything is possible and shouldn't be ruled out."

He nodded and turned to stare at the now blank TV screen. "So, is there anything? Does unmarried mean closeted? Was he Jewish? Muslim? Hell, was he a hateful prick someone would want to get revenge on? Ties to white supremacy? Weopanized Christianity?"

The captain smiled. "You want me to do your job for you?"

Jackson scrunched his face again. "Got it. I'll start digging."

He turned to the door and found it open, their resident techie, Laura Berch, standing in the doorway and still holding the knob. She smiled at him. "Maybe this will help. I finally got his phone unlocked."

Jackson didn't smile back, but he took the phone from her as he squeezed past her out of the room.

"You're welcome," she called behind him.

He took it to his own desk and sat in his chair. He checked the messages first, looking for any hate mail or obvious clues. "Holy shit," he said.

"What?" his partner said from the desk across from his. "What do you got?"

"Probably gonnaherpasyphylaids from taking it in the butt," a cop to his left said; he looked one donut away from a heart attack.

Jackson snapped his fingers in the man's direction. "Quiet, Stacks, the grown-ups are talking. It's impolite to interrupt." He looked back at his partner. "Whoever blew Edgar's mind texted him first."

"Holy shit. Anything we can use?"

Jackson scrunched the right side of his face. "I don't know. I mean, there's enough to know for certain this was a homicide, but it doesn't point fingers. It looks like Edgar was ignoring it. Some of the messages are read, but he didn't respond to any. Perhaps he thought he was being trolled, or maybe he knew more and was just trying to ignore it. I'm gonna have to dig deeper into the phone, look for emails and social media posts, anything that could point to who our perp is. Manny, can you go to his place and see what you can find there?"

"Yeah, I'm on it." Jackson's partner got up. He came around the desk and looked over his shoulder at the phone in his hands. "You gotta be shittin' me," he said upon seeing the countdown that led to the head blown emoji. "He told Edgar he was gonna blow his head off, and the poor bastard never saw it. The last messages are unread."

"Maybe it's like the broad on that superhero show," Stacks said as he sipped a coffee and spilled it on his baby blue shirt. He cussed and quickly put the cup down, drawing tissues from a box nearby to press on his shirt. "Maybe your perp has that super power where she can look people in the eyes and blow their heads off."

Jackson turned and shot him an angry look. "What did I tell you? Let the grown-ups talk. Superpowers aren't real, pal."

Manny Santiago patted him on the shoulder. "I'm gonna get over to Edgar's place."

When he walked away, Jackson went looking for Laura. When he found her, he took her arm and startled her. Immediately, he let go. Handed her the phone. "He said he was going to do it, and then he did it. What kind of tech could do that?"

She looked at the phone and then met his eyes. "I-I don't know. But I'll find out. Just…give me some time."

Jackson nodded, took the phone, and went back to his desk.

MANNY PULLED UP in front of Edgar's house, a red brick house with a classic stoop and an attached garage. The house was only one story. He got out of the car and walked to the front door, knocking. No one answered, but a dog barked from within. "That's as good as a warrant to me," he said. "Only an asshole would let a dog starve."

He popped the locked door open and stepped in. The barking dog was a Pomeranian, and it ran over, shaking and started licking his ankle. "Hey, bud," Manny said. "What's your name?"

He bent down and looked at the dog's heart-shaped tag. "Rambo. Wow, okay. Maybe you're a little dog with a big spirit, huh? Or maybe your daddy just liked movies."

He went to the kitchen, which was remarkably clean, and found the dog food. He filled Rambo's bowl and patted the hungry animal on the head before standing.

Manny headed for the bedroom. He went through the cabinets and dressers, the closets, and the TV stand. All he discovered was that Edgar was a meticulous guy. It seemed like his whole life was that damned Price Slashers grocery store. He had paper after paper with numbers and employee schedules, budgets, and inventories.

He was frustrated and sat on the couch to rub his temples. Rambo came over, jumped up on the couch with his thin, tiny legs, and lay on Manny's lap like he'd known him for years. Manny looked down at him and frowned. "Who killed your daddy, Rambo? Do you know?"

His phone went off, and he answered. "You're not gonna believe this," Jackson said. "We've got another one. Captain wants you over there."

"Where?"

"The damn Price Slashers where Edgar was Assistant Manager, dairy aisle to be specific."

"Co-manager, actually. They're above assistants. I've been through everything in this guy's place, and it's all that damn store, Jack. What I didn't find was anyone who could take this absolutely awesome little dog."

"He had a co-worker he seemed pretty close to. They texted a lot.

Gal named Bonnie. Feed it and lock up, and I'll give her a call."

Manny hung up and pouted as he was forced to move the dog from his lap. "You be good. We'll find you somewhere nice, or I'll take you home with me, okay?" The dog lay its head on the couch but rolled its eyes up to look at him. "Man, you're killing me. See you soon, Rambo."

Manny ran out to his car and sped off toward the grocery store, which he never shopped at, because he felt they were overpriced. He hated that there was another murder, but he liked the fact that it gave a motive. Leads were good. Whoever was behind this they were going to catch him.

His ENERGY SIZZLED out like a blown circuit as soon as he stepped foot on the dairy aisle. "Christ," he said, putting a fist to his mouth and turning away.

An extremely pale young man who Manny was willing to bet wasn't as pale an hour ago, frowned, and nodded at him. "Yeah, I had to get all the customers out, though, uh…the ones who were hit are still outside being tended to by the first responders."

"Do you know who she is…was?" Manny asked him, trying not to look back at the headless body surrounded by blood spray and meat chunks. Even without looking, he could hear the wet remnants of the woman's skull and brains dripping off the shelves onto the egg cartons.

"That's Bonnie, sir… Our store manager."

Manny sighed. "Shit. Sorry, Rambo."

"Huh?"

"Never mind. What's your position here, kid?"

"I'm the customer service manager, Bryce. Am I…am I next?"

Manny frowned. "I hope not. Help us catch this guy so there is no next. Someone offed your store manager and co-manager. Who would want them dead?"

Bryce stared intensely into Manny's eyes as the rhythmic blood drip continued behind him. "Are you serious? This is a grocery store. The turnover rate is super high. Tons of people have been fired or quit. There are irate customers, some of them regulars. Shoplifters who have been caught and prosecuted. There are people who wanted promotions who watched other people get them just because of who they knew. There's probably hundreds of people who it could be."

Manny sighed. "Well, then, go to your office, find a pen and a piece of paper, and start making me a list. Write down everyone you can think of."

"Really?"

"Do I look like I'm joking?"

The young man grumbled something, but he turned and headed for the front office. Manny already felt like throwing up, and the flies that left the vegetables to buzz around the corpse didn't help. Still, he strapped on a pair of gloves and went and knelt beside the woman. He dug in her pocket and pulled out her phone. It was locked with facial recognition.

"Fuck. Couldn't be a thumb print?" He shook his head and called the office. "Laura. Hey, babe. It's me. I got another phone I need you to get into. It's locked with facial recognition, and the vic doesn't have a face to recognize."

"I can get in. Just bring it to me. And don't call me 'babe'. It's not professional."

"You're literally my wife."

"Not at work."

He sighed. "Fine. We need to see if she had a laptop or something, too, maybe a tablet. Then you can dig through for anything that could tie her and Edgar together outside of this store." He hung up, took the dead woman's phone with him, and headed up to the office where Bryce was still working on his list. "I'm gonna need the tape."

"Camera in that aisle is a dummy. A lot of them are actually. They're just meant to deter people, not actually catch them."

"Fantastic."

"Please find who did this. I don't wanna die."

"I'm not gonna let you die, kid."

"Promise?"

"Yes."

Bryce's head exploded and coated Manny with crimson gore. He wiped it from his eyes so he could see. The headless boy and his squirting, ragged neck stump were still seated at the desk, pen in hand, though the paper he'd been writing on was soaked through and unreadable. "Fuck!"

Captain Lewis, Jackson, Laura, and a freshly showered Manny were seated in a circle in the captain's office. "All three people were warned," Lewis said to the group. "All three missed the messages. Is that a clue or a psychotic coincidence?"

Jackson growled. "Who knows? No one answers their phones for numbers they don't know, text or voice. There's so many scammers and trolls these days, you can't even blame 'em."

"Sounds like he's voting for coincidence," Manny said. "But it could be a clue. Maybe someone felt like they were always ignored, and that's

271

why they used this method for their vengeance. Bryce was making me a list of possible suspects, but it got ruined when he…"

"You sure you're good?" Captain Lewis asked. "Maybe you should take a few days. We can get you counseling."

"I'm just still trying to process it," Manny said with a shake of his head. "One moment I'm talking to the kid, looking him straight in the eyes. Next moment, his brains and skull fragments are caught in my hair. How the fuck does that even happen?"

"That's for me to figure out," Laura said. "The captain's right through, babe. You should go home and get some rest, maybe go see your mom."

Manny stared daggers at her. "Did you just call me—? Wow. Motherfucker. You're right. I'm going home."

He stood up and stormed out.

Captain Lewis gave Laura a quizzical look. "What was that about?"

Laura frowned. "I think he's just stressed. I'll talk to him when I get home."

"Make sure he follows up with the psych, please. I called her earlier. She's expecting him."

Laura nodded.

"M.E. says no explosives or residue anywhere on the bodies," Jackson told them. "So no shots, no explosives… Whatever this guy is doing, it's something with those phones. In each conversation, he counts down and ends it with that goddamn emoji."

"Yeah, but it's definitely more than that," the captain said. "I could text you both the same things right now and you're not going to explode."

"I'd prefer you didn't try it, though," Laura said with an awkward laugh.

"Just figure out how he's doing it because I don't think he's done."

"We need to alert the surviving managers," Jackson said, rubbing at his face. "If there's an assistant or other customer service managers, maybe a district manager or a perishable merchandiser… Any one of them could be next."

"Go do it," Captain Lewis said, and while you're at it, find out who wants all these people dead. Someone has to know something."

Jackson nodded. He got up and left the room. The moment the door shut behind him, his phone was in his hand, texting Davis to tell him he would be home late.

JACKSON FORCED A smile when the door opened. "Hi. I'm Detective Mewes. I'm looking for Elton Longhorn. He's not in any trouble. I just need to speak with him about a case. Is he available?" He showed his badge.

The woman in the doorway frowned. "He had a management meeting at store 114…um… Holiday Rd. The new megastore. All the Price Slasher bigwigs were supposed to be there."

Jackson's eyes widened. "What time was that meeting? Have you spoken to him?"

"Why? What's happened? Why do you seem so alarmed? Is he in some kind of danger?"

"Mrs. Longhorn, please answer the question."

She looked almost dazed and shook her head, her eyes on the clouds. "I uh…um… I don't know. I always expect him late after these meetings. I don't know for sure."

"Madeline, who is that?" a male voice asked from behind her.

"It's about your father, Jim. It's the police. Would you like to come speak to them?"

Silence. She shook her head. "My stepson. Blended families are complicated. Do you want me to try to get a hold of Elton?"

Jackson nodded. "That would be great."

She called him and paced around on the top step of the porch. Jackson took a step back and watched. Then she lowered the phone, met his eyes, and shook her head. "He didn't answer, but if they're in the middle of the meeting, that's not unusual."

Jackson scrunched the right side of his face. "Do me a favor and have him call me if you see or hear from him." He handed her a business card.

"Of course," she said. "Should I be worried?"

"I don't know," he said all too honestly.

When he was back in his car, he yanked out his own phone. His instinct was to call Manny, but he stopped himself, thinking of all he'd been through, and called Lewis instead. "All the bigwigs for Price Slashers are in one place. A management meeting," he told her when she answered. "I'm on my way there now. The Holiday Rd. megastore."

"Shit. Okay. I'll send backup. Hurry. I have a bad feeling."

Jackson hung up and pressed the gas pedal hard. The captain wasn't the only one with a bad feeling.

"HOLY SHIT! I'VE GOT IT!" Laura shouted as she barged into the captain's office.

Captain Lewis looked up from her desk and frowned. "You should be home with your husband."

Laura blinked like she'd been slapped. "I'll check on him in a little bit. I just… You have to see this… Fuck. Look, I told him not to call me babe at work because he doesn't call me babe like a husband. I am not sure he's even straight and he says it in like a gay best friend kind of way and I've wanted to have the talk with him but things have been so crazy and then that kid died in front of him and I was like, it can wait, and then without thinking, I called him babe because I was concerned and he got righteously pissed and I was afraid when I went home he would confront me about it and then it would force me to be honest and we would have to have that dreaded conversation at a really inappropriate time. So I thought, well, let me try to figure this case out since I didn't want to go home. I'm awful, aren't I?"

The captain swallowed. She took a deep breath. "Well, that was a lot. You don't think Manny and Jackson…"

Laura shook her head. "No. No, they're more like brothers. I think Manny is still in the closet. I've found…things though. On his computer and his phone. It's really complicated."

"Maybe he's bi. Liking men doesn't mean he's not into you or loves you any less, Laura."

She blinked like she was stunned again and diverted her eyes. "Maybe, but like…is bi real? I've heard so many people say it's just a cover or a cop out. I don't want him to pretend if I'm not what he wants."

Chief Lewis sighed heavily. She stood from her desk. "Yes, Laura. It's real. Not that it's any of your business, but I'm bi. I've known for sure since I was eleven. I think the conversation you've been avoiding is one you really need to have. It might actually make things a lot better. Now show me what you've found."

Laura opened her mouth to say something, but closed it and nodded. She left the room, and the captain followed. When they reached her test room, she gestured toward a human dummy in the center. She handed the captain a pair of headphones. When she put them on, Laura donned her own pair and hit a button on her phone. A cellphone attached to the dummy started to vibrate. The dummy's head exploded and shot fake blood onto the wall. They took off the headphones and looked at each other. "Okay," Captain Lewis said. "Do you want to tell me what the hell that was?"

Laura held up her hands, but her face was beaming with a smile. "Okay, so, have you heard of Exploding Head Syndrome?"

The captain looked at her with confusion. "I thought you were going to tell me it was some kind of sonic sound weapon, but you went with a sleep disorder?"

Laura looked struck again, but shook it off. "No, sonic weapons are fiction. They can blow up dry skulls, but the brains and blood prevent it from killing a living person. I mean, you would have to use something at like 240 dB for hours and hours—maybe *days*—to actually kill them. Definitely couldn't work in the time it takes to buy a coffee, even when they're shorthanded."

Captain Lewis shook her head and threw her hands up. "So what is it?"

Laura's smile widened. "Well, every phone had a late-night phone call days prior to the explosions. One of those calls led to a voicemail that was obviously listened to, and the others were answered."

"Cut to the chase."

"The voicemail had a subliminal message. It pushes people into waking dreams. A sudden, almost narcoleptic waking sleep. Exploding Head Syndrome is when you hear a sudden bang and see a flash of light and *believe* you're exploding, but you're not. It's not actually dangerous at all, just disturbing."

"Laura…how did they die?"

"Right. Well, the exploding head emoji is a trigger. It activates the sudden sleep. It's so instant that no one even has time to notice. It could happen mid-sentence, while driving, making a sandwich, whatever."

The captain sighed. "And something in the message also makes the false brain explosion turn real. It's hypnotic suggestion tricking their brains into blowing their own fuse."

Laura's mouth fell open. "That was my big reveal. I can't believe you stole my moment. I worked forever on that."

"You took too long." Captain Lewis frowned. "Also, what was the point of the headphones or the dummy?"

"That was just for effect. They always do stuff like that in the movies."

"Christ. Go see your husband and talk to him. You need to stay far away from this case until it's over."

Laura's mouth opened again. "What? Why?"

The captain sighed again. "Because as smart as you are, you listened to that message, which means the subliminal trigger is now in your head and you're in serious danger until we can get someone to put you under and remove it."

"Shit."

"Avoid texting for a bit just to be safe. One stupid emoji in a joke conversation could make you go boom. If you need to talk to someone, call them."

Laura's eyes went wide. "But it's 2025! No one actually talks on the phone! This is horrible!"

JACKSON GOT TO the store, and his bad feeling intensified. The parking lot was full of cars, but there wasn't a single person outside. "Maybe the store was closed for the meeting," he said out loud as he unbuckled his seatbelt.

He approached the front of the store and saw a sign on the door that echoed his thought. For some reason, it didn't relieve him. The automatic doors were locked from the inside. He frowned and knocked. "Police!" he called. "Please open up!"

Management meeting or not, that should have done it, but no one came. He tried again just to be safe, but it was still eerily quiet.

Sighing, he popped the lock. It wasn't hard. He tugged the doors open just enough to slip through and closed them again behind him. The lights were on and the aisles were well stocked, but there were no cashiers at the register, no stock boys on the aisles, no baggers getting carts. It was a ghost town.

Where the hell is the meeting? "Police!" he called out, drawing his gun. "Is anyone in here?" He moved slowly up the middle aisle toward the back of the store. "This is Detective Mewes! I need anyone who hears me to come out where I can see them!"

Silence. He reached the back aisle and stared into the meat market. There was not a drop of blood to be seen. Everything was sanitized, spotless. Not seeing blood where it belonged made him fear even more, seeing it where it wasn't.

He pushed his way through the swinging back doors. There were brightly colored signs with arrows pointing toward the meeting room. He was on edge, looking at all the tall pallets of groceries and lurking shadows. When he reached the meeting room, he could already see the portal window in the door smeared with red.

Jackson tightened his grip on his gun and pulled the door open.

"Jesus," he said when he laid eyes upon the room.

There was a large oval table with an array of gourmet snack foods in the center. Every seat was occupied by someone without a head, except one. The table, the walls, and the ceiling all dripped with red and brown gore. Some of the bodies had slumped or slid halfway out of their chairs before getting caught on an arm. Others, though, were still upright, their arms on the table. One was even holding a cracker that now contained a chunk of his or someone else's brain. At the head of the table was a thin man covered in blood, smoking a cigarette.

Jackson knew he should speak, but all he could do was stare at this man. He took a step forward and raised his gun. A chunk of discarded skull crunched under his foot. His phone went off and he jumped. Without taking his eyes off the man who didn't seem in a hurry to go anywhere, he dug out his phone. He put it to his head, holding his gun toward the only other living person in the room. "Yeah."

The ceiling dripped blood in a metronome-type rhythm. Drip. Drip. Drip. Drip.

"Backup is almost there. I sent Laura home to Manny, but before she left, she discovered how the killer is doing it." She filled him in much quicker than Laura had explained it to her.

"That's insane," Jackson said, staring at the man who just sat where he was, smoking his cigarette without a care.

"We just need to figure the *who* and we can close this case."

"I think I have the who taken care of," Jackson said. "I gotta go."

He hung up and stuffed the phone back in his pocket. "Why?" he asked the man at the head of the table.

"This isn't my seat," the man said. "I switched with Regina after everyone went pop. I didn't think she'd mind." He gave a sickening laugh. "Get it."

"I wish I didn't," Jackson said. "It's over. The cavalry is on the way, so tell me why you did it."

The man reached over and stubbed his cigarette out in another man's geysering neck stump. "You know…last year at this very same meeting, I brought my special potato salad, my mom's recipe. She passed. Cancer. But I always loved her potato salad. It felt special to me to share it with everyone. They criticized it. They laughed. They talked about how we needed to have these things catered."

"You killed all these people over potato salad?"

"No!" the man screamed. He bounded from his chair and slammed his palm on the table. Jackson jammed his gun in the man's direction.

"Back down! Sit!"

The man sat and lit another cigarette.

Drip. Drip. Drip. Drip.

"The potato salad was just a testament to how shitty they were. They don't care whose recipe it is. They don't care who died or from what. Human beings are numbers to them. If they die and people actually fucking have, they just roll them out the door and replace them. They celebrate the fact that they're all evil sociopaths. They look for it. There are people who work their asses off that earn these positions and actually deserve them, and get stepped on and used because they're not big enough dicks. There was a guy named Carter who worked doubles and triples for them, sometimes in three different departments in one day. He worked nineteen fucking days straight, and when he finally got one, they called him in. I was there when they interviewed him for an upcoming promotion. They did it in front of a manager who was a friend of his and counted on him. They asked him to say in front of that manager that he would leave him high and dry with nothing. They demanded he prove how willing he was to step on people and hurt people to rise in the company. They said, 'We need to see how hungry you are.' He wouldn't do that and asked them later if they could speak privately and more professionally, and they said no. They told him he had his chance and blew it because he wasn't cutthroat enough. This whole fucking company thrives on evil. Well, you fucking know what? Now, if they want to stay in business, the people who actually earned their spot are going to have to be promoted and actually given their chance. It was the only fucking way this business was ever going to change. There were just too damn many of these assholes."

"The hypnosis, the subliminals. How did you get everyone's phone numbers?"

The blood-soaked killer laughed. "Every single store has a 'Manager number list' with their names and cell numbers on it in case you need to call another store for something. That's how fucking invincible these people think they are. I tried to speak up, to add some humanity to this company, but I was ignored, laughed at, shut down. The only reason I'm even a manager is because my Dad was one of them, and they saw me as part of the Price Slashers family. They never would have taken me otherwise. They would have stepped on me like everyone else. I thought maybe having someone at the top with an actual fucking conscience would make a difference, but it didn't. I was one tiny fish in a lake full of evil. But not anymore. I did that."

"You sure did. Now you're going to rot in prison if you don't get the death penalty. Was it worth that?"

"To actually change things and set things right? To give the people who actually work for it and earn it, their fair shot? Abso-fuckin-lute-ly."

"Well, good. I'm glad you see yourself as a hero. You can let those delusions keep you company for the next forty years."

"Say what you want. If you didn't work here, you didn't see it day in and day out, you didn't live it, I don't care. Anyone who has…will understand. Maybe they won't agree. Maybe they wouldn't have done it themselves, but they'll understand."

Not a moment later, the room was swarmed with officers. The man, whose name turned out to be Reed Hader, didn't resist in the least as he was cuffed and led outside.

It didn't feel like a victory to Jackson, though. Maybe these people weren't perfect. Maybe they really were a bunch of assholes. But they were people. People with families. Everyone always failed to see the gray areas: the kids who weren't bad but probably would be now, the husbands or wives who would die from grief, the parents who would have to bury their children. The damage goes so far beyond the initial death. Hatred, grief, pain… They trickled outward like ripples in the water when you threw a pebble into a pond. A drop of red from the ceiling smacked him in the face. He wiped it off and finally holstered his gun.

Jackson took his phone out, his eyes on the boardroom full of headless corpses, and he called Davis. "Hey, honey," he said when the phone was answered. "I'm gonna have a world of paperwork, but then I'm coming home and I'm staying there for a while, days, weeks maybe. I'd really love if you could take off work too and stay with me."

"You got it," Davis said. "Whenever you get here, I'll be here, arms open and waiting."

"I love you," Jackson told him.

Drip. Drip. Drip. Drip.

"FIN!"

John Schlimm

"FINI"

John Schlimm

If you were to use a very large scalpel and carefully slice and peel away the mottled, dark-grey top, dorsal skin, and a surface layer of the pale, white underbelly, the thirty-foot, five-thousand-pound gliding predator would have looked spectacular. Like a Betsey Johnson x Peter Benchley collaborative deep-sea installation constructed of muscular flesh and trillions of rainbow cupcake sprinkles.

His spherical eyes—with menacing, deep-blue irises and large, round pupils—readjusted constantly between the shifting low-light, murky depths and the illuminating rays when he got closer to the surface. His gaping, five-foot-span mouth, rimmed with multiple rows of hundreds of razor-sharp, serrated teeth allowed a steady, inward flow of marine life, fulfilling one-half of his sole destiny to eat and reproduce while continuously moving lest, ironically, if he ever stopped he'd drown.

As the unmatched killing machine stealthed through the dark, briny water fifty miles off the New Jersey coastline, his two-foot, Y-shaped brain, weighing just under three ounces resembled a confetti-studded sculpture or whimsical accessory that Betsey would have sent down the runway this season. After forty-four years on earth, this great white shark's evolutionary neuroplasticity—a remarkable trait he shared with the human brain to rewire by regenerating neurons—finally glitched. It convulsed, seized, causing his eyes to widen and his jaws to slam shut, snapping a young dolphin in half.

The infinite spectrum of microbeads, microfibers, and nurdles embedded in the aquatic brute's body finally hit maximum overload. But instead of killing this great white, the four decades of ingesting primary and secondary microplastics finished rewiring his complex brain to now narrow in on a new target, something smaller but just as colorful as the shards of toxic debris polluting his massive body.

A newly-energized and lethally-motivated serial killer was reborn, as he ferociously whip-cracked his caudal fin, picking up speed and heading for the nearest shoreline.

The Saturday after Labor Day

"I can't believe I let you persuade me into wearing this swimsuit," former NFL linebacker Jackson Maloney chided his husband. He was 6'4" and towered over most people he met. Great for the field.

And for the bedroom, where he would devour his much smaller husband.

Tanner rolled his eyes. "I thought it would be cute for us to have matching swim trunks on our honeymoon," the interior designer teased with a boyish grin. "Besides, the design perfectly complements your yummy, chocolate-brown muscles and my Kate Moss-heroin-chic, lily-white frame."

Jackson loved how extra his new husband could be, so if wearing matching swimming attire bearing every emoji a person could name made him happy then so be it.

"Okay," Jackson said, playfully surrendering. "But did you really have to get the pairs with the eggplant emoji on the crotch and the poop one on the ass end?"

"This is the year of the emoji, *again*," Tanner said. "Thanks to Vineyard Fins launching their collection of emoji-covered clothing, shoes, accessories—*everything*—which I've used for my clients back in the city, and also larger things like kayaks and even a custom-designed speedboat. Jenna Hawthorne is *the* designer of the moment! I hear she and her husband—tech-billionaire Brick Hawthorne—even have a home here on Lickety Island. That is, in addition to their penthouses in NYC and Boston, and sprawling estate on Martha's Vineyard where the Vineyard Fins flagship store is."

It was times like this Jackson was sure Tanner had a streak of stalker in him. It was cute, but also concerning. "I still think emojis are cheesy," Jackson said, ignoring the stalker vibes and instead leaning down to kiss Tanner on the forehead, "but whatever my hubby wants, I'm happy to oblige!"

"Well, we have two hours before we need to check out of our love nest and head back home," Tanner said, "and since we're already in the hottest swimsuits of the season, I'll race you down to the ocean to jump a few final waves, and maybe see what else happens to swell up!"

"That's one way I might get to lose this damn suit," Jackson joked, launching into a sprint.

Both men dove into the crest of a large wave. Once past where the water was breaking, Jackson stood in neck-deep water while Tanner wrapped his arms and legs around him.

"Can you believe we're finally married?" Tanner asked. "It doesn't feel real."

Jackson replied by giving his husband a long kiss as the salty water swished around them, causing them to sway in what felt like a dreamy scene from a romantic comedy—sunny, cloudless-blue sky and lyrically-keowing seagulls overhead included.

Sixty feet away, the great white locked in on his targets, the colorful shapes triggering his eyes, and infuriating his newly-ignited instinct to destroy. At forty feet, had the newlyweds been paying attention, they would have seen the six-foot, grey dorsal fin slice up through the water, then at twenty feet splash down to the right for a sideways attack.

"I hear Zac Posen, Christian Siriano, and one of the Kardashians just bought homes here," Tanner said, grasping his husband tightly. "And word has it that George and Amal were also spotted house-hunting over on Anchor's Away Lane."

Jackson laughed and shook his head. "You are such a star-fuuuu . . ."

Over his husky husband's shoulder, Tanner saw half of the wide-opened mouth with its hundreds of triangular teeth emerge a few feet away. He released his grip, inadvertently shoving his husband into the jaws as he pushed and kicked back in a panic.

The great white clamped shut on Jackson's muscular torso and legs, igniting an explosion of blood, guts, and brown skin. The twenty-mile-per-hour impact of the beast's snout slammed into Tanner, shattering ribs and pushing his small body up and to the side.

Gagging on mouthfuls of chunky, blood-infused seawater, the new widower saw the fin glide out, then in a sharp U-turn start heading back towards him.

"HELP!" he screamed, the pain in his chest searing, knowing full well that the closest houses on either side of their post-summer rental were a football-field's length away in either direction.

"SHARK! SOMEBODY HELP!"

Tanner kicked frantically and wildly paddled, but the current held him in place. The fractured chunks of rib bones were lacerating and punctuating his liver, stomach, and lungs.

"HELP! SHARK! HELP!"

The young, up-and-coming interior designer's words were swallowed whole by the morning's refreshing sea breeze and singing seagulls, just as he was when the great white made him disappear in a single gulp.

"THESE AFTER-LABOR Day visitors are worse than the summer crowd," Lickety Island's only realtor and life-long resident Martha Adams ranted. "They come here looking for discounts and bargains without an ounce of respect or empathy for us lifers."

Sheriff Cass Sparrow, also a life-long islander, stood with the realtor—who was attired in a Vineyard Fins short-sleeved polo covered in a dizzying menagerie of emojis: 🦞, 🐚, 🦑, 🦐, 🦞, 🦀, 🦀, 🐠, 🐟, ⛵, and ⚓—in the bedroom of the rental cottage. It was located on Lost Tuck Beach, so named for the fabled fisherman Tuck Wilder who went missing after setting sail from there in 1854.

"I'm still not sure why you called me," Cass said. She had the weekend off, which meant precious, quality alone time with Laurie, her wife of 25 years, who owned Lickety Island's only jewelry store in town. When Martha called like a raving maniac, the two had been laughing their way through preparing a fresh seafood lunch, with Lickety Isle Brew lagers on ice to wash it all down.

"I want this couple arrested, and I want you to personally do it, not that doofus of a deputy you have!" Martha said, motioning to the clothing and other items strewn around the master suite and causing her custom-made Vineyard Fins emoji charm bracelet to jingle. "Their check-out time was noon and here it is 1:00 p.m. and they're nowhere to be found."

"Not sure who you're referring to, but neither Deputy Chuck or Deputy *Rufus* is a *doofus*, they're just young and new at the job," Cass said, defending her seconds in command. She then switched gears and asked, "Anyway, did these renters pay you?"

"Yes, I always demand payment up front," Martha answered.

"You know how folks are today, especially these new outsiders coming from places like New York, Boston, and LA," Cass tried to reason. "They probably caught a last-minute, private helicopter out of here to destinations unknown, on a whim. Especially since they left their wallets behind, which is strange, but I still don't think it's anything to be concerned about. I've seen much more bizarre antics than that this past summer."

Had either woman looked out the sliding glass doors leading from the bedroom down to the beach at that moment, they would have caught a glimpse of the glistening dorsal fin glide by. The great white swallowed the few remaining pieces of Jackson Maloney and was now heading up the coastline in search of his next meal. He was insatiable, and already famished again, while the reenergized inferno of rage burned deep in his belly and brain. The beefy, pro-football linebacker and his twink, interior designer husband were only the first course.

"I have my next *off-season* renters waiting at the Stowaway Diner in town to move in here for the next week," Martha fumed with a grunt. "I guess I'll just have my cleaning lady bag up all this junk and toss it in the garbage."

Cass saw that the so-called junk included two Vineyard Fins towels. One bore a range of furniture-based emojis, while the other boasted sports-related ones.

"I'd maybe hold onto the…um, junk…for a few days in case they come back," Cass said, "but yes, go ahead and prepare the space for your next renters."

Martha agreed with another grunt, then yelled to the lady from Lickety Island's Housecleaning Co. to get started and to make it fast.

Cass saw her chance and slipped out, heading back home where she could pick up where she and Laurie had left off: making lunch and enjoying their quiet Saturday at home.

"PENELOPE, PLEASE SLOW down," elderly Hispanic nanny, Marcela Aguado, called out to the seven-year-old spoiled brat running ahead of her down the path to the private beach. "My legs don't move like they used to."

"Hurry up!" Penelope yelled back, continuing to sprint until she reached the water. She looked out to see if there were any dolphins or seals. Usually they loved swimming along her beach. Not today.

Catching up, Marcela set down the jampacked Vineyard Fins tote and Penelope's Vineyard Fins beach chair. Both were covered in the smiling-face-with-sunglasses emoji and hearts—♥🦈❣️🖤♥🖤. Emojis were "in", so she'd been told, and anyway, Penelope liked the cartoony things.

"Do you like my new suit?" Penelope asked, striking a pose and flicking her long, curly Bergdorf Blonde-hair. "My mother let me design it myself! She said she's going to call it The Penelope and sell it in her stores next summer."

Marcela pretended to care, looking over the suit dotted with pink-ribbon emojis, as well as 🍸, 🦐, 🐕, 🦋, 🍫, 🔍, 🍶, and 🥟. It was overwhelming and busy. She hated it.

"These are all my favorite things!" Penelope continued. Her child-size Vineyard Fins sunglasses were shaped like cutesy, mouse-face emojis.

"Yes, dear, very nice," Marcela lied, hoping to humor the child and shut her the fuck up. She had taken off the adult-size, mouse-face sunglasses—a gesture from Mrs. Hawthorne to help her "further bond" with Penelope—the minute she was out of the fashion mogul's view.

"My little brother Benson got to design his own emoji swimsuit, too," Penelope blathered on. "His has his favorite boy things all over them, like baseballs, soccer balls, skateboards, yo-yos, video-game controllers, money bags, toolboxes, alien monsters, and pickup trucks."

Marcela rolled her eyes, reaching into the tote and pulling out a towel that matched Penelope's bespoke swimsuit.

"How nice," she said.

"I wanted to also get microscopes like I use in school and taxis like I see in the city on mine, but mother suggested tubes of lipstick and diamond rings instead," the child said.

"You best get in the water, unless you want that other layer of sunblock I promised your mother I'd apply," Marcela said.

"Not today, Satan!" the brat spewed, then turned and ran into the ocean, letting the bubbly-white remnants of a smashing wave fizz and wash over her.

Kids these days, Marcela thought and stifled an eye roll.

The child never paid attention to anything going on around her that didn't involve her. Such as the peek of dorsal fin about fifty feet in the distance, heading her way. All she cared about were those stupid fucking emojis, and yapping on and on, even now as she waded further into the ocean.

Marcela spread out Penelope's towel, laying a second one on top for when the child emerged, screaming about how she was freezing. Next, she opened the child's chair where a bundled-up Penelope would sit and enjoy her afternoon snacks and mint-flavored bubble tea that, for now, would remain in the smaller Vineyard Fins emoji-covered cooler bag. Marcela then finally pulled out the book she was currently reading, *The Old Man and the Sea*, and settled into the sand.

Marcela heard the vague cry of the child—such an attention-seeker—and ignored it with a slight wave. She was going to read this book, goddammit, and that little pest wasn't going to ruin it. Thankfully, Penelope stopped calling, and Marcela was able to read in peace.

She couldn't remember how long it had been since she had glanced up from the novel, but when she did, Penelope was nowhere to be seen.

The veteran nanny stood and called out to the kid. Had Penelope been pulled out by a wave? Maybe she ran back up to the house? Was she playing hide-and-seek like she often did, disappearing for hours? Marcela desperately scanned the private beach—known officially as Hawthorne's Lickety Cove—from end to end. There wasn't another soul around.

What the aging woman's vision also didn't register was a small, fading red slick of fleshy morsels on the water's surface where schools of fish now greedily dined, and further out the flash of a huge caudal fin before it submerged. And what she couldn't possibly know is that the great white shark was really growing tired of these small, albeit colorful, bites, and was determined to find something bigger and bolder to decimate next time.

For the second time today, on her weekend off, Cass had been directly called and her official presence as Lickety Island Sheriff requested. At least she and Laurie had finished their homecooked lobster rolls with all the trimmings. And luckily, she was only halfway into her second Lickety Isle Brew lager when Brick Hawthorne had called and demanded she come at once to their beachfront estate—Hawthorne's Landing—on Anchor's Away Lane.

"Did you see Penelope pulled out or go under?" Cass asked the child's nanny, who was sitting on a couch in the sun room that ran the length of the house in back. Hovering tensely inches away were the child's parents, tech-billionaire Brick Hawthorne—a Clark Kent-handsome descendant of *Scarlet Letter* fame who had made it big himself in Silicon Valley—and his wife Jenna—a chiseled, brunette Barbie and Founder, CEO, *and* Chief Designer of Vineyard Fins.

"Penelope did not drown, Sheriff," Jenna protested, before Marcela could answer. "We've told you repeatedly, our daughter is a champion swimmer."

Cass stared at the woman, whose sundress was covered in sunshine and flower emojis. It was disgusting, among the worst items of clothing she'd ever laid eyes on, and clearly one of Jenna's designs. Just like the one Marcela had already described Penelope wearing when she last saw her head into the ocean for a swim.

"A riptide could easily pull out even Michael Phelps," Cass said.

"Are you trying to crack a joke, Sheriff Sparrow?" Brick howled. "Because I don't think any of this is one bit funny."

"No, sir, I wasn't," Cass tried to explain. "I was only making the point that even the strongest—"

"I've heard enough." Jenna interrupted. "I demand you arrest Marcela immediately!"

"*Arrest her? For what?*" Cass asked, confused and beginning to lose her patience.

Jenna turned to her husband. "Too bad the cameras aren't capturing all of this for the audition tape," she said to him. He nodded back.

The Vineyard Fins founder then returned her attention to Cass. "I expect you to arrest her for obviously trafficking our beautiful, precious daughter to some awful smuggling ring of perverts, who get off on doing unspeakable things with children."

"MRS. HAWTHORNE, I WOULD NEVER . . ." Marcela scowled, losing her temper at the ridiculous allegation. *This* was the thanks she got from a family she had faithfully served for sixty years?

"I don't want to hear another word out of your mouth," Jenna said, silencing the nanny. "So what's it going to be, Sheriff? Are you going to arrest this woman, or do we need to call our friends in Washington?"

Cass's brain was spinning like a Tilt-A-Whirl. After navigating several summers with the new super-wealthy crowds coming to her fare hamlet thirty miles off the New Jersey coast, not much surprised her anymore. But accusing an old nanny of human trafficking when the child either ran away and was hiding or lost, or was on the ocean floor being nibbled on by crabs, hagfish, and other hungry marine life—that was next-level insane.

Attempting to diffuse the irrational situation from spiraling further, Cass asked, "Mrs. Hawthorne, what did you mean when you mentioned audition cameras?"

"What?" Jenna snarled, then announced with a flick of her fair, "Oh, I'm in serious contention—a natural shoo-in, they say—to be cast on the new series *The Real Housewives of Boston*. In fact, I'm in talks to anchor the whole show—you know, like be the new Kyle Richards or Bethenny Frankel, only of Beantown, which will also include our life on Martha's Vineyard and I imagine here on Lickety, too."

Cass wanted to seriously scream, "ARE YOU FUCKING KIDDING ME RIGHT NOW?" and punch this arrogant, entitled, narcissistic lunatic. But she didn't. Instead, she took a brief moment to compose herself, looking around the room—three walls of which were covered with paintings by a young new artist/chef in New York who was doing a collab with Vineyard Fins for the company's emoji line. There were framed graffiti-style, food-based emojis: 🍔, 🍕, 🍟. It went on and on. Cass thought she might vomit.

She then looked out the back wall of windows down to the beach and cloudless blue sky, devilishly thinking how she could really slam this bitch with a single revelation. Over the summer, Lickety's premier realtor and gossip Martha Adams had told her about Brick spending a very cozy weekend in this very house with a closeted, A-List movie star, known for his action-hero films, while the lady of the manor had been in LA opening a Vineyard Fins store.

"Um, excuse me, Sheriff, are you going to arrest this monster or not?" Jenna demanded, pointing at Marcela on the couch.

"I won't sit here and take this after everything I've done for this family!" Marcela said, starting to stand from the couch.

Jenna shoved the old woman down. "First of all, you're fired!" she screamed. "And second of all, Brick and I will make sure you spend the rest of what's left of your pathetic life behind bars."

"Now hold it," Cass said, stepping between the two women.

Four miles up the beach from Hawthorne's Landing, and just two miles out, the great white was circling a fishing boat. At one point, the shark dove down fifty feet, then raced upwards at fifteen miles per hour, banging the bottom of the boat, causing it to raise up and lean precariously. The three, drunk fishermen on board were tossed to the deck, but when everything calmed and nothing more happened, they chalked it up to a rogue wave—albeit one none of them saw coming—and cracked open another round of Lickety Isle Brew IPAs.

For his part, the great white simply grew bored of the old trawler—a dirty white boat bearing the name *A Pirate's Life for Me*. It was a reference to the 1967 sea shanty, and was painted in large letters and various colors along both sides. The bright colors were what first caught the aquatic serial killer's attention, but the closer he got he realized it wasn't what he was wired to seek out and destroy. The head-first ramming of the trawler's bottom was more out of mischief and annoyance over wasted time than it was sinister.

"Your father and grandfather, God rest their souls, would be ashamed of you, Mr. Hawthorne, and this wicked witch you've married," Marcela spat.

Jenna lunged forward, but Cass held her back.

"Get the fuck out of my house, you nasty old bitch," Brick said. "And don't forget you signed an iron-clad NDA!"

"Look, your daughter is missing, possibly drowned," Cass told the couple firmly. "Time is of the essence right now."

Marcela stood and stormed in a straight shot through the formal living room, grand marble-tiled foyer, and out the front door.

"Are you going to just let her get away with this?" Jenna yelled, glaring at Cass. She tore at her necklace, a large, sparkling lemon emoji pendant, and hurled it at the juice-box emoji painting, leaving a gash near its spraypainted straw.

"Sheriff Sparrow, our daughter has not drowned," Brick insisted. "I agree with Jenna, you need to arrest that monster for obviously trafficking Penelope."

It was hopeless, and almost certainly tragic.

"Okay, let's do this," Cass said, seething. "We'll wait twenty-four hours. If Penelope doesn't return by then, I'll inform my deputies, *who are currently on duty and will be for the full weekend*, to file a missing person's report. But I still think—"

"You're not paid to think, Sheriff." Jenna scowled. "And I won't have those bozos, Deputy Chuck Wagon or whatever the fuck his name is, and Deputy Rufus handling our sweet daughter's trafficking case."

"Huh?" Cass replied, shaking her heard. "His name is Deputy Chuck *Wiggins,* and he and Deputy Rufus are both more than capable of handling a missing person's report."

With that, Sheriff Cass Sparrow officially had had enough. She followed the nanny's lead, stepped around the couple, and headed for the door.

"Sheriff Sparrow," Brick called after her. "Before you leave, we'll need you to sign a non-disclosure agreement."

Cass stopped, digested what she had just heard, then continued out the door, muttering, "Fuck you!" She sure hoped some of that ice-cold Lickety Isle Brew lager was left when she got home.

Twelve miles further up the shore, just off Amity Plains Beach, the great white quivered along the full length of his thirty-foot body, then upchucked the spoiled Hawthorne brat—spewing her out in a bile-green soup of unidentifiable chunks. Watching and pointing from the shore, the beachgoers were entertained by a flock of gulls diving towards the water, feeding on what they assumed was a school of unlucky fish.

Lickety Island's first and only serial killer was then ready for the third course of his feast. Hungrier than ever!

"I DON'T KNOW how you kept your cool, babe," Laurie said, leaning back against the town sheriff in their backyard hammock. "I would've nailed that bitch in the nose if I saw her talking to anybody like that, especially an old lady."

Cass laughed, taking a sip of her Lickety Isle Brew lager and welcoming the wonderfully woozy buzz overtaking her.

She knew her wife's bark was worse than her bite, but she loved that go-get-'em spirit. The two had celebrated their twenty-fifth wedding anniversary back in April. They had lived in this small, inland cottage a mile from downtown for almost as many years, having moved in two months after they were married at sunset on Lighthouse Point Beach at the southern end of Lickety. They met when Laurie was vacationing on the island, which back then had only one inn called The Shaggy Sailor and was ignored by the bulk of summer residents and visitors who much preferred Nantucket, Martha's Vineyard, and The Hamptons instead. It was love at first sight for them both.

They loved their cozy, little island paradise. Though in recent years since it became a trendy stopover for trendsetters and droves of young, new millionaires and billionaires, it was challenging to keep it that way.

"But what about the Hawthorne girl?" Laurie asked, sipping her own lager. "I mean, you don't think it possibly could've been traffickers, do you?"

"No," Cass answered. "Those people are out of their minds! After I left, I called Chuck and Rufus and told them to be prepared to file the missing person's report when we hit the twenty-four-hour mark tomorrow afternoon. But sadly, I'd bet that kid's body washes ashore before then."

Laurie shivered and snuggled closer to Cass. "Just awful."

Cass turned the beer can in her hand. "What the *fuuuuck* is this?"

"I know, so dumb, right?" Laurie laughed. "It's a collab that Lickety Isle Brew is doing with Vineyard Fins."

"Ugh," Cass said, rolling her eyes.

"See, the emojis on mine—the one, the blue ball, and the crescent moon—means once in a blue moon," Laurie explained. "And let's see… The two smiley faces, checkmark, and pill on yours means laughter is the best medicine."

"How, pray tell, do you know that absolutely useless bullshit?" Cass asked, taking a sip. "Are you now the emoji whisperer?"

Laurie laughed again. "No, I asked my niece and nephew this afternoon when I zoomed with them back in Pennsylvania."

"Hey, I thought you were inviting Kara over tonight," Cass said, changing the topic and referring to their friend, who was an artist and owned the Lickety Surf & Kayak Shop.

"I did, but with the full moon tonight, she wanted to kayak offshore a bit to take some photographs for her upcoming gallery show," Laurie replied.

"Oh, cool, can't wait to see them," Cass said, gulping down the rest of her beer and shimmying her butt to get the hammock swinging. "*Annnd*, I'm looking very forward to having you all to myself tonight." She gently kissed Laurie on the forehead.

Ten miles from the couple, the fuchsia sun was sinking near the hazy horizon out beyond the empty stretch of Salt & Pepper Beach. Kara Dornin relished the solitude of the pristine shoreline there. She pushed her kayak out into the low tide and maneuvered herself into it. Her camera and snacks were stowed in a waterproof bag inside the kayak.

Soon, Kara was a quarter mile out, and, fortunately, the water was calm.

Forty feet below her, the great white cruised, drawing invisible bullseye circles around the mysterious creature above him on the surface as it moved further and further out to sea. This was a new prey the shark had never seen before that was becoming more tantalizing by the minute.

Full moons meant cold air and colder water, but that didn't bother Kara. She had come prepared in a new wetsuit and kayak.

She knew others found it cheesy, including her dear friends, Cass and Laurie, but she loved emojis. And this summer, Vineyard Fins had nailed that game.

Kara had run into Jenna Hawthorne recently while they were both at the Squirrely Beach Gallery where the series of graffiti-style emoji paintings by the up-and-coming NYC artist and chef were on exhibit. After explaining what she does—owning the island's only surf and kayaking equipment rentals shop—the next day Jenna sent over the emoji-patterned wetsuit and kayak. They were samples that Jenna asked Kara to test out for possible tweaks before they went into production next year.

The sun looked like it was only mere inches above its own shimmering reflection on the ocean as Kara steadily paddled out about a half-mile from the shore. The emojis covering her wetsuit and kayak looked dreamy in the rose-colored light, and were also reflected in the still water as if they were melting and flowing outward in an enigmatic feat of performance art.

A dorsal fin slid out of the water fifty feet behind Kara, making a beeline for the artist and shop owner. At twenty feet, the shark dove out of sight, causing barely a ripple.

Kara laughed, thinking of what Cass and Laurie would probably say when they saw her wetsuit and kayak. Both were adorned in an all-over, wavy pattern of emojis that, when you really thought about them, made little sense together: 🎪, 🚂, ⛺, 🪐, 🎲, 🎸, 📫, 🤠, and the only thing that even remotely rang true: 🦈.

Kara pulled her camera out, adjusted the settings, and focused it towards the horizon to capture the neon-pink ball melting into the water.

"FIN!"

The great white continued diving, down to fifty, then sixty, then finally seventy-five feet where it shifted gracefully into a sweeping U-turn. Like a five-thousand-pound missile, the voracious serial killer shot upwards, engaging all muscles while his maladapted, microplastic-infected neurons fired spasmodically.

Kara framed the fleeting, arched sliver of blazing, pink sun in the seconds before it would disappear for the night. So gorgeous!

As her finger pressed the shutter button, Kara's kayak was slammed from the bottom with the force of a bullet train, twisting her around to face the distant shore, jarring every muscle, organ, and bone in her body, ripping apart her groin, her guts, shoulders, arms. Her spinal column buckled and snapped with the crunching of the jaws, her neck tore apart, leaving her conscious only a second longer to see her camera flying through the air towards the rising full moon and a crackling flash of emojis popping on her wetsuit as she and her kayak cradled in the ginormous jaws of a merciless terminator.

The Sunday after Labor Day

CASS STRETCHED OUT in her beach chair and checked her watch. It was noon. Perfect, that would give her a few more hours of peace and quiet before she knew the missing person's report for Penelope Hawthorne would be filed and ignite the inevitable shitstorm.

But for now, she was determined to enjoy the time she had left with Laurie and the other beachgoers on Jersey Shore—a place mostly frequented by the local, year-round residents—that so far hadn't fallen prey to all the touristy bells and whistles. Unfortunately, Cass thought,

301

looking around, even the locals had fallen prey to the summer's hottest trend. She was in a sea of a different kind—swimsuits, towels, totes, umbrellas, frisbees, volleyballs, coolers, water bottles, and rafts all emblazoned with dumb Vineyard Fins emojis. One middle-aged man even had full chest and back tattoos of palm-tree emojis. It looked like a Care Bear had barfed all over the beach.

And lining the beach's parking lot, tall flag poles displayed an LA artist's Vineyard Fins collab installation of giant flags bearing assemblages of world-flag emojis—a monstrosity that Cass tried to keep out of eyeshot.

"I'm going for a swim, babe," Laurie said, jumping up from her own chair and giving Cass a quick kiss.

Cass watched as Laurie—not in a Vineyard Fins suit—jogged to the surf, then dove into the swell of a large wave where dozens of others were enjoying the water.

"Hey, Sheriff Sparrow, look what we found down the beach . . ."

Twelve-year-old twins, Presley and Bear Brody, approached Cass with a chunk of…something…covered in those damn emojis.

"What is it?" she asked more to herself than the boys.

"Hey, I recognize that," the Mayor, Sally Rizzoli said, approaching Cass and the boys. "It's part of the kayak that Kara Dornin showed me. The one Jenna Hawthorne gave her to do a test drive. She had a matching wetsuit, too."

Cass suddenly recalled that Kara was out kayaking last night, and then realized that they hadn't heard from her this morning about joining them here at Jersey Shore.

"How could this have happened?" Cass again asked herself more than anyone else.

The answer came in a mad rush—

"FIN!" a nearby child yelled and pointed to the water, followed by a rippling explosion of frantic screams along the shoreline.

Cass bolted out of her chair.

To the far right, several feet out into the water, she saw the six-foot dorsal fin speeding into the swimmers. It suddenly leaned to the right, its jaws exposed.

"SHARK!" Cass screamed. "GET OUT OF THE WATER!"

She watched the great white cruise in a wavy line, chomping down on anyone in his path—several teens, the mayor's wife, a grandpa, realtor Martha Adams, a kid on a yellow raft…

"GET OUT OF THE FUCKING WATER!" Cass yelled again, running towards the massacre, pushing her way through the frenzied crowd—half of whom were also rushing to help while the other half had their phones raised, capturing every second.

Cass waded into the bloodbath, searching for Laurie while pulling kids and adults in and dodging severed hands, arms, feet, legs, and heads, and fragments of shredded swimsuits and rafts covered in Vineyard Fins emojis.

She finally spotted Laurie about ten feet in front of her. "LAURIE!" she screamed. "SWIM FAST!"

Cass tried to get closer to her wife but the waves kept pushing her back.

Finally within arm's reach, Cass grabbed Laurie's hand and began to pull. But then a hysterical man—the one with the chest and back emoji tattoos—grasped onto Laurie's back. Cass tried to pull them both closer to her.

The span of triangular, serrated teeth broke the surface behind Laurie and the man on her back. Cass screamed. The man released his grip on Laurie, dipping to his left away from her.

Cass watched, helpless, as the great white clamped down on her wife's head and torso, the force of the attack knocking the sheriff backwards. He then pivoted to his right, ripping the couple apart and bolting back out to sea with a trail of Laurie's blood in his wake washing over Cass.

CASS RAGED DOWN the long wooden dock at Lickety Island Marina with a score to settle. She passed a disorienting array of old fishing trawlers mixed in with multi-million-dollar yachts bearing names like *Punta Playa*, *Billion Dollar Baby*, and *You Can't Afford Me*. Her former Lickety Island High School classmate, Dexter X. Warrenton—a trust-fund-baby-turned-eccentric-adventurer-and-collector known as Dex X.—was close behind her. She had called him, knowing he'd have what she needed in a pinch. In the meantime, she instructed Deputies Chuck and Rufus to close all the island's beaches.

Finally, the sheriff found what she was looking for: the Vineyards Fins new, custom-built, thirty-foot speedboat. Even from a distance, Cass could see the vessel's exterior and interior were covered in water-themed emojis and, oddly, flying saucers. Across the back, the boat's name was scripted in bright red: *The Scarlet E.*

Reaching the boat, Cass wasted no time jumping aboard, startling Brick and Jenna Hawthorne. Dex X. followed close behind her.

"I need your boat!" Cass told the couple. "It's police business!"

"Like hell," Brick growled. "Get the fuck off before I call the police!"

"I AM THE POLICE, ASSHOLE!" Cass yelled back, slugging the tech billionaire in the face. She heard the splintering of bone as his nose broke, and he rushed backwards for safety, instead falling over the railing and into the water.

Dex X. let out a raucous cheer! He was rich, too, but he was old money—dating back to Lickety Island's original settlers, including his great-great-great-grandparents—and found the obnoxious attitudes and activities of the new rich so ridiculous and tacky.

"What are you doing, you psycho?" Jenna demanded, then turned her attention to the sheriff's disheveled, grinning sidekick. "And who's this homeless man you brought on my boat?"

Brick was splashing and cursing in the water, complaining that his thousand-dollar shirt was all wet.

In thirty seconds flat, Cass explained what had happened at Jersey Shore and how that along with the disappearances of the couple at Lost Tuck Beach, Penelope, and Kara, she believed the great white shark doing all this was somehow being triggered by the emojis everywhere. She also believed *The Scarlet E* could be used as bait to catch and destroy it.

"You've got to be fucking kidding me," Jenna screeched. "If you think you're going to lay the blame on me for—"

"Either you get off this boat right now, or head out with me and Dex X. to get this motherfucker, *or* I'm sending you over the side the same way your husband went," Cass said, starting up the boat. "And by the way, Dex X.'s family has more money than you. As in came-over-on-the-Mayflower-rich!"

Brick climbed a ladder out of the water, and stood on the deck, dripping wet and holding his nose. "Jenna get off that boat right now!" he demanded.

"Oh, shut the fuck up, Brick," Jenna said, sitting down and sizing-up Dex X. with a new appreciation. "I'm not going to let some shark pin this massacre on *my* brand," she said. "Plus, it'll be great to talk about when I'm cast on *The Real Housewives*."

"I won't have you running around out there like some common vigilante," Brick yelled.

"Oh, you mean like you were, running around this summer like a common whore with that actor while I was out of town opening my West Coast Vineyard Fins shop?" Jenna spewed. "Newsflash, he already has a secret husband tucked away in Maui, so he was just using you, but for what I don't know. You're a boring lay!"

"YOU BITCH!" Brick yelled.

"Not to mention this thing *ATE* your daughter!" Cass said, trying to circle the talk back to the more pressing emergency.

"*Yes, and that,*" Jenna conceded.

"You ready, Dex X.?" Cass asked, rolling her eyes and beginning to throttle up.

The rumpled fifty-three-year-old held up three grenades that were part of his contraband collection of weapons. "Just say when!" he answered.

"Oh my god, are those real?" Jenna yelled as *The Scarlet E* sped out towards the horizon.

Five miles out to sea, the Vineyard Fins emoji speedboat floated while its three passengers sat in awkward silence. Cass kept forcing thoughts of Laurie out of her mind until this job was finished, albeit she'd kill the monster with her bare hands if she had to in her wife's honor.

"Why do you choose to look homeless if you're wealthy?" Jenna asked Dex X.

Cass wished she had punched her when she had the chance at the start.

"It's my vibe," Dex X. replied. He then unzipped his pants.

"DEX!" Cass yelled.

Jenna started covering her eyes, then saw he was showing-off his Vineyard Fins boxers covered in biohazard and radioactive emojis.

"Not you, too!" Cass exclaimed, as all three laughed for the first time.

"At least someone has taste," Jenna mumbled in Brick's direction, then walked to the stern.

"Check this out," Dex X. said, handing her a grenade.

"Picture replicas of this as a purse covered with fire, fire extinguisher, bomb, sparkler, comet, rocket, and collision emojis for next season's collection!" Jenna said excitedly, turning the grenade over in her hands. "I could even do an entire capsule collection around it."

"You've got to be fucking kidding me!" Cass replied, then pivoted, saying, "I asked him to bring them so we can use them to get this asshole shark. We just need to wait until we see it coming in our direction, wait for it to open its mouth, and then pull the pin and toss one in."

"*Easy peasy*," Dex X. said, raising an eyebrow and running a hand over his wild, sandy-blonde curls and five-o'clock scruff. "I did once help catch a twenty-foot anaconda in the Amazon. Damn near lost my hand."

"I could vomit," Jenna declared. The Vineyard Fins designer then examined the explosive more seriously and asked, "How does this thing work?"

Cass just then realized Jenna was in a blouse and pants covered in gold-coin and pink-purse emojis.

"Jenna, don't stand so close to…" she began to warn.

The great white lunged, plopping his open mouth onto the stern, causing the speedboat to tilt back and upward. Jenna fell, screaming, ass first into his mouth. The grenade flew from her hand and disappeared into the water with a *plunk*, wasted.

Cass and Dex X. leapt forward to help, but it was too late. The shark and Jenna were submerged within seconds.

"HOLY FUCK, that thing is the size of a semi," Dex X. cried. "We're doomed! We need to get out of here!"

"I need you to calm down," Cass said—as much to herself as to her old friend—while scooping water out of the boat. "Help me get this water out."

Minutes later, the boat was rammed from the bottom, cracking it in half, and tossing Dex X. overboard. The second grenade bounced down from a helm seat and into the water between the two halves of *The Scarlet E.*

"DEX!" Cass yelled, clinging to the steering wheel with one hand while tightly fisting the final grenade with her other hand.

Dex X. was catapulted several feet out of the water, yelling, "YIP-PEE-KI-YAY!" while his lower half was in the shark's mouth. Before Cass could react, he was slammed back down onto the water's surface and pulled under.

The speedboat's stern half—inscribed with *The Scarlet E*—was now sunk and out of sight. And the bow half was tipping upward and would soon also vanish, along with the Lickety Island Sheriff in it.

Cass started to climb the near-vertical bow, eventually reaching the pointy top where she was greeted by large prince and princess emojis that no doubt represented Brick and Jenna Hawthorne.

About fifty feet out ahead, she saw the slick, six-foot dorsal fin emerge and slice through the water coming her way at about thirty-miles per hour while the wreckage she was clinging to kept slipping down.

Cass thought about Laurie—the love of her life—and knew what she had to do.

The fin was about forty feet away now.

The sheriff shimmied up on top of the bow's pointed end, straddling it.

The great white was twenty feet away.

Fifteen.

Ten.

As the monstrous serial killer rose out of the water, mouth opened, Cass clutched the final bomb, stood, pulled the grenade's pin, and using the bow's pointed edge as a launching pad she dove head first through the jaws, penetrating the shark's mouth and jamming the grenade as far down his narrow throat as possible.

Five seconds later, while the great white was still lifted out of the water, he exploded in what looked like a tractor-trailer-size pinata bursting with flesh, blood, guts, and trillions of microplastic, rainbow sprinkles.

FROM A HUNDRED feet away, the great white's thirty-five-foot, six-thousand-pound male partner raced forward, then circled where his mate had just died. Having defied known science at the time, the two male sharks had bonded when they reached sexual maturity at age twenty-six, some eighteen years earlier, and had been inseparable ever since.

After a few minutes, the seven-foot dorsal fin of the enraged killing machine slashed through the Atlantic Ocean, undeterred, bolting northward towards Montauk where rampage and revenge would be his for the taking, and eating.

CONTENT WARNINGS

This book contains body horror. 'Sculpting' contains trans body modification, 'The High Road' contains male rape and discrimantory language. 'Molly, From Data Analytic' contains suicide.

All the stories contain aspects of bodily dismemberment.